HERE SO far AWAY

HERE
SO far
AWAY

Hadley Dyer

HARPER TEEN

An Imprint of HarperCollinsPublishers

HarperTeen is an imprint of HarperCollins Publishers.

Here So Far Away
Copyright © 2018 by Hadley Dyer
www.epicreads.com

Library of Congress Control Number: 2017951265
ISBN 978-0-06-247317-2

Typography by Heather Daugherty
18 19 20 21 22   PC/LSCH   10 9 8 7 6 5 4 3 2 1
❖
First Edition

For my dear dad, William Dyer

Love set you going like a fat gold watch.
—Sylvia Plath, "Morning Song"

THE STARS GO WALTZING OUT

ONE

August 1992

Life's a bad writer, my father used to say. I think he meant that most of us would write our lives differently, given the chance. If I could choose one year to rewrite, it'd be my senior year of high school, and I'd probably start with that first shack party. Or I might go even further back and make Sid stay in the valley. I always wondered how it would have worked out if the five of us had stayed together. Who knows, maybe Sid could have been the one to stop me from making such a mess of things.

Sid left early on an August morning. He came out of the house wearing his Eddie Murphy costume from the previous Halloween: leather pants, leather jacket with the sleeves pushed up, gold chain, no shirt. Natalie and I cracked up because we knew he was trying to keep us from getting emotional, Lisa burst into tears for the very same reason, and Bill blurted out that there wouldn't be black kids at our school anymore, since Sid had been the only one.

Lisa was so mad at Bill for ruining the moment, she hardly spoke to him for a week. The freeze-out might have lasted longer, but somebody's grandmother died, god bless her, leaving a ramshackle saltbox overlooking the bay that was perfect for a shack party. Most of her stuff had been moved out already, but there were still a few chairs and whatnot, and the taps ran and toilets flushed, which made it a five-star. When I arrived, half our school was packed into the little house, and two different Skid Row songs were blaring from competing ghetto blasters.

"Georgie Girl!"

Lisa's boyfriend, Keith. We didn't know each other well enough yet for him to be calling me that, but he had a joint in his hand and probably knew where Lisa was, so I smiled and pushed my way over to the staircase where he was sprawled.

"I'd offer you this, but Lisa says you're insane when you're high," he said. "You punch people or what?"

"Only until they're unconscious. Where's Lise?"

"Living room. Hey, Joshua's back in town, if you're looking for some action."

I fluttered my eyelashes at him. "But Joshua and I aren't married."

Keith sat up and leaned toward me, and I could see how

bloodshot his eyes were already. "Why do girls always have to be in love to have sex?"

He was too stoned to be having this conversation with his girlfriend's best friend, and I said so.

"I'm just asking."

A flash of Lisa's red hair in the next room. Keith had red hair too, and neither of them seemed to know how much the twin vibe creeped everyone out.

"No offense," I said, giving his cheek a pat as I turned to leave, "but most of you suck at the sex part, so there's nothing else in it for us."

I crowd-paddled to the living room past town boys, farm boys, mountain boys. A bunch of them were measuring their heads with a TV cable. "One more year," I said when I reached Lisa.

She didn't have to ask what I meant, just handed me a sticky bottle of Long Island Iced Tea and a plastic cup. "A wise man once said, if you can't make it better, you can at least make it blurry."

"Which wise man was that?"

The sound of peeing from the other side of a closed door answered, so loud it seemed to be hitting the bowl from a very great height.

The door swung open. Bill was only five eight with sneakers on and had a way of walking with minimal bounce, a gliding slouch across a room. Back then he was slightly overweight and this side of slovenly, but he had honey-colored curls that no girl could resist touching and absolutely nothing embarrassed him. He was the opposite of Lisa, who was small but ridiculously strong, with huge, kinky red hair that was moussed, diffused, straightened, and sprayed to sculpture-like perfection. She carried herself so confidently, yet would be mortified by the badly timed squeak of a vinyl seat.

Bill held out a china mug with a picture of Prince Charles and Princess Di on it for me to slosh in some booze. "What?"

"Did you find that in the bathroom?" Lisa said. "You don't even know what it was used for."

"Let's toast," I said quickly, before Bill could bug Lisa with a crude joke. "To Nat and her brave battle with the Double Dragon." (She was locked in her bathroom for the night after eating a funky pizza slice.) "To Sid and his tight leather pants—especially the leather pants. To a bitchin' senior year. And to the five of us being together again next year, somewhere far from here."

Lisa waved her cup vaguely toward us. "Yeah, Nat, Sid, cheers. Do you believe in love at first sight?"

"No," I said, using the neck of the bottle to guide her cup into a more upright position.

"I do. But, George, he's not looking at *me*."

I twisted around and saw Joshua Spring angling himself into the living room.

The history here is that Joshua Spring was in love with me

and had always been in love with me. It started on the first day of first grade when he trailed Lisa and me into the schoolyard at lunchtime. I reckoned he had one of two possible agendas: showing us his bird, as Dougie O'Donnell and Patrick O'Connor had done when they cornered us at recess, or stealing my Han Solo action figure. Instead, he took a plastic ring with a heart-shaped sapphire from his pocket and pressed it into my hand. Then he bolted, leaving a trail of big muddy footprints to his hiding place behind the hippo slide.

You can see under a slide, right? The only reason his head seemed to disappear into the hippo's nostril was because he was so tall for his age. We decided that Joshua Spring was too dumb to pay any more attention to and ignored him until he moved away a few months later, after his parents split up. Every time he came back to visit his dad, he was several inches taller—and still in love with me. It was like a sickness, and by the time we got to high school, I think he kind of hated me for it.

Now here he was, hanging out with a bunch of stoned jocks, including Keith, Lisa's boyfriend and Joshua's default best friend whenever he came back to town. Joshua was another half foot taller since I'd last seen him, easily six three, and he was genuinely, astoundingly *hot*. He had a jaw, for Christ's sake. Most of the boys at our school didn't have jaws yet, especially the jocks, with their baby fat and thick jowls. Their faces just sort of slid into their necks. And from that look Joshua gave me before turning away, I knew that however old I got, even when I was eighty and my boobs were dangling by my ankles like old-timey Christmas stockings filled with one orange apiece, Joshua would be there waiting for me. Hotly.

"He has a girlfriend," Bill said.

Lisa stared at him. "Impossible."

"Fact."

"Who? He just moved back."

"*Back* back?" I said. "Permanently?"

"Christina with the face," Bill said.

"Can't be serious," Lisa said. "Keith hasn't said anything about it. If they are together—*ish*—technically, you can't become boyfriend-girlfriend in only a week, and—"

"*Dude*," Bill said. "When's the last time George talked to that guy? Him looking this way doesn't mean they're hooking up."

I shrugged. Because Joshua was now standing in front of a crumbling fireplace that had a mirror built into the mantel, and I knew that he could see me behind him, and he was watching me watching him watching me.

I was leaning against a sideboard in the dining room, drinking directly from the bottle of Long Island Iced Tea, when Joshua finally made his move.

"Where are Lisa and Keith?" he asked. Super-laid-back. As though he hadn't been giving me lingering looks for an hour.

I nodded toward the corner, where they'd stacked themselves on a kitchen stool. "Brother-sister quality time."

"I'm never going to get used to that." He took the bottle from me, sniffed it. "Jesus. It's like plane fuel. What did you cut it with? Tap water?"

"Yup."

"You want some of this home brew instead?"

"Nope."

I knew one thing about the Spring family's home brew: no one tried it twice.

"That would be a good nickname," he said. "Home brew." His hair was bronze colored, his skin a similar shade from his summer tan. "I guess that's stupid." He handed the bottle back.

"No, it's just, you're the most uniformly colored person I've ever seen."

"I know. I'm like a big beige crayon."

"Not beige. Camel? Bile?"

If you want to get a hot boy to headlock you, and I'm not saying I did, that's how you do it.

"Hey! Stop putting the moves on my guy!" Christina yelled from the kitchen.

I didn't know much about Christina Veinot: eleventh grade, popular, probably one of the Veinot Dairy Veinots from Veinot, a little ferrety in the face. But I could tell she was only partly joking and magnificently sloshed, center of gravity up in her head, makeup running, hair wet against her T-shirt. Bill had started a game of bobbing for beer caps in the corroded sink.

"We were fighting over you," I said. "You're so pretty."

Joshua and I were reclining against the sideboard now. His arm felt hot against mine. I knew we looked good together, my dark Irish coloring contrasting with his beach boy glow. Lisa and Keith were grinning at us with unabashed glee.

Christina seemed to be contemplating a comeback as she stood there, head bobbling around. Then she threw her arms up and screamed, "*Whoo-hooo!*" which made everyone else scream, "*Whoo-hooo!*" and *that* was a shack party. That really was the best we could come up with when we all put our heads together and decided to have a good time.

"Whoo-hooo," said Joshua, raising his bottle of home brew. His mouth grazed my hair as he leaned over and murmured, "You want to get out of here?"

"What about . . ." I nodded toward Christina.

"Oh, we're not . . . We're just hanging out."

I glanced at my watch. An hour left before curfew. If I couldn't find someone to drive me home for midnight, I'd be facing the Sergeant. Or would I? My father was—well, let's say, under the weather. Maybe he wouldn't be waiting up.

"I've had only a few sips of this," Joshua said. "I'll get you home on time. Promise."

We drove to the shore, where we lit a fire and huddled together against the cold wind coming off the bay and ignored time passing. Yeah, he said something mildly ignorant about Kuwait and, yeah, something that might have been racist about Saddam

Hussein, and yeah, okay, we ran out of things to say about two minutes after that, but he was sweet and he was gorgeous and he smelled like woodsmoke and strawberry gum and boy, and he looked at me like I was the only girl there had ever been.

Which is when I began to worry that he'd heard about my slutty period in eleventh grade. Nothing serious, a bit with the *whooring*, as Lisa put it: three guys at East Riverview, our rival high school. I'd wanted to lose my virginity with minimal fuss. Not that I wouldn't have preferred it to be with a special someone who could make it beautiful and meaningful and full of harps and fireworks, but since there was no special someone, and not much chance of one appearing out of the fog, I wanted to get it over with. That led to crashing some parties on the other side of the county line and meeting Leon, whose most winning quality was that he was someone I didn't have to see every day. And that led to a couple of bonus boys to confirm that the problem with sex wasn't Leon's undescended testicle but that sex was overrated. At least, sex with guys from East Riverview.

The new moon was bright in the sky as Joshua pulled me close. I'd made out with lots of boys, but hadn't felt anything like real love, not since Han Solo. I'd convinced myself I wasn't built for it, that I'd never understand a ballad. Now it was like every line of our story had been writing us to this moment by the sea, the formerly heartless girl in the arms of the perfect guy, who had been in front of her the whole time.

Soft at first, it was a whisper of a kiss, like a strawberry secret.

And then: like getting rammed with a deli-sized bologna.

"I'm so sorry," I said, after audibly desuctioning my very wet mouth from his and dabbing it with my jacket sleeve. "I'm still hung up on Leon."

The name just slipped out.

"Leon."

"You don't know him."

"The guy from East Riverview?"

"Um . . ."

"The guy who used to go to basketball games dressed like a woodchuck?"

I'd forgotten about that. Leon had been East Riverview's mascot in junior high. Or was it that East Riverview didn't have an *official* mascot but he came to the games dressed as a wood-chuck anyway? Even after they asked him to stop.

"Different Leon," I said. "I'm sorry, I think you got the wrong idea."

He was swallowing a lot. Oh, he was going to cry. Oh, he *was* crying, tears running down his cheeks, ragged breaths. He sobbed and sobbed and *sobbed*. I started casting around for a piece of driftwood so I could do the humane thing.

"Joshua—"

He was up and running, his giant footprints a good six, seven feet apart in the sand. After I smothered the fire, I found him in his car, face buried in his arms against the steering wheel. He mumbled something that sounded like "Just get in."

We sped down into the valley much too fast, gravel pummeling the car like bullets. "I love this car," Joshua said. "I *love* this car. I'm going to frickin' *die* in this car."

"We're *in* this car!"

He swerved severely and I screamed. "Rabbit," he said.

We didn't speak again until he pulled up in front of my house. "Joshua . . ." The light in my parents' bedroom snapped off. "Let's pretend this never happened. I promise not to tell anyone if you don't, okay?"

He tried to smile, eyes glistening with a fresh tide of woe that he was barely holding back.

"Okay, good. We're going to have the best year. You'll see."

I made the mistake of deciding the phlegmy sound was Joshua Spring agreeing with me.

TWO

"**L**eon," Lisa said. "Of the thin lips. And one ball. *Really.*"

We were having tea with Bill and Natalie in our usual booth at the Grunt, an old-school diner with blueberry-colored walls and mismatched dishes from every decade but the one we were in. Nat was leaning on Lisa, still fragile after her bout of food poisoning, which hadn't stopped Bill from ordering a jumbo root beer float and hoovering it down in front of her. Not that Nat ever looked sturdy. She was skinny, white blond, and tree-limbed, all long bones and sharp corners.

Lisa eased her off and scooted out from behind the table to come around to my side. She began sniffing me like a police dog searching for clues: down my hairline, along my cheekbone, around my ear, up again. She *always* knew when I was holding out on her, and she loved inventing new ways to make me crack. I did not flinch, I did not flinch, I did not flinch—until her tongue darted out and flicked my nose.

"*Ugch*," I said, palming her face away. "Alright."

"Alright?"

"Alright."

"Say it."

"I'm not hung up on Leon."

Bill pawed a paper napkin out of the dispenser and passed it to me. "Keep licking. See what else she says."

Lisa slid back into the booth beside Nat. "First of all, I can't believe you thought anyone would buy that. And second—me and you, Keith and Joshua, two best friends dating two best friends? Don't you get how perfect that would be?"

"You could date *us*," Bill said, indicating himself and Nat.

I didn't like it when Lisa called us best friends in front of the others, though it was true. You might think of your friends in tiers, but you don't have to remind them of it.

"You're my fourth–best friend at best," Nat said to Bill, lowering her head to the table.

He wagged his straw at her like he was erasing what she'd said. "On the bright side, George has just become the big fish that every guy in school wants to haul into his boat, if you know what I mean. If you don't know what I mean, I mean this bitch, right here, is now so ungettable that everyone wants to get her. And if you don't know what I mean by *get*—"

"We got it," Nat said. "While I was sitting on a toilet with a bucket on my lap, George was rejecting the hot new guy—and it only made her more popular! Bravo, life!"

Bill and I weren't doing a good job of holding our faces in check. In fairness, it wasn't always clear when Nat was trying to be funny.

Lisa glowered at us and stroked Nat's hair. "You shouldn't have led Joshua on if you weren't interested," she said. "Keith is so pissed."

"How did I lead him on? By standing next to him at a party? Letting him drive me home?"

"Leaving his girlfriend behind without a ride, kissing him . . ."

I'd been betting that Joshua wouldn't tell Keith any of it, never mind the kissing part, and I could see Lisa was doubly pissed that I hadn't told her myself.

"You said she wasn't his girlfriend. *He* said she wasn't his girlfriend."

"Duh. He lied," Bill said.

I guess I knew that, but I didn't have to admit it.

"Well, that is *news* to me. Also, technically? He kissed me. Which was . . . it was . . ."

Lisa was giving me the eyebrow, not blinking, not getting it.

Sid would have. Bill did. "Bad breath? Biter? Did he lick around the outside of your mouth?"

Nat propped her head up on her arm to look across the table at him. "You really have to break up with Tracy."

"Not Tracy. Remember Becky, the cocker spaniel from hockey camp? My mouth, my nose, my *ears*." He leaned over until his face was nearly touching mine. "So, what was it, little snake darts? Nasty *hiss-hiss* coming at you? *Hiss-hisssssss—*"

I shook him by the shirt collar until he was all hissed out. "Anaconda tongue, you jackass."

"That's it?" Lisa said. "Oh—phew!"

"No phew," I said. "How did we get to phew?"

"You can rehabilitate a bad kisser."

"Hell no," Bill said. "You can take mediocre to okay, and you can get from okay to some approximation of the fundamentals of good, but you'll never get from bad all the way to good. Right, Nat?"

"If you ain't got no rhythm, ain't no one gonna teach you to dance."

"Exactly. Homegirl."

"*Geo-or-or-orge*," Lisa groaned. "We're talking about a love story more than a decade in the making. Are you going to walk away because of one bad kiss?"

In a word: "Yup."

"That's cold-blooded, even for you."

"But good news for the Face," Nat said. "Who, by the way, is coming over."

I twisted the soreness from my morning run out of my back and glanced behind us. Christina was leaving three tables of Elevens, who all watched as she strode toward us. She was a tiny thing—pipe-cleaner legs, dirty-blond hair down to her waist, razor cheekbones. She could cut a person. Would. And I had sort-of stolen her sort-of boyfriend in front of half the school. That was a big shack party.

We were starting senior year as the reigning popular group, as you define it at a country high school. We'd inherited it. In eleventh grade, pre-Keith, Lisa had dated a senior, captain of the basketball team, and the rest of us got pulled along with her. They graduated, we got bumped up, she dumped the old captain for the new captain, simple as that. We were set to be the most benevolent and boring ruling class of any high school ever. We weren't bullies, didn't get up in anyone's face. People *liked* us. We spent most of our time doing exactly what we were doing at that moment—making each other laugh and/or ganging up on someone for their own good—and we collectively gave only enough of a crap about where we stood not to give it up.

But the new Elevens cared. They were a large group, slitty-eyed girls and thickheaded boys. Always posturing, always too loud, always lip-curling, slow-moving, filling as much space as possible. They could not wait until we were out of the way.

I wasn't worried about what this Joshua stuff might mean for us, but I could sense Lisa's nerves the way she could sniff a lie as I exhaled it. She was, after all, my top-tier friend, and she'd been looking forward to senior year since kindergarten, when she started transforming herself from a frizzy-haired bundle of ugly duckling into the second coming of Molly Ringwald,

Breakfast Club edition. Plus, she and Keith had gotten caught between me and the Tongue and the Face. So when Christina stopped at our table and said, loudly enough to be heard by her friends, "What's wrong, George? Sex injury?"—I wasn't having it.

I stood up so I was towering over her and stretched my back again, nice and easy. "Yeah," I said, "but, baby, I'm good to go again if you are."

It wasn't one of my better lines, but in the pause that followed, I learned something about Christina Veinot: she wasn't up for a quick comeback. That left her with pretending to laugh or being humorless and earnest, and her group didn't do earnest. They learned that from us. She went with a small head shake and faint smile, like we were a couple of gal pals exchanging quips. "Well, say hi to Joshua for me," she said, the hardness gathering again behind her eyes.

It didn't take much—just a fragment of movement, just the suggestion of a step in her direction. "George!" Lisa said.

But I was already sitting down, having gotten what I wanted from the Face.

She'd flinched.

"You have no filter," Nat said as we watched Christina retreat to the ladies' room.

Bill finished noisily vacuuming up the last of his float. "*George* has no . . . Dude, you've never had a period that I did not know about."

"Not having a filter means you say everything," Lisa said. "George will say *anything*."

That's what made them a little afraid of me, the Elevens, what made me the enforcer of our group. The girl version. I mean, I was wearing a delicately beaded yellow cardigan over my Tito Jackson T-shirt.

"Only to the Elevens," I said.

THREE

I dreamt all night about eating wet, sour sausages, and when I woke up, with a start, realized I'd forgotten to brush my teeth. I did remember to wear my running clothes to bed, the surest way to get my arse out the door on a Sunday morning, but the gloomy sky outside my bedroom window was begging me to burrow deeper into the covers.

"George? George!"

I leaned in the doorway of my parents' room. The Sergeant was sitting up in bed wearing an old RCMP training depot T-shirt, his reading glasses, and a skirt of newspapers.

"You can't get out of bed to yell at your beloved daughter?"

He glared as he swung his leg out from under the covers and thunked it on top of the papers. The skin sewn over the place where his foot used to be was chafed and purple, angry-looking.

A double row of black stitches circled his leg, just below his calf.

"You can't put a nice sock on your stump for your beloved daughter?"

"My cast fell off," Dad said. "Now, if you're all wrung out of concern, go over to the dresser and get that stack of bills and the checks and a pen. And my cigarettes."

In my defense, had I said something more sympathetic, Dad would have batted it away. We were alike in that respect, two cats who only wanted to crawl under the bed and be left to suffer alone. He didn't seem to be in pain, though who could tell? For weeks he'd walked on a foot that was dying before he would admit where the smell was coming from.

"How does a cast fall off?" I asked as I collected everything. "Were you dancing the shimmy?"

"The swelling went down all of a sudden. I was taking a whiz when I felt it slip. It was grab it or graffiti the wall. I protected the wall."

"Had to be a hero."

"Your mother's fond of that wall."

I placed his things on the bedside table and took in the leg situation. Though the skin was irritated, the stump itself had a surprisingly soft look. It was flattish across the bottom with rounded edges, like a Nerf baseball bat. "Dad," I said casually, lest a cat claw shoot out from under the bed, "do you think it's okay for it to be out in the open like that already?" He'd been home from the hospital for just over a week.

"We're waiting for the doctor to call back and say whether the local ER can put on a new one or we have to drive into the city." He pointed to the end of the bed. "Sit. We're overdue for a discussion."

For the past thirty-two hours I'd been nursing a false hope that for once Dad would let something slide, as though they'd removed his personality with his foot. "If this is about Friday night, I missed curfew by five minutes, max," I said, perching on Mum's side, which was tucked in already, her slippers neatly aligned with her bedside table.

"It was twelve twenty-seven and that was not Lisa's car. You think things are going lax around here because I'm short an appendage?"

My eyes drifted back to the stump then to the crusted-over cut on Dad's forehead. He'd fallen getting out of bed a couple of nights earlier, having forgotten the foot wasn't there anymore. It was hard to fathom how you could fail to remember such a thing, even while groggy on meds, even for a second.

"Well?"

"Joshua Spring drove me home."

"Ah, the Springs. I had to pull his mother over twice for driving under the influence."

"Just because his mother—look, he drove me because Lisa has a one-o'clock curfew, like a normal person. He has a girl-friend."

Sort of.

Mum appeared in the doorway, carrying a stack of linens. "His father had a wife, but that didn't stop him from getting frisky with the dental hygienist," she said. "Oh, Paul, I can pay those bills. You're supposed to be resting."

"I'm *sitting*. Aren't you supposed to be going somewhere with those sheets?"

Mum looked down at the linens in her arms. "I am."

When she'd gone, Dad said, "I'm giving you Abe. As soon as I can talk your mother into taking the Honda."

I almost rolled off the bed. Borrowing my parents' cars required heavy negotiations unless I was driving to work, and Abe was Mum's baby, a secondhand 1975 Lincoln Continental Town Car. It was a ridiculous vehicle—tan colored, size of a small apartment, impossible to park—but Mum was convinced it was safer than Dad's little Honda, even though she was always clipping things with that wide-ass hood.

"I don't know what to say."

"You don't know what to *say*?"

"I mean, thanks. Really, thanks."

"Well, let's face it, kiddo. You'll be doing a lot more of the driving while I'm laid up, helping your mother and brother. It's only fair. But no more missing curfew. You have a car and no excuses. And hear me now: no bringing babies into this house."

"Wha—Where would I get a baby?"

"You get pregnant, you're on your own. I'm not your aunt Joanna, running a day care for her offspring's offspring."

"Oh my god, Dad!" The unexpected sight of the empty cast lying on a chair in the corner of the room brought my voice down a few octaves. "I was only a half hour late."

And my slutty phase was ten months ago, thank you, not to be revisited.

"Kids your age, on the brink of being sprung from high school, they decide the world has nothing left to teach them. This is your idiot year. You'll never be stupider in your life." He lit a cigarette. "Do me a favor and fetch that ashtray from the guest room before the rest of me gets incinerated."

I paused at the door. "Is that what the hospital did with your foot?"

"No, they mounted it on the wall."

Before his surgery, the only place my father was allowed to smoke was in the basement with the door closed. There wasn't supposed to be an after location.

Mum was making up the bed in the guest room. "Did you know that Dad is smoking in—Who's coming over?"

"No one," she said. "I'm moving in here for a while."

"Why?"

"Because your father is smoking in our bedroom. Don't fuss about it, hey. The doctor doesn't want him quitting just yet."

"I'm pretty sure he said that smoking could damage his blood vessels. Oh, and kill him."

"And later he said he'd never seen someone go through a more violent withdrawing than your father when he was in the

23

hospital. Now. George."

Now period George period meant *Pay attention.*

"Dad's got pain enough. We're not putting him through *detoxivacation*"—not a typo; this is how my mother talks—"at the same time. Soon he'll be able to make it down to the rec room, and then maybe he'll be in a mood to quit."

Mum raked a hand through her hair, which was dark and wavy like mine but coarser and aggressively pruned into a no-nonsense, silver-streaked cap. Her attention had drifted to the window. "Should have done something different in the garden this year. One day I'll rip the whole thing out and start over." She sighed. "I say that every year."

Down the hallway, a loud thud. "George!" Dad bellowed.

"Go on, see what he dropped," Mum said. She handed me the gigantic spleen-like ashtray I made for Dad in first grade. "And give him this before he gets ashes on the bed. I'll be there in a sec."

My younger brother, Matthew, was lying unconscious on the carpet of my parents' bedroom. "Did he see the stump?" I asked Dad, nudging Matty with my toe.

"What do you think?"

"I think he might have seen a stump."

"Jesus, Mary, and Joseph," Mum said, pushing past me into the bedroom. "Did he faint, Paul? What are you two doing, just watching him?"

"Here, put him on the bed with me," Dad said, clearing

away the newspapers.

"I don't think bringing him closer to it is going to help."

"It's what they call exposure, Marlene. He has to confront his fears. What would you rather, drag him all the way to his own bed?"

When Matthew came around, next to Dad—who'd tucked his leg back under the covers—he was the yellowy pale of raw chicken. At fifteen, my brother had a Victorian constitution that was unlike anyone else's in our gene pool. He passed out at the sight of blood. He'd been known to pass out at the *thought* of blood. Or vomit. Or mucus. Or earwax. Or hair in his food. He fainted at the hospital watching Dad get prepped for surgery. Later, in the cafeteria, remembering Dad getting prepped for surgery, his pupils one-eightied and he slid gently under the table.

"Did you dream?" I asked him. Matthew had once said that being out for a minute or two was like being asleep for hours, with vivid dreams, sometimes nightmares.

He shook his head and pointed in the direction of Dad's leg. "Are you going to take it out again?" he asked.

"I'm not cruel," said Dad. "Don't mean it ain't *there*. Aw, son, don't start crying now."

"I can't help it. It's so unfair."

"What is? The partitioning of my foot and myself?"

He looked at Dad incredulously. "*A pebble*."

My father cut his toe on a sharp pebble at the beach. He

didn't notice it at first because the feeling in his feet wasn't great from the diabetes, ignored the cut when he did find it, ignored the infection that developed in the cut, ignored the gangrene-like symptoms that spread from the infection, and then faster than you can say *transtibial amputation*, the doctor was telling him the whole foot and ankle had to go.

This was the first time his bad habits had seriously caught up to him. He'd been living like he was on a campaign to do himself in as quickly as possible without using a traceable weapon. Smoking? Check. Buttered donuts? Check. Exercise? Please. And he got away with it too. He passed every health test those Royal Canadian Mounted Police threw at him, year after year. You'd think getting diabetes would have smartened him up, except, so what? Have your slice of pie, or three, since Mum's already shoving a needle of insulin into you. On the days he'd let her, that is, because he didn't like the side effects and often couldn't be bothered. Then he gave himself a teensy cut.

"Fair is for sports and the application of the law and not much else," Dad said. "Life's a bad writer, son. So this is what's happening. I'm going to pay the bills. Your mother is going to drive me to one hospital or another—"

"Local," Mum said. "I called the doctor again. But we'll have to go into the city Friday afternoon."

"I'm paying the bills. Your mother is driving me to the local ER. George is getting ready for work. And you, son, you will practice the tuba, as you always do, get ahead on your recommended reading list for school, as you always do, moon-walk through high school, graduate at the top of your class, and save us all."

That my father talked like this about Matthew all the time, that Matthew didn't even *have* a curfew because he was too reliable and socially awkward to need one, had gnawed at me forever, but for once I didn't care. Because a Friday afternoon trip to the city meant my parents would stay over with Aunt Joanna and her offspring and her offspring's offspring so Mum wouldn't have to drive home in the dark. And there was already talk of a shack party next week, and I desperately needed to kiss someone to replace the memory of Joshua Spring's tongue. And I now had a car.

FOUR

After I polished all the windows and threw open the wooden shutters to let in the sun that was burning off the rain clouds, I stood on the steps of the hundred-year-old lighthouse, took a cigarette pack out of my pocket, and thought about the day when my friends and I would move far away from the valley, with its pastoral, old-world charm and soul-sucking tedium.

There wasn't a drop of water to be seen: the north mountain stood between the lighthouse and the bay. Farmland stretched in all directions, across the valley and up the slopes. It was as though the lighthouse had gotten lost on its way to the ocean, or maybe took one look at the eighty miles of volcanic range blocking its path and given up. In fact, it had been brought inland from a tiny island that was eroding. Some historian types had it taken apart and moved it to this fallow plot, then put it back together again with the help of the East Riverview shop classes. I was the keeper, the only staff member, with volunteers from the heritage society filling in the gaps.

I pulled smoke deep into my weary lungs and held it for as long as I could stand it. I'd gone overboard on my morning run, the kind of workout that turns you uniformly red from the neck up, ears and all, and you're still dewy with sweat when you get out of the shower. I was trying to run off the seven pounds that I'd gained over the summer—the corner pockets of flesh that had appeared on the insides and outsides of my thighs, which my scrawny brother was too happy to remind me about every chance he got. I was also trying to run off the sting of what Lisa had said at the Grunt, but her words ricocheted back at me with every step: *cold-blooded, cold-blooded, cold-blooded. Even for you.*

It hadn't pricked at the time, but was slowly working down like a splinter, past Joshua, past all the other disappointments with all the other boys, to a more sensitive place. Because the truth was, I didn't miss Sid and it had been worrying me. I mean, I *did*, but not the way I thought I would, the way you were supposed to miss someone you'd been hanging out with since seventh grade. I missed him like my favorite TV shows in the summertime. Sure, it was better when he was around, but I knew we'd be together again, and I could go a whole day, even two, without thinking about him. I didn't say this to the others, just nodded like a robot when they talked about missing Sid and said, "*So much.*"

I'd called Nat from work to ask if she thought I was cold-blooded. You had to be certain you wanted the answer when you asked her about these things because she always left you a bit clenched. "You don't do big feelings," she'd said. "You hate ballads, sappy movies. The last time I saw you cry, you'd caught your hand in a car door."

"I have feelings. You're the one who always pokes me with your bony elbows if I try to hug you."

"Yeah, but you never lose your head. You probably need to if you're going to fall in love." She sighed. "Anyway, that's what I told Lisa when she called to talk about you."

Typical.

"What did she say?"

"She said you don't want to be a member of a club that will have you as a member. Woody Allen."

"Woody Allen quoting Groucho Marx."

"*Point being*, if Joshua didn't like you, you'd be all over him. You just like the chase. Oh, and Bill said—she called Bill too—he said that's true, but no one would think it was a big deal if you were a guy and we should lay the hell off."

The closest farm stood on a ridge above the lighthouse, and through a stream of exhaled smoke, I could see a man winding his way down from it. He drifted in one direction, then the other, occasionally ducking into the tall grass. Was he searching for something or hiding from it? I scanned the fields, but the only unusual sight was him.

As I watched this silent film, I thought again about what Nat had said. Was that my thing, catch and release? Or was I too sane for love, if that's even possible? I took another drag from my cigarette and forced myself to remember the kiss and the moments leading up to it. Maybe Lisa was right; maybe it hadn't been so bad. Maybe I should give Joshua another— I gagged as the memory of his tongue reached the back of my throat.

Sputtering smoke, I saw the man was close now, approaching the lighthouse through the waves of grass. He was almost severe-looking, dark and angular, but an overgrown haircut and beard softened the edges, as did the rosy sunburn across his nose. Slightly taller than I was, midtwenties, I guessed, with an expression that was somewhere between concerned and amused.

He was not from the valley—that I could tell at a glance. A flare shot through my chest. It felt like fear, but it wasn't fear.

"Light," I said. By which I meant *Lighthouse is open, if you happen to be interested in touring this lovingly restored local landmark,* but *light* was all I managed to croak out.

"Life?" he said.

"Yes." I cleared my throat. "I am choking on life."

"Sounds like a line from my high school diary."

The cute response would have been *Best thing I ever read,* but I was reminded of something Sid said when he heard I used to fantasize about being the fourth Pointer Sister: "Sometimes you don't meet a person a minute too soon." I stubbed out my cigarette. "Sorry."

"Sadly, that is true," he said mildly. "Do you work here?"

"Did you want a tour of this lovingly restored local land-mark?"

"Actually . . . I was wondering if you'd seen a pig."

"Ever?"

Don't ask me why; just my smart-ass reflex.

"More like, in the last twenty minutes. I'm after one that's gone AWOL."

His voice was a little raspy, like the feeling of running your hand along a plane of unfinished wood.

"Ah. No, sorry."

"Man, I don't want to sound paranoid, but I think he's *hiding*," he said, scanning the fields. "I usually have to sneak up on him."

I resisted the urge to ask how often he lost this pig, and instead offered to take him to the top of the lighthouse to see if we could spot it from the lantern room.

The lighthouse had a narrow, three-story wooden tower attached to an octagonal-shaped building that housed the old diaphone fog signal. From a distance, it reminded me of a lady in a bright white dress with an extravagant bustle. The heritage society had restored the interior to its original condition and then some: hand-woven rugs, wrought-iron banister, grand-father clock, an adorable potbellied stove in the keeper's quarters.

"This is impressive," he said as we climbed the curved metal stairs, our footsteps echoing through the tower, and it was, especially up in the lantern room, where the sun blazed in as it set between the mountains.

"Behold—the hay," I said, tapping one of the diamond-shaped windowpanes. "Very dangerous at night. Not to mention the potatoes. The apples. Over yonder, the corn."

I was aiming for witty and had landed somewhere closer to Lisa's father after a couple of wine coolers. So I was grateful when he said: "Have you ever lost a vessel?"

"I crash them into the corn all the time."

"I think I've heard your siren song. That's home, the farm-house on the ridge."

"And you live there with this pig?" I asked.

"Why do you sound surprised? Don't I look like a local?"

"Uh . . . yup."

"Damn, I thought I was pulling it off. How did you know? Is it the threads?" He was wearing a checked shirt with the sleeves rolled up, jeans, Converse, and the leather-brimmed lighthouse keeper's hat that he'd plucked from its hook downstairs.

"I dunno, you can just tell. You don't have an accent."

"Neither do you."

"I live in town." Like our village was so much more sophisti-cated than the surrounds. "We have a *traffic light*," I added in the poshest voice I could muster.

"I think you're saying I couldn't even pass for a townie. Out of curiosity, where would you guess I'm from?"

I pretended to give him the once-over, but really, what did I know? I'd never been anywhere. "Hard to say."

"If you had to guess—"

"Away."

"I come from *away*?"

"My nan would say you're a Come From Away. But then, she also thought Catholicism was a cult."

He leaned in. "Isn't it?"

Yes, I liked him. I liked how he played along with my late grandmother's casual bigotry, how talking to him was like a good tennis rally, how he purred with energy that made it seem like he was moving even when he was not moving. He was cool yet curiously eager to blend into a place where bean sprouts were still considered ethnic food, and his absurdly blue eyes were as round and bright as a toddler's. And so when I spotted the pig trotting from one cluster of trees to another, I did not say anything quite as helpful as *There's the pig.* I said: "Where *are* you from?"

"Out west originally, but I've lived all over. And now I'm here."

He didn't offer a reason why. Did people like him just decide one day to become people like us? The only Come From Aways I knew were the parents of Doug O'Donnell, former first-grade flasher, present senior-class stoner.

"That was a trick question," I said, "if you're not from any-where."

"Afraid so. Tell me, Captain—"

"Keeper—"

"Tell me, Keeper, what would happen if I flipped that switch over there?"

"You'd turn on the lantern. . . ."

He flashed a mischievous smile and glided toward it, his eyes never leaving mine. I waited until he had his hand on the switch.

". . . and *blind* us. You have to flip it and run."

The switch was for a small lightbulb on the ceiling. The real lantern switch was wired down to the service room, but you had to leave the lighthouse to see the effect, and I wasn't ready to let him go yet.

He slumped. "If you can't play with the big toy, what do people do for fun around here?"

"Depends on what you mean by *fun*. Shunning outsiders?"

"Talking is nice." He took off the cap and handed it to me, and I felt the flare in my chest again. "How about Long Fellows? Is that a good place?"

I shrugged, made a noncommittal so-so face. Did he think I was old enough to get into a bar? Bill claimed I could pass for nineteen, the drinking age Down East. He was always trying to get me to pick up liquor for him, but when your dad's a cop, you know how to measure risk. I drank, but not too much, stayed away from drugs, although that was more because my friends couldn't stand to be around me when I was high.

How old was he anyway, this Come From Away? Twenty-five? He wasn't nearly as tall as Joshua or as stocky as Bill, but he

was more *present* than any boy I knew, more substantial somehow, and as I watched his shirt pull about the roundness of his
shoulders as he leaned against the window frame, I thought—

You are the one
Solid the spaces lean on, envious.

Sylvia Plath.

"Are you worried about something?" he said.

"Just thinking."

"About what?"

"Poetry. I read some great stuff in your high school diary."

He grinned. "Are you a poet?"

"God, no. Do I look like a poet?"

He studied me. "As a matter of fact, you do."

I kissed him. Stepped through the beam of sunlight that had
turned the lantern lens into a giant gold jewel and kissed him.
Even as I felt his whiskers against my skin, his lips on mine,
his tongue, blessedly, nowhere, it seemed impossible that I was
doing what I was doing, but from his startled look when we
pulled away, I knew that I had.

I also remembered that I'd been smoking and probably had
potbelly-stove mouth.

"Sorry, I needed to replace a bad sensory memory," I said.

My heart was thudding so hard it felt like my shirt was
moving.

"How bad is bad?"

"It made me hate being a mammal."

Now he was laughing. "Oh man, did you tell the guy?"

"Of course not!"

"So, he's still out there, thinking he's okay? What if he goes his whole life and no one tells him? Wouldn't you want to know? I'd want to know. At least, I think I'd want to know."

I had a feeling he thought that if he kept talking we wouldn't have to deal with the question of what happens next. I didn't even know his name. He was a complete stranger, a grown-up. And yet I had a hankering to do something insane—*more* insane than kissing him—to grab him, climb him, bite him till he bled.

"Oh, there he is! The pig!" And with that, the stranger sprinted down the perilously steep staircase.

I couldn't see anything piglike, near the trees or anywhere else, was sure he was trying to escape me, that I had literally repelled him back up the mountain. But as I stepped out of the lighthouse to watch him bounding through the fields after the invisible pig, he turned, cupped his hands to his mouth, and shouted, "See you at Long Fellows!"

FIVE

When Dad first joined the RCMP, my parents had to relocate every few years and never knew where in the country they'd end up. Which might sound exciting, but we're talking rural detachments, from the northern wilds of Nowheresville to the windswept grasslands of Greater Middle of Nowhere. Then, some luck: Dad was transferred to a detachment in the valley, so they got to start their family close to where they grew up, and Matthew and I got to spend our formative years visiting Nan on Sundays, which is probably why Matty is still today a nervous wreck. She dropped her teeth into everyone's glass from time to time, but she definitely chose his the most.

Lisa and I met in a skating class when we were five, added Natalie in fourth grade, and the boys in seventh grade, and through all those years we thought that I was always on the verge of leaving, that my family could be transferred to Who Knows Where at any time. But Dad stayed at that detachment for almost nine years, and then he went to another valley detachment, and in the end, it was Sid who moved, just because his parents wanted to try living somewhere else, and Vancouver is about as different and far away from the valley as you can get. It seemed the only way the rest of us would get out of there, including me, was by making sure we had somewhere to go.

Which is why Lisa and I were in Veinot that afternoon, a town with five traffic lights and a mall with a bookstore that stocked a grand total of one book about theater. She was hoping to be chosen as the director of the school play to help her application to a program at Aurora University next year.

"I'll give you five bucks if you ask the old lady at the counter for *The Joy of Sex*," I said. "Got it right here in my pocket."

"Ten," Lisa said.

"I don't have ten."

"Well, do you have lip balm? Because I can't find mine." She was elbow-deep in her gigantic purse, like she was trying to birth a farm animal.

"You aren't going to leave without paying for that."

A young clerk was standing at the end of the aisle. He pointed to the book that Lisa had tucked under her other arm as she rummaged around in her bag.

"No," Lisa said. "I mean, *yes*. Yes, sir, I'm going to pay."

She was now holding the book out as though it was

radioactive. As bossy as Lisa could be with her friends, she was way too fragile outside of the bubble wrap of our group to take on an adult, even an adult wearing seven layers of Band-Aid-colored pimple cream over his forehead acne and a name tag that read "Brenda."

I swiped the book from Lisa and speed-walked over to the clerk, giving his sleeve a conspiratorial tug. "Hey, buddy, she just found out she's really sick," I whispered. "Not the best time to accuse her of stealing."

The clerk's hand went to his forehead. "I didn't mean to . . . My boss asked me to check because we've been losing a lot of stock to high school kids."

"We go to Aurora," I said. "The theater program?"

"Yes, of course—"

"Besides, if she wanted to steal something, would she take . . ." The book was called *Observatory Direction*. It looked impenetrable. "Do you think someone who would read a book like this would steal a book like this?"

"No, of course. Of course not. I'm so sorry."

I took the five-dollar bill out of my back pocket and put it in his pink-smeared hand.

"It's more than five, but . . ." He waved the bill in Lisa's direction and said, with too much pep, "Sorry for the misunderstanding! Hope you'll be alright!"

I hurried Lisa out before she could decide she felt bad for him. "If you said what I think you said, you're going to hell," she said. "And not regular hell, the hell below that."

"The furnace room of hell?"

"The hidden bunker under the furnace room of hell."

She was still a little nervous as we wandered the makeup and perfume aisles at Thompson's, and being overly cautious about keeping her hands fully visible. None of the clerks bugged us, but none of them offered samples either, even though we were practically the only customers, and they were standing around with samples in their hands. A Clinique clerk, with bangs so teased and stiff they seemed varnished, tapped her red fingernails loudly on the cash register.

Lisa peered into the makeup case in front of her. "George? Uh, what time do we have to be at the hospital?"

"What time . . ."

"Chemo starts at six, which means what for prep?"

She was somehow managing to act like she was unsteady on her feet and trying to hide it. I covered my smile with a cough. "Five thirty," I said. "But you know they're always running late."

"Let's not hurry, okay? Let's try to enjoy *today*."

The clerk straightened up and tugged on the hem of her jacket. "Would you two girls like some lipsticks to take with you? What about nail polish? We've got *very* cheerful new colors."

"Oo-de-lally!" Lisa said as we left the mall, a pound of samples clacking inside her bag. "Now we can go to the bunker below the furnace room of hell together."

"Like we always dreamt!"

"Hey, listen." She bumped me with her elbow. "Will you be my stage manager? If I get the play?"

"Why wouldn't you?" Lisa had earned it, taking any backstage job she could get in every single school production, including the lip-synch battles and that traveling hypnotist who turned twelve kids into a flock of chickens. And though only seniors were allowed to direct the play, she'd had the chance to direct a whole bunch of things at this fancy theater camp that she and Sid had gone to the previous summer.

"Someone else might submit a better proposal," she said. "Anyway, will you?"

"Is that props and stuff?"

"Yes."

"Are you asking me because you think I have a natural talent for stage managing?"

"Yes."

"Are you really asking me so I'll make sure everyone listens to you?"

"Yes!"

"Okay, cool. Sure."

We wandered over to Pierre's, a chain of secondhand clothing stores. You could practically see the stench of BO rising from the clothes piled up in the raised wooden bins, but there weren't many other options around, unless you wanted to dress like a secretary or somebody's mum.

It had taken me years to find a vintage-based uniform that I liked and Lisa approved of. Sneakers or boots, always. Jeans, almost exclusively, in various states of wear, with an inverse relationship to the frilliness of the top: new for a well-worn blazer; ripped for a dainty cap-sleeved blouse. I put my hand on a polyester cruise shirt with a palm-tree pattern. "You want Old Lady When She Was Young and Chic," Lisa said.

"What's this?"

"Old Lady."

"Maybe that could be my thing. I don't have a thing."

"I don't have a thing either."

"Yeah, you do. You're all theater and *look at me expressing myself I'm so expressive.*"

"Whatever are you talking about?" She was doing some kind of veil dance with a large beige girdle.

"If I wore this top, people would say I'm quirky."

"Don't take this the wrong way, but the only quirky thing about you is wanting to do it with Tom Petty."

"Speaking of hot guys . . ." I'd been trying to get up the courage for three days to tell her about what happened at the lighthouse, the longest I'd kept anything from her. She wouldn't approve of what I'd done, plastering myself to some stranger's face when there was a perfectly good Joshua Spring to tickle my tonsils, but I couldn't tell anyone before I told Lisa, and if I didn't tell someone soon I was going to lose it. Each night when I curled up in bed, I cradled the memory of the stranger like a new toy, though it was beginning to seem less like a memory than a dream.

"We might need one of these next year," Lisa said, holding up a Noel University jersey. "What's wrong? Why are you smiling without your eyes?"

"Nothing—"

"Bullshite. You look like a stuffed elk."

"It's just, you don't want to go to a university up the highway, do you?"

"It wouldn't be so bad. We'd know lots of people, and they have a great theater program."

"As great as Aurora's?"

"Sure. Well, almost. And their sports teams are definitely as good."

"Basketball, maybe." Wait. "Is Keith planning to go to Noel?"

"No. I don't know. If he gets in."

They'd only been dating for two months. We'd been talking about moving to the city together forever. Aurora also had a history of science program that Nat had her eye on, a hockey team the boys approved of, and for me—it was in the city, and since I had no idea what I was going to do with the rest of my life, that was all I needed.

"It's not like we'll be stuck at home," she added. "We can still live in the dorms."

"You think the Sergeant is going to cough up for residence

if I can stay at home and drive that car he gave me?"

"You could live in that car. It's big enough."

"We could *all* live in that car."

I smiled, this time with my eyes, I hoped, but my warning gauge was still quivering in the yellow zone.

"Forget I mentioned it," Lisa said. "It's way too early for us to be thinking about this. Who knows what could happen in a year?" She picked up the girdle and slingshotted it at me. "Were you going to say something about hot boys?"

It no longer felt like the right moment to describe how the stranger's hand had tentatively touched the small of my back when I kissed him, how I could still feel the weight of his thumb pressing lightly on my flesh through my shirt.

"I was going to say that we should hit the mall again, see if that cute guy who gives free drinks to redheads is working at Orange Julius today."

Lisa plopped her bag on top of the wooden bin. "I'll give you five bucks if you can convince the lady at the register that you were wearing that shirt when you came in." She plunged her hand into the bag and pulled out her wallet triumphantly. "And a thousand more if you promise never to wear it again."

Keith and Joshua were hanging out in the food court with some guys from the school basketball team and the county swim team, which Joshua had joined. "It's like how you can entertain a kitten all day with just a cardboard box," Lisa said as we watched them from behind a pillar flicking straws and ketchup packets at one another.

"Seriously!" one of the basketball players was yelling. "This dog had balls as big as my TV set, I *swear*."

"Did you know they would be here?" I asked.

She shook her head. "I *swear*."

"Let's go over." I peeled off the horrendous shirt, which I still had on over mine, and crammed it into her bag. "If we act like the other night was a big deal, it'll be a big deal and it'll suck at school next week."

"I don't think that's a good—"

I was already walking away.

"Hey, guys," I said. "Whatcha doing? Planning your prom dresses?"

"Go to hell," Joshua said.

He tried to storm off, but he was so big and the space between the tables was so narrow that his arm caught mine, knocking me sideways. He walked on.

I stood there for a second as everyone stared at me, Lisa with her hand over her mouth. Then I followed him, my sneakers squeaking on the fake marble floor, grasped his elbow, and yanked.

I was usually pretty good at comebacks, which sometimes made me think I was smarter than I actually was. Much like how my long, wavy hair compensated for the plainness of my face, so naturally I was hugely vain about it. No, I'd never been in an airplane, never met a Jewish person (I think?), wasn't entirely sure if Mongolia was a real country that just sounded like a made-up place, but I could be quick, and quick can make up for less than clever.

Not this time.

"I don't *think* so, asshead!"

Joshua turned around, eyes dark with rage, and it dawned on me that he could hurt me if he wanted to. Then he blinked and the first tear dribbled through his long bronze lashes.

Shocked, I let go of him and he ran. He ran straight into a lady carrying a tray of drinks, and left grape soda footprints in his wake.

The rest of the guys started howling, even Keith.

Fucking boys.

SIX

"See you at midnight," Matthew said.

I laughed. For the record, not because I planned to end up at Long Fellows that night. Oh, I'd thought about it—not going to the bar but the fact of it, sitting beside the highway east of Veinot, luring a Come From Away with its semiliterary name. If only I had a fake ID, I might have been able to manufacture a chance encounter, but I had no excuse for strolling past the farm up on the ridge that wouldn't be obvious and desperate.

As predicted, Mum and Dad had decided to stay overnight at Aunt Joanna's in the city, a two-hour drive away, and as predicted, there was a shack party to celebrate the end of the first week of school. I was driving Nat, so I wasn't drinking, but I wasn't coming home before I had to either.

"What makes you so sure I won't tell Dad you missed

curfew?" Matthew asked, peering into the pot of chowder that Mum had left simmering for us on the back of the stove. She had also set out two bowls, two napkins, two spoons, and a note reminding us that there was bread in the breadbox. (There was always bread in the breadbox.)

"Because you're not a tattletale."

"I'm not lying if he calls and asks if you came home on time."

"Say you don't know. Say you went to bed early and didn't wake up when I came in."

"But what if I didn't go to bed early?"

I tried rolling the sleeves of the fitted green tweed blazer that Lisa had found to go with my sloppiest Levi's. Better down, she'd say. I rolled them down. "You're in tenth grade now, buddy. You gotta learn to handle this stuff."

He scowled a pretty scowl at me.

Anyone who thinks that being attractive isn't an advantage in life, let me introduce you to Matthew Warren, a brainy, frail young fellow of fifteen who was growing up in a place where, for boys, size and athletic ability were the only currencies accepted. I had height and hair, and the rest was makeup and attitude. Matthew had refined features: large brown eyes, perfectly arched brows, and very white, very straight teeth. There was something almost glossy about him, the way light reflected off his surfaces. Being pretty—and you would have said he was pretty, not hot, since he hadn't sprouted hair below his eyebrows yet—meant that people thought of him as quiet and shy, not scrawny and awkward. He wasn't weak, he was unthreatening. He wasn't nerdy, he was smart. And he knew the trick to preserving all this was to say as little as possible at school, which made him slightly mysterious. But in another year or so, once everyone in his grade was driving and going to shack parties, he would be exposed.

"Do you want to come?" I asked. "Check it out?"

He scrunched his well-sculpted nose. "Nah. I'm going over to Tim's to play Super Nintendo."

"Suit yourself. Just don't not come because you're chicken."

"Why would I be chicken?"

"The Elevens?" His wince told me I'd nailed it. "You'd be with seniors."

"Yeah, but you won't be around all the time, and I don't need some of those guys knowing my name."

I reviewed the week with Nat on the way to the party. Mr. Gifford, who we'd had for economics in eleventh grade, was teaching a new class called Modern World Problems, and what with everything going down in Somalia (famine), Bosnia (genocide), and Nicaragua (earthquake), it seemed unlikely to make him cheerier. Someone was pregnant already—one of the headbanger girls—and Doug O'Donnell had been kicked out of class twice. The first time was for having bong breath at nine in the morning, the other for standing on his desk after Miss

Aker delivered a moving sermon on the power of poetry.

History and French were the only classes that Joshua and I had together, but it had been hard to avoid him all the same. He didn't exactly blend into the crowd, and we kept making accidental eye contact. I noticed he'd started focusing on the tops of the lockers as he navigated the hallway, rolling over the occasional tenth grader who got in his path.

Since there was no shack to be had that weekend, the party moved out to the quarry, which was basically a gigantic sand pit. "What are you going to do if Joshua comes?" Nat asked as we turned onto the dirt road that would take us through a patch of forest to the pit. Drunk kids were stumbling out of the parked cars that lined the shoulder.

"Oh, probably make him cry."

At that moment my headlights lit up Lisa walking with Keith and Joshua. She hadn't told me they were coming together. After what happened in the food court, did she honestly expect that we were all going to hang out?

I realized then that I should have told her about the stranger. If she knew I'd thought of him approximately ten thousand times over the past week, she'd understand what a lost cause this thing with Joshua was—not because I was being my usual heartless self, but because no matter how hot and adoring he was, no matter how perfect it would be if two best friends dated two best friends, nothing Joshua had said or done since the first grade had filled me with as much hope as hearing the stranger say, *See you at Long Fellows!*

"I changed my mind. I'm not staying," I said, pulling over. "Bill's driving. He can take you home."

"Is he bringing Tracy?"

"I think so."

Nat made a noise that was somewhere between a retch and a squawk.

"Then go with these guys."

"You can't avoid Joshua forever. You'll never get to be around Lisa."

"He'll get over it eventually," I said. "Right now, I can't take him losing it again."

"Couldn't you . . ." She sighed and tugged on her denim miniskirt. It was a warm night, but Nat was always cold and I hadn't been able to talk her into a jacket or tights. Now her thighs—or as Bill called them, her skin-dipped femurs—were covered in purple blotches. "If I were you and Joshua was all over me, I'd pretend to like him. At least I'd have a date for the prom."

It's not like that hadn't occurred to me—faking it. Please. I once convinced Bill for a whole day that I wore glasses (an old pair I borrowed from Dad's dresser) and always had, just because. But I didn't know how you were supposed to fake *feelings*, and anyway, once someone has told you to go to hell, it's probably too late.

"Here." I shrugged off my blazer and passed it to her, then

reached into the glove compartment, took out a set of keys on a hot-pink feather chain, and handed them over too. "Go have fun. If you want to try your luck with the Tongue, you have my blessing. And give Lisa her keys for me?"

She'd left them behind in Modern World Problems. I was forever rescuing Lisa's keys.

"Yeah, alright. Thanks for the jacket."

"Are you okay?" I asked as she got out of the car.

Nat pulled the blazer over her thin sweater and leaned in. Her lemon-scented hair lay against the green tweed like finely sheered white ribbons. "I'm okay," she said. "I just wish someone would look at me the way Joshua looks at you."

Eleanor Roosevelt said that you should do something every day that scares you. You say she wasn't talking about sneaking into a bar. I say you can't prove she wasn't.

Long Fellows could pass for a small hockey arena from the outside, with its aluminum siding and tiny windows. Even after I ditched Nat, I hadn't meant to land there, idling in the orange lights of the parking lot. But that word, *cold-blooded*, had taken occupation of my head again with the slamming of her door. It followed me through town, back onto the old highway, into the next town and the next. I couldn't outdrive it like I couldn't outrun it.

I wasn't cold-blooded. I had kissed a stranger at the light-house. I wanted to do it again. And then what? I thought, not-so-gently rapping my forehead on the steering wheel, will you date this grown man? Bring him home and introduce him to the Sergeant? Do you think he's sitting at the bar dreaming of pinning a corsage on you before the prom? Lisa was wrong: I wanted to be a member of a club that *wouldn't* have me as a member.

Maybe, *maybe* if I saw him one more time, I could get him out of my system.

I cataloged the risks as I tugged open the door to the bar and crossed a dark, crowded, smoky room with black walls, a sticky floor, and "Sweet Home Alabama" thumping on the sound system. I could get booted for underage drinking. I could spend hours listening to "Sweet Home Alabama" on repeat and he might never show up. He could show up, take one look at me, and head for the hills again. But whatever came, it would evaporate into the night. I was more than twenty miles from home at a honky-tonk bar off the highway that no respectable person—in my parents' eyes, anyway—would go to. I probably wouldn't see any of these people again. As long as the bartender didn't call the cops on me, no one had to find out.

"Pint of Morgan's, please."

"You got ID?" the bartender asked.

"Not on me." I leaned into the bar. It was as sticky as the floor. "Come on, I've been here a million times."

"No, you haven't."

"Sure I have." I mouthed a little *Whassup?* to an imaginary acquaintance in the corner. "Remember, we had that whole conversation about—about draft beer."

"No . . . Hang on. Are you the one who always pays more for two half-pints because they stay colder than one full pint?"

"That's me. Half-Pint. That's what my boyfriend calls me. I call him Home Brew."

Nice touch, I thought.

"So why did you order a full pint?"

"Because you won that argument."

He considered this, then brightened. *"Drink faster."*

"Drink faster. *Classic.*"

He poured me a Morgan's. "I'm cutting you off at two, and don't show up without your ID again."

"Does a whole pint count as one or two?"

"One," said a voice behind me. I thought, briefly, it was the stranger, but when I turned around all I could see was a wall of hair. It separated into a group of long-haired dudes pushing through the crowd toward a small stage. Great. Would they be doing heavy metal covers or new country covers?

Another beer appeared at my elbow.

"From the gentleman at the end there," the bartender said. "That's two of two."

I peered down the bar.

Oh.

No.

The "gentleman" had to be fifty. He did not have all his teeth.

"What's the matter?" asked the guy on the stool beside mine. He looked like he belonged to a biker gang: long, curly black hair, shiny and crisp; bushy beard; leather jacket that was too tight around his gut.

"Am I supposed to go over and talk to him now? The guy who bought me the drink."

He leaned over and checked him out. "No."

The biker guy gave the gentleman a salute that seemed to mean both *thank you* and *piss off.* "Come on, Half-Pint. Band's about to start."

I was uneasy as I followed him to a table. Did sitting with the biker guy mean I was now *with* him? He was slightly terrifying, with his furrowed expression and a large circular burn scar on his temple that suggested something deliberately pressed against it. One hand was wrapped in a thick, dirty bandage. "Barbed wire," he said. "Maybe I was somewhere I shouldn't have been."

"Does it hurt?"

"Let's see." He slammed it against the table, making me jump. "Yep."

The biker guy's name was Bobby, and he'd founded the band when he was sixteen. They were based in the city but played bars and campuses all over. "Mick there on the left is filling in for me tonight," he said. "Hope he's good. He's a friend of a friend who happened to be around."

Among the long-haired and long-bearded dudes onstage was the Come From Away, tuning an acoustic guitar. His eyes were even brighter under the stage lights, his hair mussed and shirt rumpled like he'd traveled all night to get to the gig. Now I knew his name: Mick.

Bobby was leaning back on his chair legs, missing nothing. "I think I've seen him around," I said.

"Don't bullshit a bullshitter, Half-Pint."

Thankfully, the band started to play. It wasn't metal, wasn't country, wasn't exactly rock or blues. It was a twang and a rumble and a steady, easy beat, and as they hit the bridge of the song, unexpectedly, between the second verse and the chorus, Mick looked up from his guitar, directly at me, and it was like a door opened, blowing winter air over my skin.

At the end of the set, Mick stepped up to the center microphone. "Thanks for letting me join you tonight, all you long fellows," he said. "Before we go, another for the drunks at the back. But we need Bobby since this one is still new to me."

Bobby pushed back his chair.

"And bring your friend," Mick added, turning to tune his guitar.

"Let's go, Half-Pint. You'll know the words."

Of course I knew the words, like everyone else in this corner of the world. As soon as the first chord rang out on Mick's guitar, they flooded my head. But that didn't mean I was prepared to sing to a packed bar. I'd never sung in front of an

57

audience, other than carols in the elementary school Christmas pageants, and yet somehow there I was, onstage next to Bobby, still clutching one of my two pints, blinded by the stage lights and vibrating with panic.

Bobby's voice was incredible. He may have looked like a biker but he sang like an Irish rover. He gave me a gentle push toward another mic as he rounded the first chorus.

> *For when I am far away*
> *On your briny ocean tossed*
> *Will you ever heave a sigh*
> *Or a wish for me?*

Beyond the lights, people were nodding and hooting and whistling. I whistled back. I whistled the entire next verse, the room growing still as I trilled the familiar melody. Oh, sure, Bobby could sing like an Irish rover—but I could whistle like a goddamn nightingale. It was the only real talent I had, and until then, it had been hard to imagine a more useless one.

Bobby joined me for the chorus and we did the rest of the song together, my whistling rising above his baritone. I couldn't see Mick, but I could feel the thump of his foot on the floor behind me.

In the movie version of my life, I will raise my pint triumphantly as the music ends, setting off a roar from the crowd. They will demand an encore, something from Motown, naturally, and the entire bar will sing along. In reality, I was having a hard time shaking off the panic, despite the sloppy but enthusiastic applause.

I felt a hand on my arm. "That was amazing," Mick said. His smile faded with the stage lights. "Or a really shitty thing to do to you."

It all suddenly felt very precarious, the revelation that I was underage imminent. If there was any movie moment in the making, it would be someone who knew my parents parting the throng with shouts of "*J'accuse!*"

"No, it's cool," I said unconvincingly.

"I'm sorry. You struck me as fearless." Reading the question on my face, he added, "You made a strong first impression."

He placed his guitar on its stand. "Let's get a drink. That beer looks like it's warm."

"I should probably go. I have to be up early tomorrow."

This was not remotely true. They were touching up the paint at the lighthouse, so I didn't have to go in at all.

"So do I."

He took the glass from my hand, set it on a speaker. Waited.

"Okay," I said. "But you'll have to buy."

SEVEN

He sat in the chair cornered to mine and slid a beer across the table toward me. "Were you the guy who said that a full pint only counted for one?" I asked.

He nodded. "Are you really nineteen?"

"I'm really twenty."

"I guess I've hit that age where everyone born after 1969 looks like a kid to me."

"Please. You're barely old enough to be my babysitter."

"Not barely. You know, we've . . ." He swirled his finger around his mouth. "But I don't know your name."

"Sorry about that."

"Don't be sorry. Scared the shit out of me, but . . ." I was sinking in my chair as though I could hide behind my pint. "Anyway."

He fiddled with the broken end of a dart that was lying under the edge of the ashtray.

"George," I said.

"Short for Georgia, Georgina?"

"It's my middle name. Frances George."

My father had been so sure I was going to be a boy that he didn't allow my mother to talk about girls' names and wasn't prepared to change course after I was born *sans le schlong*. He let Mum tuck a girl's name in front of it, but no one called me Frances.

Mick grinned.

"Shut up. Frances isn't so bad."

"I know. That's my name. Probably spelled differently."

"Your name is Francis? Your mother named you Francis."

"Yeah—she did."

"I thought everyone was calling you Mick."

"Short for McAdams." He nudged my elbow with his. "Did you ever tell that guy he was a lousy kisser?"

"Uh-uh."

"It's none of my business, but you should know that guys don't start getting better until—well, until they're old enough to be with women who are old enough to tell them that they need to do it better."

The beer was soothing my nerves. Or maybe it was how our arms touched as we leaned in to hear each other and his breath fell on my cheek when he talked, how his shin grazed mine whenever his leg got jiggly under the table. "In case you're worried, you're more than fine," I said. "Although you do like a run-on sentence."

"You're fine too. And a bit young for me."

"Live a little, Francis."

I pulled out my cigarette pack. He took it from me and lit two, passing one of them back. The cigarette was slightly moist from his mouth.

"Lived a lot, Frances," he said. "Trying to rein it in now."

We talked until the light flickered for last call. About how I couldn't play the guitar after two years of trying to teach myself because I couldn't get past the F or B-minor chords. Old-school country music composers that I'd never heard of but now wanted to listen to. How the colors of the sky at sunset—lilac, amber, coral, sometimes scarlet—reflected in the still waters of Lake Victoria in Kenya, a place I knew nothing about and now wanted to visit. About why I preferred to be called George and he preferred to be called Francis but ended up being called Mick wherever he went, and how "George and Francis" sounded like storybook characters who would get lost in Manhattan in one book and go on a safari in another. About how we'd both marry Tom Petty, given the chance, but would settle for Gord Downie of the Tragically Hip. Somehow I managed three good jokes and didn't let on that the reason I'd never gone anywhere and done anything was because I wasn't old enough to be in the room where we were sitting.

"One more?" he said, the lights flickering again.

"I think I've had enough."

"You couldn't be a cheaper drunk."

I'd been nursing a warm pint for an hour.

A wide arse encased in tight, acid-washed jeans pressed against the edge of our table as one of the rougher-looking lady dart players made out with a guy who may or may not have been my toothless friend. It was hard to tell from that angle and with her entire head in his mouth. "Sorry," she said over her shoulder to us as they shoved off, obviously going home together.

"I live with an old man, the owner of that pig," Francis said to me. "Puts a damper on my social life."

He was telling me this, I understood, to explain why he couldn't invite me back to his place. What could I say? Not that I lived at home, that's for sure. That I lived with someone too? He might think I meant a guy.

"I should go," I said. "It's late."

I was feeling awfully wobbly, given how long I'd made that last pint last and was supposed to be driving home, and I wondered whether it would be better or worse when I stood, but I couldn't bring myself to be the first one to push back my chair, to move out of the halo of warmth around us. Francis didn't get up either, just tossed the broken dart piece into the ashtray.

"Yo, Micky! Half-Pint!" Bobby yelled from across the room. "You want to go stand on the bottom of the sea?"

The incoming bay tide can overtake a man on a galloping horse, my mother says. I always picture a rogue wave rearing up and snatching anyone in its path, dragging them back into the sea, which is not how it goes. Point is, the water level rises fast.

"What's fast?" Francis asked.

"In total, say, six hours?"

He laughed.

"No, but they're the highest tides in the world! Every year someone needs to get rescued. People think they're okay because they seem to have all this time, and then they're cut off from the places where they can get back up to higher ground."

"People like me, you mean. Come From Aways."

"The sea will take you," I said. "She's thinking about it right now."

We'd driven to the Baptiste Peninsula in the band's van. "I probably shouldn't be getting into a vehicle with strangers," I said to Francis as we climbed into the back. "Oh well. I won't rape you."

"I notice you didn't say you wouldn't ax murder us," Bobby called from the front.

When we got down to the shoreline, Bobby wandered off to perch on a large boulder like an ancient god of leather. The other guys walked ahead, taking the only flashlight with them. Or maybe it was more that Francis and I lagged behind and so we had to navigate the beach on our own by moonlight.

The wet slapping and sucking noises our shoes made in the muddy sand were almost embarrassing. We stepped over driftwood and rocks slick with seaweed, the tree-lined cliffs looming overhead. By sunrise all of this would be underwater.

The moon disappeared behind a cloud, the stars following behind it like they were dancing into the wings, and I could no longer see Francis, who was ahead of me. We stopped walking at the same time.

"Steady," he said.

We were sort of laughing, but the darkness was unsettling. It felt as though we were drifting in space, as though the galaxy had winked off and there was nothing but infinite blackness around us.

It reminded me of the first time Dad took Matty and me outside in our pajamas to play hide-and-seek at night. "A tree's a tree whether you shine a light on it or not," he'd said. "Keep your cool until your eyes adjust. And stay clear of the skunks."

Truth is, I'd been leaving on the hall light at bedtime. If my parents turned it off, I'd creep under my bed and sometimes stay there until morning. He was trying to teach us not to be afraid of the dark. But it was night that scared me; darkness marked the time to be afraid. I'd pull up the covers, mash my head into the pillow, and then my fears would arrive like worms wriggling out of the earth. What if the Soviet Union declared nuclear war? What if I never grew boobs? What if something happened to my family?

A hand swatted my hair. "Whup. Sorry."

Then it was on my shoulder, sliding down and grasping my arm, and then I was holding on to him too and we were laughing again at our fumbling and nervousness in the dark.

"Steady," I said.

His fingers traveled up my arm, faintly brushing the side of my breast, and traced along my throat. His face was close to mine and our mouths found each other, and when the clouds parted again I sensed the return of the light but did not open my eyes, just slipped my hands under his jacket and around his back—until the explosions erupted around us and Francis drop-pinned me to the mud.

Over his shoulder, the sky was filled with pink and orange and blue flames, fiery confetti raining down into the bay. "Are you seeing fireworks too?" Francis asked. "Or did I hallucinate myself into a movie?"

"Life's a bad writer," I said, gently pushing his elbow off my hair. My underside was groaning from tip to stern from its collision with the ground, but its complaints were smothered by his body running the length of mine, the feeling of his weight on me.

"I'm sorry, are you hurt?"

"Not at all. Thanks for taking the bullet for me."

We lay there gazing at each other as the damp seeped into our clothes. I could have stayed like that all night, had Bobby not sprinted by. We helped each other up and followed him.

"What the hell are you doing?" Bobby was shouting when we reached the rest of the band, who were about to set off another round. I hadn't noticed before that the bassist—whose name I think was Tommy—had brought a big backpack with him.

"Why did you think we came out to the beach?" Tommy said.

"To experience one of the world's natural wonders?"

"No, to set off fireworks."

Bobby turned to Francis. "I didn't see this," Francis said, holding up his hands. "If you put all that away, I didn't see anything."

"Jesus, Tommy," Bobby said. "Mick is a cop, and it ain't legal to set those off around here."

That sound fireworks make on their descent back to earth? That was the soundtrack to my heart explosion, the fragments raining down upon my other vital parts. And then the questions started firing. A *cop* cop? In the valley? Municipal force or the RCMP? Did he—oh my god—did he know my dad?

"I'm not on duty," Francis said. "But, yeah, it would be better if you didn't break the law in front of me."

By the time we got back to the parking lot at Long Fellows, it was nearly three and I was as sober as sin.

Francis walked me to my car. He didn't look or move like any cop I'd ever met. Not that they don't come in different shapes and sizes, but the job hadn't taken over his body yet. He didn't pull his shoulders back, stand on his heels, assess the scene before acting. How could that live-wire energy be contained by a uniform?

"She's quite a ride," he said, stepping back to take in the Town Car.

"He," I said.

"Oh, he. Sorry."

I was too tired to explain that his name was Abe because he's a Lincoln, get it, ha-ha. Ha.

Francis felt around in his pockets. "Don't have a pen, do you? Or are you in the book?"

"Don't worry about it."

He knew something had shifted, just not why. "You don't date cops."

"Well . . . I've got a history you probably don't want to know about."

Excellent. Now I sounded like I had mental problems or a criminal record.

"I shouldn't be getting involved with anyone," Francis said. "Should stay focused on the job, settling in."

I didn't know what to say. I couldn't say I didn't like him, because I did. I liked him so much that knowing he was about to disappear was almost physically painful. But I was also very, very close to throwing up.

"Here's a parting gift," he said, pulling a stone from his pocket and placing it in my hand. It was about the size of a peach pit, salmon pink, and slightly shimmery. "From the bottom of Lake Victoria. Kind of a good-luck charm."

"I can't take your luck."

"That's okay. It's not that lucky."

"Oh, *thanks.*"

"Maybe one day you'll go to Kenya and watch the sun set over the lake. You can exchange it for a luckier one if you need to." He opened the car door for me. "Meantime, if you ever want to practice chords, you know where to find me. Or whistle."

EIGHT

It was nearly dawn by the time I snapped off my bedroom lamp. I slept fitfully, in little sips, until I was awakened by my alarm—which I'd set on autopilot, forgetting I didn't have to get up—then the phone ringing, the door slamming downstairs when my parents returned home, Matthew's voice on the stairs. "I dunno," he said. "I went to bed before she got home."

A harrumph from my father.

I hauled myself out of bed, unsteady on my feet. I'd never felt more exhausted, was bizarrely hungover, given how little I'd had to drink, but needed to put up a good front. I stopped by Matthew's room, where he was curled up with a comic and the mug of hot milk my mother made him every weekend morning. "Thanks for covering for me," I said.

"I didn't. I went to bed early so I *wouldn't* have to cover for you."

He looked glum.

"What's wrong, buddy?"

"I was talking to Aunt Joanna this morning. She called to say Dad forgot to bring home a bunch of pamphlets they gave him at the hospital."

"I'm sure she can mail them."

"No, it's not that. It's— Do you know Dad's not supposed to be home now? She offered to put him up in the city because the surgeon wanted him to stay near the hospital, but he said he had to sleep in his own bed. Now Mum has to keep driving him in."

That my father's obtuseness would require our parents to go out of town regularly might have been welcome news twelve hours earlier, but I'd vowed as I was peeling off my muddy clothes and hiding them at the bottom of my hamper that I would never leave the safety of the house again.

"Are you really shocked that Dad's not letting people tell him what to do? Besides, can't blame him for not wanting to stay with Aunt Joanna and all her grandkids. She doesn't have room for him."

To say nothing of her youngest son, Junior-Junior, aka Randall, son of Randall Junior, grandson of Randall Senior. He was between Matthew and me in age, and already in ardent pursuit of a life of incarceration.

My parents hadn't talked much about the game plan with Matthew and me, but we knew that if Dad returned to active duty it would be a big deal for his detachment. He would be the first officer in the region, maybe even the entire country, to do the job with a prosthetic limb, and the staff sergeant was keen to see him do it. Sergeant Paul A. Warren wouldn't wheel away from that. His job was his whole life, other than patrolling us kids.

"Don't think I'm going to bed early every Friday so you can stay out all night," said Matthew.

"Trust me, old sport, you won't have to."

I followed him down to the kitchen. My mother was, as usual, in constant motion. Never hurrying, never stopping, like a shark. (One of those hammerheads, with the wide-set Disney eyes and upside-down smile.) She had scrambled eggs and cod-potato hash on the stove, folded laundry in the basket at her feet, a pile of pillowcases waiting on the ironing board in the corner. She must have gotten Dad up at dawn to be home before nine.

"You're very pale, Georgie," she said.

Dad looked up from his newspaper, antennae engaged.

"Really? Because I feel great!"

Steady.

"What did you do last night?" Dad asked.

"I went to Veinot to see if there were any help-wanted signs at the mall. For when my hours at the lighthouse go down."

"Mall closes at nine."

"Then I stopped off at Nat's to loan her my jacket. And then I sat out on the porch and read. Matty was asleep by the time I got in."

Checkable with an acceptable level of risk. Uncheckable. Uncheckable.

"You weren't cold?"

"A little."

"What book are you reading?"

"*1984.*"

"What chapter did you get to?"

What was I, an amateur? Next thing he'd be verifying the bookmark location.

"I finished it."

Three days ago.

"Good for you. Now stop hovering and sit down; let your mother serve you breakfast."

The smell of the cod-hash had become overwhelming, and my skull felt so heavy and tight around my brain, it was like wearing an old deep-sea-diver's helmet. "I think I'll skip," I said. "Go up and start the rest of my homework."

Ah, but he was not fooled.

"You'll be extra hungry for those beautiful chicken livers that we're frying up for supper." My stomach acid began to burble. "Is it just me or do raw chicken livers look like Jell-O made out of—"

"*Paul*," Mum said in a warning tone. She tipped her head in the direction of Matthew, who had stopped chewing and was staring at the saltshaker as though it could transport him to a better place.

"Burnt ketchup?" Dad finished.

Matthew swallowed. "Aren't you going for a run, George?" he said, an angelic smile on his perfect face. "Consistency is the most important part of a training program. And, you know, *oink-oink.*"

"Rest is important too," I said, trying to stifle a yawn and hitch up my pajama bottoms to cover my muffin top at the same time. Dad's eyes were lasering into me again. He was about one and a half seconds away from relaunching his investigation. "But of course I'm going for a run!"

Tying my laces took more energy and brainpower than I had in my reservoir. Mum sat on the porch beside me and did the other shoe. "Iris Perry's home from the hospital. They put in the pin."

"What pin?"

"I told you yesterday. Broke her shin falling down the stairs. Bone went clean through."

I didn't know who Iris Perry was. Didn't matter. Today it was her pin, tomorrow it would be Mr. Inglis's cat's tumor, and the day after that it would be somebody's cousin's friend's something. I'd long ago put together that my mother repeated this gossip, if you could call it that, because she didn't have a lot of stories of her own to tell.

"Are you sure you're not sick?" she asked, putting her hand on my forehead. "I could pick up some Pepto for you when I get the groceries."

Oh blessed saint of ideas borne out of desperation.

"Why don't I do that?" I said. "I'll take the car over to the track and get the groceries on the way home."

"Hmm. No, it's easier to do it myself than to explain which kind to get of what."

"Wouldn't you rather be out in the garden? How many more good days like this are left?"

"I suppose . . ." She squeezed my foot. "That's my good girl."

I hit the grocery store first. As usual, it wasn't as simple as pulling things off shelves, putting them into a cart, and going through the checkout.

Yes, Mrs. Greenwood, my dad is doing well. Thanks for asking.

Sorry, Mr. Richardson, I don't think he can talk to your neighbor about the dog poop on the lawn.

Actually, Donny, Dad was kind of wondering if you could dial 911 the next time your kid sets the basement on fire instead of calling our house.

At least people had stopped showing up on our doorstep to lodge complaints, now that word was out about Dad's surgery.

Afterward, I did a loop around town to kill time. It wasn't

one of the prettier valley villages, with their quaint churches and gingerbready houses. Many of the older homes like ours had fallen into disrepair, or the lots had been subdivided to make room for bungalows and split-levels, and there must have been a sale on turquoise, avocado, and mustard siding when the newer places were going up. The downtown was filled with nondescript storefronts, too ugly to be charming and not ugly enough to be romantic like some sooty old Welsh mining village. The only big industrial building was the "new" sawmill, which replaced the original in 1920 after the boiler exploded.

While stopped at our one traffic light, I opened my door and vomited onto the asphalt. I wiped my mouth with a receipt I found on the car floor—all class—sat up, and met the eyes of our principal, Mr. Humphreys, who was in the car perpendicular to mine in the intersection, his mouth an O. (There was no mistaking the red beard and red Afro. Lisa insisted that she and Keith could never stand near him at school because they'd seem like they were all part of a lost ginger tribe.) The car behind me honked loudly, and I peeled out through the newly green light, a tad too *Dukes of Hazzard*.

I parked at the arena, rested my head on the window. How long could I snooze here before the milk went bad? A day or two? I was just drifting off, hazily considering the best way to get my cheeks red so it'd look like I'd been jogging, when a loud knocking on the pane jolted my stomach into my throat.

Bill. He had a hockey bag slung over his shoulder, obviously on his way to practice. "Hey! What happened to you last night?" he said as I opened the door.

I pushed past him to a pile of leaves, and threw up again. Midretch, I saw he had followed me and was hanging on to the end of my ponytail. "Look, I'm holding your hair. That means we're girlfriends now, right?"

"Why are you talking at me?"

"Isn't that how this works? I hold your hair while you puke and you tell me that what I'm wearing isn't flattering and how to fix it."

I gave him a quick side eye. He had on his usual plaid shirt, long white T-shirt, and baggy jeans. "Where are the rest of the *Kids in the Hall*?"

"That's it. Let me bring you over here, girlfriend. Sit on the curb."

The remaining contents of my stomach started to rise but I managed to keep them down by throwing my head back and swallowing hard.

Bill said, "That right there was worse than watching you actually throw up."

"What's with the girl talk?"

"I'm the only guy in the group now, so I'm trying to fit in better."

My eyes began to water, mostly from the effort of not vomiting. "Never mind. I am not equipped," he said. "You need a real girl for that."

"I'm sorry. I just had a bad night and I don't want to talk about it."

"Okay, okay . . . There, there." He patted my shoulder so awkwardly that I laughed in spite of myself. "There, there, there. If it makes you feel any better, Tracy and I are probably going to break up again."

Bill had been dating Tracy on and off since the eighth grade. No one knew why they were together. Bill was fun and sloppy and sarcastic and unflappable, the guy you wanted on your team for a hot dog–eating contest. Tracy had two modes: sullen and boring. She had creepy little hands like bird claws and didn't talk much, except to nag Bill. Every so often they would break up—always her dumping him, never the other way around—and we'd have this surge of hope that he'd end up with someone we liked. Then they'd get back together again. Sid had vowed to bust them up permanently, but didn't get the chance.

"Aw, *shoot*," I said.

"At least you didn't clap, like Nat. She told me what happened at the food court, by the way. So does this mean that Joshua's face has melted?"

"What do you mean, melted?"

"Indiana Jones melted. Why are you not understanding me?"

"Because I'm not Sid. I don't get your inside guy references."

"Don't you remember the end of Indiana Jones, when they throw acid into the Nazi's face and it's all like, '*Aaaaaargh* . . .'?

That's how I feel every time Tracy and I break up and I get to talk to new girls and I find a gorgeous one and garbage comes out of her mouth. When I'm crossing the room to talk to her, I'm thinking, I don't care who she is, I don't care what she is, I want to stick my head into that no-man's-land between her boobs and have a nap."

"Oh, stop with your feminist rants."

"But the thing is, to gain entry into no-man's-land, you have to have a conversation, and when it turns out she's a moron, it's like she's not even *physically* attractive anymore. The moment she starts talking about how her cat peed on her bed because it was jealous of her old boyfriend—"

"She melts."

"Like wax. Listen, I don't have anything against the guy. Joshua. I just can't figure what you talked about that night. You didn't talk like *this*, that I know."

Until a few minutes ago, Bill and I didn't really talk like this either.

"We talked about school stuff, Saddam Hussein . . ." That was all I could remember. "What do you and Tracy talk about?"

"Nothin'. Sometimes her food allergies."

"The problem," I said, "is that Joshua *thinks* he fell in love with me at first sight, and everyone else thinks I'm crazy for not feeling the same. You and me, we're probably the only ones who don't go for that insta-love crap."

"I totally believe in that crap," Bill said.

"Who did you ever love at first sight? Tracy?"

"Hell no. My hockey coach."

"Come on."

"I'm serious. And Sid."

"Are you trying to tell me something?"

"I'm saying we call it love at first sight when sex is thrown in, but there are lots of different people you meet and you click and you *know*, you know?"

"I know you miss him, buddy."

"That's the problem. Tracy asked if I'd miss her as much as I miss him."

"You lied, I hope."

"I might have thought about it a second too long."

"You wiener."

"Well, guess what? This wiener loved you at first sight too, Georgie Girl."

I shifted uncomfortably.

"Not like that!"

"Yeah, yeah. Do I have to say it back?"

"Better if you didn't now that you've made it all cringey."

"Good. I'll express it in action." I patted his knee. "There, there, there."

NINE

"It's like we're not even going out sometimes, you know?"

This was how most of my conversations with Lisa started. In the middle.

"That's so typical of Keith," I said, dragging the phone over to my bed. It was almost noon and I still hadn't slept. "What did he do?"

"I was dropping off a mixtape I made for him, and then we went into the kitchen and he—he made a tomato sandwich."

"Oh my god!" I shouted.

"No, seriously, *a* tomato sandwich. One. If it had been me, I would have been like, *Keith? What? I'm making a sandwich. Oh? Would you like one too? No, thanks. Are you sure? It's no trouble. I'm sure. Okay.*" (Lisa did this a lot, acted out all of the parts, as though no one would get it if she only gave the highlights.) "Do you think this is his way of, like, asking for space?"

Keith wasn't that deep. He was a nice enough guy but, like all her boyfriends, about as complex as a baked potato.

"Probably not. You want me to break his knees?"

"Nah. I'm just calling to see if you're okay. You know I would have told you that we were bringing Joshua to the party if Keith had warned me, right? God, this is why I keep telling Dad we need a car phone."

"I know. Sorry for taking off like that."

"What *did* you do last night?"

Lisa had always been the first person I wanted to tell whenever something important or interesting or embarrassing happened. Sometimes I started rehearsing the story in my head while the thing was still happening. But sharing what happened with Francis would make it all the more real, and I didn't want it to be real anymore. If I could go to sleep, when I woke up I could pretend it had all been a dream.

"Listened to a bunch of cool music," I said. "You know, sharpening my edge."

"Oh yeah? Which one of your three records did you listen to?"

"The one that's so cool you've never heard of it. Dude, I gotta go back to bed."

"Hang on. I haven't told you about the party."

"Can we talk about it later? Sorry, I'm so wiped." The line went silent. "Lise?"

"Something's wrong, I can tell. What is it? Were you talking to Nat?"

"Wha? No, I— We'll talk later, I promise. When I'm alive again."

"Alright. Love you."

"Like you immensely."

"Love you."

"What you said."

"Love you."

"Me too."

"Good enough."

I was drifting off when Matthew started shaking me. "George!" he whispered. "George!"

"Buddy, I *am* going to sleep, if I have to kill us both."

"The guy's here for lunch. Just tell me quick, are we supposed to go down and eat with them?"

"Who is it?"

"A cop. The new one, I think."

"What new—"

My feet hit the floor.

I caught my breath when I saw him closing the trunk of his car from Matthew's bedroom window. His hair was freshly buzzed off, the beard shaved, but there was no mistaking those angles, that coiled energy in his body, or those eyes.

I heard Matthew collapsing onto the floor behind me, but

didn't turn around, horror-struck as I was by the sight of the blood splattered all over Francis's shirt.

Mum was little but she could move, and Francis had to do some fancy ducking and maneuvering to avoid her as she fired herself out of the house and ran at him. "It's not my blood!" he said, pirouetting this way and that. "Don't—please—you'll get it all over you!"

"My god, did you shoot someone?"

"No, no! It's cow's blood," he said.

Squeak of the screen door beneath Matthew's window. "Francis McAdams, I assume," Dad said.

"I would come over and shake your hand, but . . ."

"Feel free to stay where you are. You want to tell us about this cow you used to know?"

"A call came in while I was down at the detachment this morning; a farmer said his cow was stuck in the riverbed. She was knee-deep in the muck and we had a hell of a time getting her out, which, it turns out, was because she was delivering a calf."

"My land," said Mum.

"Calf live?" My father.

"Stillborn."

"Well, hate to be the bearer of bad news, but once word gets out that you responded to an animal call, on duty or off, you'll be getting them from all over the county."

"That's what they said at the detachment. Anyway, I

thought I had a spare shirt in the trunk, but no luck, and by the time I get home and back . . ."

"Don't be silly," my mother said. "Come hop in the shower and Paul will lend you something."

"Oh, sure," Dad said. "My tuxedo is back from the cleaners."

I turned and tripped over Matthew, who had come around but was still lying on the floor. Quick inspection: he'd survive.

No fully slept, fully sane person would do what I did when I got back to my room, tearing down posters and shoving any evidence that I was what I was—stuffed animals and magazines and school trophies and photos of my friends—under the bed. I tugged the coverlet down to hide the fuzzy duck peeping out. Yeah, that would convince Francis that I was—what? Some random adult who happened to be boarding with the Warrens? *Never mind my landlords. They're old and confused and think we're related.*

I opened my window and could hear Mum through my parents' window rummaging in their closet. "You're much trimmer than Paul, so I'm afraid we don't have a lot to offer you. It might have to be this."

"That's fine, Marlene. Thank you."

I waited until I heard my mother's footsteps go down the stairs and the shower start running, then poked my head out and stared at the bathroom door. He won't open it, I thought. Slip down the hall and be done with it. Do it. He's not going to open it.

This was all within about three-quarters of a second.

I skated down the hall in my socks, sending up sparks from the rug.

The door opened.

"Oh!" Francis's face lit up for a moment before the hamster wheel in his skull began to run overtime.

I put my finger to my lips. "I can't explain now," I whispered. "Please, *please* pretend you didn't see me, that you've never seen me. I'm sorry. I have to go."

"Wait!" he whispered after me. "I need a towel."

I got one from the linen closet. In the movie version of my life, I will bring it to him, lightly place my hand upon his chest, and rest it there briefly before floating away. But really, I just hurled it in his general direction and ran.

Didn't make it.

"Georgie!" Mum said as my hand touched the front door handle. "Where are you going?"

I snatched my economics textbook from the old hutch where we tossed our keys, hats, and mail. "To Lisa's. To study."

"The new constable is here to pay his respects. We're having a sit-down lunch."

"That's okay, I'm not hungry."

"I made *pie*," she said.

In Mum-speak, that meant attendance was nonnegotiable.

When Francis joined the rest of us in the dining room, he was wearing my father's old painting coveralls. "How do I look?" he asked sheepishly.

"Like you're going to fumigate the house," Matty said.

"Our son, Matthew," said Mum. "And this is George."

"Have we met before?" He sounded genuinely uncertain.

"Nope, nice to meet you," I said.

He nodded at my economics textbook, which was sitting beside my plate. "Do you go to Noel?"

Matthew snorted.

"Next year, maybe," Mum said. "George is a senior."

Did he pale? He paled. Now he was trying to compose himself by straightening his fork and knife, rolling up his sleeves.

"Is that a tattoo?" Matthew asked.

Francis pushed his sleeve up farther to reveal a swirly pattern on his upper arm shaped like a tree.

"Dad tattooed Mum's name on his arm after their third date," Matthew said. "When did you get yours?"

"When I was living in Ireland, working in a music shop." From there he backpacked around, he explained, working for a bookbinder in Italy, a record label in Austin, a water charity in Kenya—about ten years going from one thing to the next.

My mother and brother were impressed. My father was not.

"So, that was a decade well spent," he said. "And what brought you to the force?"

"I was ready to settle down somewhere. No, that's not true. Sorry, that's bullshit."

My parents exchanged glances.

"What's true is that I spent a long time trying to avoid the family business. I thought I needed a job that was just mine and, I don't know, cool-sounding. It's fun to wander for a while, but I started feeling like what I truly want is to feel part of a community. That's what I was missing all those years on the road. So I suppose I chose police work, Paul, because I need that anchor. The weight of that responsibility."

"*Geez*," Matthew stage-whispered to me. "*First-degree blow job.*"

"Matthew!" my mother shrieked.

Now that's what not having a filter sounds like.

"Sorry," Francis said. "I've still got that rookie attitude."

I could tell Dad was not yet impressed. "Where's this farm you been living at?" he asked.

"The closest town is Veinot."

"You want to anchor yourself to a rural community, it's good to live in town. Let people see you."

"I'd planned to, but then I met Rupert." Francis leaned toward my mother. "I'm letting a room at Ironwood Farm. Do you know it? It's on the north mountain."

"Didn't it used to have a U-Pick?"

"Down to a blueberry patch and one pig now. I was hoping to give Rupert a little more time in his home, but he's not as independent as he thinks. Doesn't see too well, and the house has been let go. I don't like the idea of him being alone while I'm working long shifts, but he won't hear of bringing anyone in. Says he doesn't need a babysitter."

"You know, George works out that way. At a lighthouse. It's right in the middle of a—"

"Of a field! Down the ridge from the farm. In fact, *right* by the farm." He turned to me. "That's where we met!"

"Sorry, what?"

"At the lighthouse. The pig got loose and George helped me find him. I *knew* I recognized you."

"Oh yeah. The pig."

"I'd think you'd remember that, Georgie," Mum said.

"Until this morning I had a beard and a full head of hair after being on leave for a couple of months. My own mother wouldn't have recognized me."

His sudden pep was unsettling. "I'll get the plates," I said, pushing back my chair.

"I'll help," he said. "No, you sit, Marlene. I used to wait tables. See?" He piled the plates up his arms.

"Georgie, heat up the pie," Mum called after me.

"Do you find this funny?" I hissed, when the door swung shut behind us.

"Oh, am I not supposed to? This isn't some joke? How old are you?"

". . . Seventeen."

A knife clattered to the floor. I started grabbing things from him, filling the dishwasher.

"You told me you were twenty," he said.

"It's not like I'm twelve."

"You were *five years* ago! You know where I was *five years* ago? Five years ago I was working on a riverboat."

"Because . . . you were a character in a Mark Twain novel?"

Mum peeked in the door. "Why don't you let me help?"

"Got it, Mum. Seriously."

"Okeydoke." She paused, at a loss for what to do with herself, before backing out again.

"George, I'm twenty-nine. You're *seventeen*. What the hell were you doing at a bar?"

Now I was the one dropping utensils. Twenty-nine—that was practically thirty. Three decades. Two hundred and ten dog years.

"I dunno. Just blowing off steam," I said. The nausea from the morning was rising again. "Can we forget it? Please."

He rubbed his eyes. "Is it too much to expect you to feel sorry about the position I find myself in?"

"No, I am." And then, because it seemed necessary to state it: "Sorry. I guess this is mutually assured destruction."

We were studying M.A.D. in Modern World Problems. Supposedly, the reason the Soviet Union and America needed to point nuclear weapons at each other was so neither would fire them.

He took his hands away from his eyes and looked at me. "Mutually assured destruction means that both parties have something equally at stake."

"Don't we?"

"I hooked up with a *minor*. No. *No*. I hooked up with a minor pretending *not* to be a minor. A minor who gained entry to a bar and then offered, upon questioning, further assurances of *not* being a minor . . . We have to tell your parents."

"Great idea. Pass me that knife?"

"People saw us together—"

"Nowhere near here!"

"If your father is going to hear about it, it should be from us. From me. When it's just an honest mistake. Not a mistake that we tried to cover up."

"I've been living with the Sergeant for seventeen years—"

He grimaced at the number.

"Seventeen *and a half* years, and yet I am not a loser. Do you know why? Because I don't get caught."

"And if you did, the worst that would happen is what? You'd get grounded? Maybe lose your TV privileges? Whereas I will have made an *incredible* error in judgment before I even started this job, jeopardizing my chances of getting a permanent position if—"

He checked himself, but not in time.

"If my dad can't go back to work on a prosthetic foot."

I picked up the pie from the counter. Mum had slit a cursive *W* in the top layer of dough, as she always did for special company. It was her version of our family crest, which my dad called—and I only just got this— our "family crust."

"You know what?" I said. "Do what you want."

It took a minute for him to rejoin us in the dining room. The jovial waiter routine over, he quietly pulled out his chair and sat down with what appeared like resignation.

Mum touched his arm. "You know, I was thinking, George is out your way often. She could give you a hand with the house."

"That's kind, but I couldn't ask her to do that."

"She wouldn't mind, would you, Georgie? You could go over next week and introduce yourself to— What was his name? Rupert?"

"I mean, I have a lot of schoolwork."

Matthew snorted again.

Francis forced a smile. "Okay, well, I'll mention it to Rupert. I'm not sure how he'll feel about having such a young lady around the house." *Such* a young lady. "But thank you, Marlene."

Mum filled the rest of the visit talking about the neighbor's gout. For once, no one tried to change the subject, and by the time we'd finished the room-temperature pie, I could tell, or hoped I could tell, that Francis had decided not to say anything.

"Why the leave?" Dad asked as he and Mum saw him out. I was listening from the top of the stairs. "You said you were off for a couple of months."

"Paul!" Mum said. "That may be private."

"I don't mind," Francis said. "My father was sick and then he passed away."

"We're sorry for your loss," Mum said.

"Thank you. And I'm sorry, Paul, for what you're going through now."

"Temporary setback."

After Mum closed the door behind Francis, I heard Dad say, "That guy ain't police. He won't last five years."

TEN

Mr. Humphreys was staring at me from across the cafeteria. He was a tall man with a barrel torso and beefy forearms. He could bust up a fight between the biggest guys at school and carry them to the office by their scruffs, their legs bicycling the air. But usually he didn't need to use more than a look.

I smiled a sober and healthful smile as I joined Lisa, Nat, and Bill at our usual table.

"Bill? Sweetie?" Lisa was saying. "Enough with the plaid."

"Jeremy's wearing a plaid shirt today. And Doug."

"Grunge and new-wave Cat Stevensy. You're doing late-wave Bryan Adamsy."

"What's grunge?" I said.

Nat sighed. "How are you cool?"

Our table was the long one at the center of the room. From

that vantage point I could keep half an eye on Matty and his friend Tim, tucked into the corner as far away from the Elevens as possible, while also watching Keith in the other corner acting out an elaborate pantomime to Lisa of: *Your best friend and my best friend can't sit at a table together, so I'm going to sit over here with Joshua and Christina, but meet you on the steps after school, and do you have my calculator?* Subtle. Meanwhile, Joshua was acting super interested in setting his digital watch.

"I could go," I said.

"Why?" Lisa said. "I'll see him later."

"Could you go?" Nat said to Bill. "Find Tracy? Girl talk. Thanks."

"But—"

She turned to Lisa. "Keep facing this way. I need George to check something for me."

Bill picked up his tray. "Since I'm invisible, I'm going to go look down some shirts."

"That was harsh," I said as he left. "He's actually pretty good at girl talk."

Nat reached over and squeezed my arm. "I need you to check out Doug. In the milk line. Does he seem okay?"

"You mean sober? How can you tell? Bill said he smoked a sack of pot before gym class last week and was the last man standing in dodgeball."

"Can you keep a secret?"

"Always."

"I know *you* can. You might be a liar, but you're also a fucking fortress. I meant Lisa."

Pink blotches appeared on Lisa's cheeks. "Of course."

"We hooked up," Nat said. "Doug and me. Went back to his house after the shack party. His parents were away."

"Oh my god!" Lisa and I exclaimed at once. We swiveled around and gave Doug a good, hard gander as he crossed the room to the table next to ours. He had a loping walk, longish hair that curled under his earlobes, somehow avoiding Prince Valiant territory, and an ever-present multicolored woven hat that clashed with everything else he put on. His parents were Come From Aways, city hippies who'd bought a vegetable farm to get back to the land, and he was the wiry you get when you eat a lot of salads and carob and weed.

"He's cute," Lisa said. "I don't even mind the hat."

"There's something very . . . *amiable* about him," I said. Also pained. He winced when he sat down, gave us a weak smile as he struggled to open his milk carton.

Nat shoved a huge wad of sandwich into her mouth, like nothing in the world were more interesting than her tuna on white. "I bruised him. All over. He's *covered* in bruises." She sounded as though she were talking through a pillow.

"Didn't know you were such a wildcat," I said.

"We were only fooling around, but I'm so bony that I, like, jabbed him nearly to death."

"Do you *like* him?" Lisa said.

Nat swallowed. "I don't *not* like him. It's more like, you've got Keith. And George has—everyone else, apparently. I wanted to be with someone, even for one night."

"Oh, Nat. That's a Very Special *Degrassi* episode," I said.

"It's true. And what bugs me is, I think I like sex, and you don't."

I wasn't sure what that had to do with it, but couldn't argue with her. I liked sex in theory. I liked it well enough, you know, on my own. But my track record with guys. There was the buff jock who looked like an Adonis but whose firm, freakishly smooth muscles were about as cozy to curl up with as a pencil eraser. The scraggy guy who had a tattoo of the cross that took up the whole of his back and prayed under his breath the whole time. And Leon. Who said he had "enchanted fingers" then prodded me like he was trying to find an elevator button in the dark. Meanwhile, poor Nat. Lisa and I always thought she had an unrequited crush on Sid that kept her from finding someone else, but it was the one thing she was never honest about.

"You and me, we're not going to find the right boys here." I pushed my untouched bagged lunch aside so I could climb on my giant soapbox. "Who cares? You get good grades and will probably get into whatever university you want. Isn't that what's important?"

"Are you high?" Nat said. "I want a boyfriend."

"Guess I must be," I said. "Because I thought what mattered

was getting out of the valley and starting our real lives. But that must be the drugs talking. Yup, that must be because I'm so, *so high*."

Lisa was frantically gesturing, and I turned to see Mr. Humphreys standing behind me. "Kidding, sir."

He took out a penlight that he apparently kept in his pocket for such occasions and shone it directly into my eyes. He snapped it off. "How many fingers?" he said, holding up his hand.

I was trying to blink away the spots from the light.

"How many?!"

"Uh, three?"

That seemed to satisfy him. He went over to Doug, sniffed the milk carton on his tray, and dragged him out of the cafeteria by the ear.

Lisa and I went outside to sit in the sun for the last few minutes before the buzzer. The school was basically built on an anthill, sand breaking up the grass and giving the back fields the look of a nubby afghan. I rubbed my finger against a warm, grainy patch. It felt like a dying ember of summer.

"Is your play proposal ready?" I asked.

"Almost. Promise you'll read it before I hand it in? God, I bet there will be a lot of submissions."

"Miss Aker'll love it, and if she doesn't . . ."

"You'll kill her?"

"Sure, murder. Maybe a stern word."

Lisa unzipped my knapsack and started digging around in it. "I have to tell you something. Before you hear it from someone else."

"Whaddya need?"

"Cigarettes."

"I don't smoke."

"You do when you're stressed and you think no one's watching."

"Must be why I have the tiny, shriveled, black heart. Outside pocket."

She lit a cig—slowly, like she was buying time—and blew a tendril of smoke out of the side of her mouth. "George, I kind of told Keith something about the kissing thing with Joshua. Something like, that it didn't go so well."

I still hadn't eaten, and now my stomach clenched like a fist. Pulling her arm toward me, I took a drag from the cigarette and another. "I didn't want that to get around," I said.

"I know."

"He's friends with the Tongue."

"I know."

"Do you think he— Oh, shit. He told him, didn't he?" She nodded. "Is that why Joshua wet his pants at the food court?"

"I'm so sorry. Are you mad? Dumb question. Of course you're mad."

"Probably not as mad as Joshua," I said slowly. "He's the one who got his feelings hurt."

"I was trying to help, honestly. Keith was so mad at you for leading Joshua on—"

"I didn't lead him on."

"You didn't say anything that made him think he had a chance?"

"Like when I said he was bile-colored?"

She sniffed. My story wasn't passing the smell test, but the prosecution was light on tangible evidence.

"What if I accidentally made him think I was into him?" I said. "Can't a person change her mind?"

"Sure, but what turned you off . . . I thought if he knew it was a bitty thing, totally fixable. So I mentioned it to Keith. And then I guess I kept talking."

"About the kiss?"

"About Leon, and those other guys. To explain! I didn't know he'd tell Joshua. Or that Joshua would get back together with Christina at the shack party. Or that she would . . ."

"That she would *what?*"

"Tell everyone else."

I put my head between my knees and said—appropriately—to my crotch, "Oh my god, a few days ago I was ungettable, and now I'm the school slut."

The buzzer went off. Neither of us moved.

"I'm so sorry," Lisa said again.

"Please stop saying sorry."

"What do you want me to say?"

100

"I dunno. That you'll stop telling Keith my secrets?"

"You don't expect me to lie when he asks something directly, do you? He asked me straight out, *Who is this Leon person?* and I'm like, *Leon who?* and he's like, *The guy George said she's hung up on.*"

"Why can't you say that you don't want to talk about it?" I sat up again. "Oh, Lise, you're not becoming one of those girls who would choose a guy over your friend."

"When have I done that?"

"Well, you're talking about Noel all of a sudden."

"So? Aurora was your plan, not mine. You decided it was perfect for all of us, and it might be, but I'm not sure yet."

"Funny how you seemed sure before you started going with Keith."

She pointed an accusatory finger. "You're acting like a jealous boyfriend. Why is it okay if I follow you, but not if I follow him?"

"Don't you get it? I'm always standing up for you, Lise. Always. And you're supposed to stand up for me. But it's like . . . it's almost like it's more important to you to be popular with the jocks and the Elevens."

"You know what your problem is? You've never had a boyfriend, so you don't know what it takes to be in a relationship."

"Please! You have a new boyfriend every year, and every year he's *the one*. Until the next one. Jesus, do you think you're going to be dating Keith for more than two minutes after graduation? The guy who didn't offer you a tomato sandwich? There are millions of other guys out there—billions."

"So you don't like Keith, is that what you're saying?"

"I'm saying you'll be able to do a lot better than him when we get out of this place, maybe some theater guy who can do the directing for you while you grow a backbone."

There it was. The un-take-back-able thing.

Lisa ground her cigarette into a bare patch of sand and stood up. "Or maybe I could do better than you," she said.

SOMETHING IN THE WAY

ELEVEN

September 1992

That Saturday, one of the volunteers from the heritage society burst into the lighthouse with four women in tow. "George, these fine ladies are writers from the city, here for some weekend culture," she gushed. "I've been telling them the lighthouse has a very *storied* history."

"Are any of you writing about lighthouses?" I asked.

"Who knows what the day could inspire!" the heritage lady said, herding them along.

She took them on the Tour of No Return. Every floorboard, every nail, every windowpane and latch. "Now, we're not entirely certain, but we *think* this notch in the wall might have been made by the original lighthouse keeper. Oh, what triumph or sorrow did lead that man to leave his literal mark upon the structure of this magnificent monument?"

I was pretty sure the notch had come from someone—someone me-like—opening the door to the service room too hard and slamming the knob into the wall.

As I polished the glass in the lantern room, I pondered how long it would be before someone tried to hurl herself through it. At first, the women were just eyeballing one another and trying not to laugh. Until the restlessness kicked in. The helplessness. The despair. One of them was massaging her stomach like it was sore, which gave me the in. I put my hand on her shoulder and said, "Do you need to go lie down?"

She was confused for a second then beamed. "I have a pain!" she announced. "A terrible pain! I must go lie down in the car!"

"I'll help you!" another woman said. "In case it's something serious!" She disappeared down the steps without even looking back to see if her friend was following.

The others seemed pained too—pained that they hadn't been quicker on the draw.

I followed the two women downstairs. "It's either big-time gas or another gallbladder attack," the one clasping her belly said as they power-walked toward the door.

"We can only save the others if it's gallbladder."

Two minutes later: a loud trumpeting from the car.

"Well, it's not gallbladder," I muttered to myself.

They didn't come back in.

The sun had swung around to the west behind a veil of fog by the time the heritage lady released her remaining hostages and left me to close up the lighthouse.

I was trying not to think about how much the two escapees were like Lisa and me. I'd thought that we'd be like that forever, that we'd grow up and she'd get married and I'd travel the world and we'd end up back where we started, singing opera to Thompson's clerks to get free samples. Only, in a better mall.

You will, I told myself. It's just been five days. Four of them spent sitting awkwardly on opposite sides of classrooms, staggering our trips to our lockers, which were a few doors apart. It sucked, but it wasn't step-on-a-pebble-surprise-your-foot's-amputated suckage. Most friends fight and get over it, right? Bill once nearly knocked Sid's head off with a golf ball after Sid said the T. rex on the miniature course was a dead ringer for Tracy. If anything, we were overdue.

Cut it out, *Frances*. Think about something else.

Like the pig standing behind the Town Car in the lighthouse driveway as though it were waiting to board a bus. I was no girl detective, but I supposed this was the one that Francis had been in search of.

"Git!" I said. "G'on, pig, git!"

Because it would understand me if I sounded like a cast member on *Hee Haw*? The pig gazed into the middle distance. I clapped my hands, whistled, took a run at it.

It shuffled around to Abe's side. Stared at the door expectantly.

"Like I'm driving you. It's not physically possible for you to wedge yourself in there," I said, opening the door to check.

It did. Wedged itself in there good, settling with a smug snuffle.

The farmhouse on the ridge looked like it was floating on the mist. I had no intention of offering my services to the old farmer as my mother had suggested, had a feeling that if I was foolish enough to go within one hundred feet of Constable Francis McAdams, it would be my blood he'd be wearing next. *Seventeen*, he'd said, like it was a dirty word.

"Seventeen and a half," I muttered as I gave the pig's barrel-sized rear a shove and closed the door. Well, almost. If I were eighteen, he wouldn't have recoiled so, as if seven months would make such a big difference.

The reflection in my rearview mirror was all pig, and Abe protested as we climbed the ridge toward the farm. He could take five hundred evenly distributed pounds of people, but this was pretty arse-heavy, even for a Town Car.

The farmhouse was in the old "Queen Anne" style, or trying to be. No turret, just double-decker bay windows topped with a domed roof, like the crown of an old birdcage. It had an enclosed porch beside the bays on the front like the one we had at home, an open veranda on the side that overlooked the fields, and a single-story extension poking out from the back.

The house seemed to have been built one section at a time, grand ideas improvised along the way. But the soft yellow paint and white trim were timeworn, the roof of the weathered barn coated with rust. As I pulled into the drive, I could see the barn was built right into the slope so that you could climb up and enter the hayloft at ground level.

An old man was sitting on the porch steps. He was wearing cartoonishly baggy jeans held up by suspenders and what might have been a pajama top. "Look who got himself a chauffeur!" he declared. "Thank you kindly. Where did you find him?"

"Down at the lighthouse," I said, opening the door for my passenger, who dislodged himself from the car with a loud grunt. "I work there, if you ever want a tour."

"That's my land—or it was. Gave the heritage people that piece; most of the rest is rented out. Not the blueberry patch over thataways, and help yourself, by the way. Course, Shaggy's mind isn't what it used to be, so he can't keep it all straight."

The old man opened the porch door, and to my astonishment, the pig walked up the steps and right into the house. "Do you always let him indoors?" I asked.

"I suppose you think that's unhygienic."

"Not at all. Only . . . I'm sorry, but doesn't he go all over the floor?"

"No—he don't. He goes to the door when he needs out, like any intelligent creature."

"Sorry," I said again. "George Warren. Unintelligent creature."

His deeply wrinkled face creased even more around his eyes, while his mouth—which had the caved-in look of teeth that were missing or ground down—spread into a thin crescent of delight. "I know who you are: Sergeant Warren's daughter. My boarder was at your house for lunch the other day. Said the Warrens had two kids and one was quite a handful. You the handful?"

Son of a—

"Oh," he said. "I think you *are*."

"My brother. Killed a hundred men just for looking at him funny."

"That so? How about you?"

"Maybe three?"

He laughed.

I was holding two fistfuls of garlic mustard that I'd ripped from the side of the driveway on autopilot. My mother had a special hate for garlic mustard. "Do you mind that I'm pulling up these weeds, Mr. . . . ?"

"Rupert Fraser, but you call me Rupert. You got energy, if you don't mind me saying. The constable does too. Did you see that foot bouncing up and down?"

"He did rattle the table a couple of times during lunch." And the table at Long Fellows. I had a memory flash of his shin rubbing against mine. "Well, it was good to meet you, Rupert. And Shaggy. I could tell straightaway that he isn't—he ain't no eatin' pig, is he?"

Rupert chuckled. "No, he ain't. I'd invite you in for a longer visit, but the house isn't suitable for company."

"Some other time," I said. "I'm guessing this won't be the last I see of Shaggy."

I thought I was going to make a clean getaway, but the cop car sped past me moments after I left the driveway. He did a U-turn, turned on his lights.

I pulled over and got out. I wasn't talking to the Constable through the window like a criminal.

"That idea of your mother's," he said, taking off his hat and wiping his forehead, "I'm sorry, but it's not happening."

He looked so strange in his uniform. It was hard to connect this man, with his buzzed head and ill-fitting pants, to the one I'd made out with in the sun-drenched lantern room and the soupy darkness at the bottom of the sea. He seemed leaner, more sinewy than I remembered. I hadn't noticed before how smooth and tan and tidy his hands were. An actor's hands. And his ears were kind of big.

Bill was right: say the wrong things, melt like wax.

"I was returning the pig," I said. "You ought to put him on a leash or something."

"Oh. Thanks. There's a pen for him, but it needs repairing."

"I owed you one for not telling my parents about everything."

"I was concerned that Paul would come down like a hammer,

exceeding what I personally consider was the seriousness of the crime."

"Well, thanks."

"Not your crime, the bartender's. What he did was lax. What you did was stupid."

"*Hey.* I know you wouldn't have hooked up with me if you'd known how old I am, but guess what? I wouldn't have hooked up with you either, not if I'd known who you were. Why didn't you say you were an RCMP officer?"

"Because . . ."

"Alrighty, as long as you had a good reason."

"Because I was off duty. Because pretty soon everyone is going to know me as the cop. I just wanted to be myself a while longer and, I don't know, get a feel for the place, as a civilian."

I wished I could say I didn't get it, but I had been living in an RCMP officer's house my entire life. Things would be different for him now.

He glanced over at the farmhouse, then back at me. "No. I knew you were too young for me. Even if you were twenty, you would be too young. But the first thing you said to me was funny." He slapped his hat against his leg. "And I wanted to hear what else you had to say."

With that, he got back into his car, pulled another U-ey, and drove away.

TWELVE

When I got back from my morning run, soaked with sweat after forty-five punishing minutes to nudge another half pound from my thighs, Mum was sitting at the kitchen table, bills and bank statements spread out around her. Dad was across from her in his wheelchair, his face a brick wall.

"Are we satisfied?" he said.

"Not exactly. You been drawing on our savings."

"I sent a little Joanna's way. To help with the new grandkid."

"Mortgage payment's higher than I thought."

"You thought wrong. Happens."

Mum tried to smile, but now her lips were pressed together so tightly they'd disappeared, like they always did whenever she was nervous or mad at Matthew and me.

"Dad, don't you have whatchacallits? Benefits?"

"I'm still bringing home the bacon. Course, we don't know what job I'll be going back to, if any."

"When will you find out?"

"How about you give me a minute to learn how to walk on the prosthetic before you make me run?"

"Right. Sorry."

My parents had never really talked about money in front of us kids before. We didn't waste it, but no one seemed to seriously worry about it either. Mum cut out coupons, like everyone else's mother did, bought new clothes for herself about as often as we updated our furniture, which was when something wore out completely, but I'd always thought that came from having grown up in a big family in a cabin on the south mountain. Dad once told me that the pipes sometimes froze and if my granddad couldn't afford to get them fixed for a while, which was usually the case, Mum and her brothers would have to cut a hole in the ice to collect drinking water from the river.

The dryer timer buzzed. Mum pushed back her chair and rose stiffly, taking small, urgent steps across the kitchen like she was trying—well, like she was trying not to crap her pants. Had I ever seen Mum look that worried before?

"Don't let her get you worked up about this," Dad said as she went down the basement stairs. "This is exactly why you have savings, so the money is there if you need it."

I sat in Mum's chair and took a big gulp of the lukewarm coffee she'd left behind, wiping my mouth on the collar of my damp T-shirt and wishing I could peek inside the blue bank books with their silver embossed logos. I wasn't sure how much was in my university fund or how much I needed, but since my parents had been matching every dollar I handed over to them since I'd started working at the lighthouse, I assumed we'd have at least the first year or two covered before I even stepped foot on a campus. "Dad, if you can't go back to work, will we have to live off my school money?"

"It's not like I'd retire. I'm footless, not brainless. But no, we're not touching that."

"Will it be enough?"

"You'll be fine for tuition, and for books, student fees, and all that. I just don't know how exactly we'll manage residence. Unless you go to Noel and live at home."

"Dad, I don't want to be a jerk—"

"Never a promising start to a sentence—"

"But it doesn't seem right to choose a school because it's the closest."

That was a big fat reason *not* to choose it.

"It would be different if there was some special program you wanted to do and you had the grades to get in *and* it was a hike from here. Then we could talk about getting a loan, though you know how your mother feels about debt. You don't need a fancy college if we're talking about a run-of-the-mill degree."

"There *is* a special program that I want to get into."

There was no special program; I just didn't want the idea of

Noel too fixed in my father's mind. What let you see the world? I zip-lined through the possibilities like I was taking a word association test: explorer—tour guide—flight attendant—pilot—air force—soldier—war correspondent—

"Journalism," I said. And conveniently: "They offer it at Aurora."

"So you'll apply to Aurora."

"Yeah?"

"I'll say it again: I don't want you to worry, kiddo. But let's think before you send out applications willy-nilly. You could spend money on fees that won't amount to anything."

"Maybe if you did your physical therapy," Matthew said quietly, "you could be back to work sooner than you think."

I hadn't noticed him hanging on the swinging door between the kitchen and the dining room.

"I do it when you're at school," Dad said, gathering up the paperwork. "Perhaps you two might deign to head that way before the next millennium, so I can get on with it."

Since we didn't have much homework that afternoon, I decided to take the Bickersons back to Pierre's with me to finish my clothes shopping.

"*Aargh*," Nat said, kicking the car door closed as a strong breeze whipped half of her hair out of its bun. Another gust brought the whole thing down. Now she was windmilling her arms like she was trying to punch everything in the universe.

"Are you fighting the wind?" Bill said.

"You go to all this trouble to get yourself put together and then it has to mess it up every time."

"Your hair was already falling out of its thingy."

Only because Nat had spent twenty minutes pulling out selected strands one by one so that they framed her face just so. She swatted her bangs out of her eyes. "Stop defending it!"

Bill gave me an exasperated look. Nat had been especially Natty for the past week, partly because of my fight with Lisa, partly because of what'd happened with Doug, who she was avoiding. And when Nat got to cranking, she tended to crank on Bill, who was Teflon enough to take it.

"Who doesn't resent the wind?" I said, pushing open the door for them.

Bill gave Nat a little shove inside. "That should be the title of your autobiography."

Nat wasn't a big fan of Pierre's so her mood didn't improve as we sifted through the bins. "Have you heard from Sid?" I asked.

"Couple of postcards."

"Only one for me."

Course, I'd only written to him twice.

This wasn't surprising. Sid's parents sent him to a different camp every summer and we wouldn't hear from him the whole time he was gone, but then he'd be back and it was like he'd never left. He was like a windup toy: you could drop him anywhere and he'd keep on walking.

"Bill calls him sometimes," I said, watching him try on ladies' hats in the next aisle over. "He says it's . . ."

"Awkward."

"Yup."

Which *was* surprising, if nothing new, because Sid was so fun and animated in person. Lisa's favorite thing in the world used to be when we'd reenact Andy Garcia's love scenes with Sofia Coppola in *The Godfather Part III*, Sid emoting like hell, me channeling a block of Swiss cheese. But get him on the phone and he'd keep drifting off, like he couldn't focus on you if you weren't in front of him.

"This made a lot more sense before he moved," Nat said.

"What do you mean?"

"Before it was two guys, two girls—"

"Three girls."

"You're a boy-girl hybrid, so you cancel yourself out. Now it's one guy, two girls, and you. Sid's gone, you and Lisa aren't talking, and even if you were, you can't hang out with Keith when Joshua and the Face are around, and how's that going to work? What if Sid leaving was the beginning of the end?"

"The end of *what*?"

"Us. Our group. What if we only worked when we were all together?"

"Stop it," Bill said, marching into our aisle. He'd gotten himself done up in a Jackie O. pillbox hat, a faux Chanel jacket, and

Minnie Mouse gloves, and he looked positively stricken, clutching his pearl-encrusted collar.

"Okay," Nat said. "Don't get your pearls in a knot. I'm just saying—"

"Stop it!" He started blowing in her face, sending her wispy white bangs flying.

"You stop it!"

Bill took off his pillbox hat and dumped it in the bin beside him. "I can't lose my best buddy, my girlfriend, and my whole damn group."

"Wait, Tracy dumped you again?" Nat said.

"Well, no. I dumped her."

"Dumped her *how*?"

"You want the transcript?"

"But you never break up with her," I said. "Ever."

"So, yeah, the thing is . . . The thing is she said I was spending all my time running between you girls, and something about taking her for granted, and something-something you have to choose, so I chose."

"You chose us?"

He nodded.

"You chose us," Nat echoed.

"And Lisa." He gave me a meaningful look.

"And Lisa," I said. "I'll fix it—promise. I mean, with just you two losers, how would I know if I should get this green shirt or that green shirt?"

"Neither of those shirts is green," Nat said. She retrieved the hat from the bin and perched it on her head. "So, Bill, maybe we could, uh, study together some time? You know, since my study partner moved away."

To put this into context: Nat and Sid could be competitive about grades, and spent hours together cramming for tests and talking smack about how lazy Bill was because he didn't have to work at all to get straight As. Which meant that Nat was making an excuse to hang out with Bill in his time of need, and, as my mother would put it, for once she turned over the hem to hide the stitching.

"Sure," he said. "We could do that. Just as friends?"

"Get over yourself. Someone's got to keep an eye on you. Now that Sid's gone, there's one less person to stop you from getting back together with your ex–T. rex."

THIRTEEN

I said I would fix it, and I meant it.

As usual, Nat had located a raw nerve and pressed her finger on it. Maybe we only worked as a five, and even if we could work as a four, what was going to bring us back together? Bill and Nat had made it sound like it had to be me, but I hoped they'd had the same conversation with Lisa. One of us just had to make the first move.

Our school held eight hundred kids, from seventh grade up, smaller schools feeding into it like tributaries. There were those who could walk down its hallways in a resplendent burnt-orange satin blouse with puffed sleeves and a little tie at the collar and have their stock rise with every laugh, and there were those who could not. Not to brag, but I was in the first group, so I had my icebreaker, found in one of the bins at Pierre's.

I also had a large slab of my mother's famous gingerbread that she let me take as a pick-me-up for Bill, but when I dropped into the seat in front of his in homeroom, he was already covered in crumbs from Nat's mother's famous date squares. "If I knew how much nicer mothers are to the dumpers than the dumpees," he said, mouth full, "I'd have broken up with Tracy a long time ago."

I'd learned the dangers of slagging Tracy off when it might be a matter of seconds before Bill got back together with her, so I handed him the Tupperware container and said, "Whatcha wearing, cowboy?"

His shirt had pivoted from Bryan Adams to the Lone Ranger.

"Lisa." He tore a page out of his binder and used it as a napkin. "She took me shopping last night after I got back from shopping with you guys. Hope she finds that thing you have on as funny as you think she will because I can't keep doubling up on all this girl stuff."

"So far everyone else does."

We had Miss Aker for homeroom, followed by English during first period. Lisa arrived a few minutes after the buzzer, flustered and waving a permission slip. She slid into a desk a few seats behind me and didn't look my way.

Miss Aker—she of the prematurely white hair, long dresses, and practical socks 'n' sneakers—said, "Now that you're here, I can share our news. I'm delighted to tell everyone that Lisa has been chosen as the director of this year's school play." Spattered applause. "We thank the two other applicants for their efforts. Lisa, perhaps you could share your proposal and the changes to the production this year."

Lisa stood up, already turning pink because she was allergic to public speaking. That's when she noticed me and my shirt. Her mouth went slack, like her brain couldn't compute what she was seeing, and then she seemed *annoyed*, as though I'd distracted her on purpose. She gave her head a shake, centered herself again. "So I went to see this theater troupe in the city, and it got me thinking about the different ways you could adapt a classic poem like 'Evangeline.' At first I was like, *As a musical?* Then I was like, *No, with movement and acrobatics and miming—*"

"And puppets and black light and kids from the short bus!" Doug said.

Miss Aker pointed to the door. "Office. It's the *nineties*, Doug."

No one but Miss Aker heard what Lisa said after that. Space needed to be gazed into; elastics weren't pinging themselves. Lisa really did need someone to be the heavy. She also clearly needed someone to tell her that giving Longfellow's "Evangeline" a circus vibe was a bad idea.

". . . Jennifer P. will do costumes, Jennifer C. will do makeup, and Christina Veinot is the stage manager. Christina suggested it would be good to have an even split of juniors and seniors working on the play this year, and Miss Aker and I agreed."

She did not agree. I could see it in the way she sat down again, eyes forward to avoid making eye contact with anyone.

Tradition dictated that the Elevens ran the Christmas talent show and only did small production tasks and supporting parts in the play, graduating to bigger jobs in senior year. Lisa had paid her dues and so had all the other seniors who wanted to work on the play. Now she'd given half of it over to the Elevens, just because Christina had told her to.

Bill gave my back a can-you-believe-it jab.

"Onward!" Miss Aker shouted over the buzzer for first period. "To begin, I have a special poem that I'd like to share. It was written a long time ago by a local poet, someone who prefers to remain anonymous."

"Is this person in the room at this moment?" Mike asked.

"I cannot reveal the author, but it's a terrific example of confessional poetry."

No one was buying the secret-author thing. Miss Aker used the same poem every year and always presented it with the same little speech. Rumor was she had a suitcase full of rejection letters from literary magazines.

"Mike, start us off. Read the first stanza, please."

It was about two boys who hung out constantly. They raced all over town on their bikes, turned grass blades into reed instruments, shared a crush on the same girl, and wept together when they came upon a dead dog on the bank of a creek. But when they turned thirteen, they suddenly stopped being friends, *the reason buried like a bone.*

I liked it, in spite of Bill's second, harder jab. It was plainly put, to the point. I didn't understand writing something that had to be translated into real talk, especially since it seemed like no one ever agreed on the meaning. The only poet I'd gotten into was Sylvia Plath, whose poems were often savage and almost always interesting, even if you didn't know what she was on about half the time.

> *I think I am going up,*
> *I think I may rise—*
> *The beads of hot metal fly*

"Who here has been friends for a long time?" Miss Aker said.

Bill practically shouted, "George and Lisa!"

I turned around to glare at him. He gave his cowboy collar a smug little tug, and I vowed he'd soon be rolled in a rug. (Who says I'm not a poet?)

"Perfect. Let's hear a few memories of your friendship, girls, see if we could mine them. Lisa, what's your earliest memory of George?"

After an uncomfortable pause, Lisa said, "Probably that time she blew a gasket in kindergarten because the teacher couldn't find her Minnie Mouse hat."

It was a minor fit, and *not* her earliest memory of me. The earliest, for both of us, was a skating recital of "The Farmer in the Dell." Lisa played the Black Cat. I played the Cheese. At five, I was so small that my parents worried I had a growth disorder, but I could skate well for my age. I *was* the Cheese, *le grand fromage de la dell*! I skated frontward, I skated backward, I wiggled my yellow-costumed behind adorably. Then the Brown Cow ran me down and I fell. The audience went, *Awww*. Because *of course* the littlest one couldn't stay on her feet. I knew I looked like a baby, and was grateful when the Black Cat with the luminous blond lashes and orange curls bubbling out of her hood laughed heartily, like I'd done it to be funny, and watched me get up all by myself. Years later I asked why she didn't help and she said, "Because you didn't want me to," as though that would have been obvious to anyone but her.

"We once snuck down to the basement to watch *Nightmare on Elm Street* on the VCR," I said. "She started sleeping in her parents' bed after that."

"How old were you?" Miss Aker asked. "Nine? Ten?"

"Fourteen."

"George swallowed a marble because she wouldn't admit she'd thought it was candy."

"Lisa throws up if she runs through deep snow."

"George thought a harbinger was an eating disorder."

"Lisa laughed so hard she thought she'd peed her pants, but she hadn't." The laughter that had been bouncing around the classroom died down. "There was this big brown dot on the back of her pants, though."

Lisa's face as the room erupted.

It would have been kinder to smack her. How could I hit her

so hard where it hurt? Because she'd gotten me into a corner is how, and being willing to say anything, if not everything, was how I fought my way out of corners. She'd said it herself. Except usually I wasn't fighting my own fight. Usually, I was protecting the person I'd just knocked out.

"Okay! Very revealing and extremely regrettable!" said Miss Aker. "So let's move on. I want you to partner up, pull your desks together, and brainstorm a poem based on your shared memories. Lisa and George, you should have different partners since you've . . . purged yours already. Who would like to partner with George?"

Four guys were on their feet at the same time—Bill, Derek, Jeremy, and Mike. Bill stared down the others.

"Told you," he said as I turned my desk around. "You're the girl all the guys want to get."

"Especially now that I've gone from ungettable to notorious slut. So why am I partnering with you, if I could have any guy I want?"

He flexed his biceps, strong-man-style. "I've got muscles." He said it like *musculls*. "I just look soft because of the Dorito layer on top. Anyway, hardly anyone buys that story about you and the East Riverview guys. It sounds too convenient, that they all *happen* to go to a different school."

"Life's a bad writer, buddy."

That was as far as we could get before the weight of what had happened fully settled. I glanced over at Lisa working with

Shelley-with-an-*E*, the yearbook editor. She had her back to me.

"I didn't think one fight would screw things up this badly," I said.

"It didn't." Bill reached under his desk for the Tupperware container with the breakup cake. "But it's good and broken now."

FOURTEEN

Dad was asleep in his recliner, still wearing the jogging pants he'd slept in the night before. I dumped my knapsack onto the carpet next to his prosthetic and myself onto the velour chesterfield beside him.

We were broken, Lisa and me. *Good and broken,* Bill had said. As in, broken up. She'd already asked Nat if she could get some stuff from me, like a sweater and a mixtape one of her exes made her. She wanted me to know we were done.

I'd never had a breakup with a boy before, let alone a best friend, and didn't know all the rules and procedures. Crying was usually part of it, but I was too stunned to cry. Not calling was also important, that I'd learned from magazines and my friends, and it seemed to be true whether you were a dumper or a dumpee. You had to let the other person come to you, and if they didn't, so be it. Calling always, always made it worse. Except it wasn't clear how both people not phoning was going to get you anywhere. Was that the point? To keep you from fooling yourself into thinking you would be able to stay friends? And what was the friends' version of staying friends?

I was sure that if I called Lisa, she wouldn't pick up, not only because she understood the rules better than I did, but because she was really, really mad. I was mad too. She'd started that fight in front of the whole class. She had, not me. Still. It was crazy to want to make it so final so fast. I stared at the stucco ceiling, knowing that I was seconds away from calling because I was lousy at doing nothing; the kid whose mother had to duct-tape mittens on my hands to stop me from scratching when I had hives.

Dad stirred in his chair. "Hey-o! *That's* a shirt," he said at the sight of my orange top. "Did you see the message on the pad in the kitchen?"

I sat up. "Lisa?"

"No, your boyfriend."

It was Rupert Fraser, wanting to know if I'd like to help out around the house and farm as Mum had suggested, only he offered to pay me. "Six dollars an hour," he said when I called him back. "Up to fifteen hours a week, let's say. Less if you like."

I couldn't flatter myself that Francis had decided he wanted to hang out, but where else would Rupert have gotten the idea to hire me? Then Rupert said, "Mick will be working a lot of long hours."

"You call him Mick?"

"What do you call him?"

"He introduced himself as Francis."

Sort of.

"Hoity-toity. I've been thinking you'd be good company for an old man while he's gone. Though I got to warn you, I can be quite a handful. . . ."

So the idea was that Francis and I would dodge each other. Fine. Rupert was offering more than the heritage society paid me, and that would make up for my lighthouse hours going down now that it was the off-season. The more hours I worked, the less likely it would be that I'd end up at Noel, and the less time I'd have to think about why that would be even worse than I'd originally thought.

I went over to Ironwood Farm after school the next afternoon, feeling sullen and sooky in my nonvictory of having gone all day without trying to talk to Lisa or accidentally-on-purpose catching her eye. She made it too easy, acting all sunny and chatty and working the hallway like a minister's wife at the Christmas tea. In the milk lineup, she threw her head back and laughed so hard at something Bill said that he took an involuntary step back. Even though I knew she was putting it on—just like I was pretending it was totally normal for me to be hanging out at the skateboarders' table—it still sucked that she wanted everyone to think she didn't care. Like juggling at a funeral, except the body was still warm.

I couldn't get to the farm fast enough. Mindless labor, money in my pocket, and a legitimate excuse to tell Bill and Nat that it was cool if they wanted to go to the basketball game with Lisa because look at me already moving on to new things. I was so relieved to have somewhere to go, until I crossed the threshold of the house.

Francis wasn't kidding: it was filthy. Cobwebs, clutter, torn linoleum. As I did a tour around, checking inside and under things, I could see where he'd started tackling it. The kitchen counters gleamed against the stained wallpaper. The ancient stove top was as clean as it was going to get, but the oven was crusted over.

"Now, seeing this from the outside, you'd think this house smells like a pig farm, but it don't, right?" Rupert said.

I'd smelled a house like this before. There was a bona fide cat lady in town who had at least fifty semiferal cats, and I rang her doorbell on a dare from Lisa when I was eight. I glimpsed floors so worn that they had actual holes in them, and the smell of mildew and unwashed old person and unwashed clothes seemed to be carried on the dust floating from the ghostly layers that covered every surface. That house had undernotes of cat pee, whereas this one had the earthier scent of pig manure.

"It's a tad *poinky*," I said, though I couldn't see any poo piles.

Maybe Rupert was tracking it in on his shoes.

But underneath the grime, the house seemed like it had been at one time a comfortable, welcoming place. The furniture was faded but colorful. In the living room, a formal red chesterfield that looked like it was from the first half of the century was kitty-cornered with a green one that was straight from a 1970s basement bong room. Old family portraits and hooked rugs hung on the walls with randomly tacked up album covers, mostly bluegrass and Celtic folk music. Suncatchers hung in most of the windows.

I peered into an ornate copper birdcage that had been recently polished and had fresh newspapers lining the bottom. A beautiful blue parakeet was sitting on a perch. "Hello, pretty boy," I said to him. "Say pretty boy, pretty boy." The bird remained absolutely still. "Come on, pretty boy."

I whistled a dandy tune to him. He turned slowly on his perch until his back was to me.

"Wilfred's a dick," Rupert said.

The second floor wasn't much cleaner than the first, but it had less junk. The master bedroom might have even been pretty, with its cheerful blue-and-yellow floral wallpaper, iron bed frame, and lace curtains, were it not for a filthy crib-sized mattress on the floor.

Beside the back stairs was a small, empty room overlooking the blueberry patch—meant for a maid, perhaps, or a baby— and the one next to it was plainly Francis's. A twin bed with a buttoned headboard of stuffed green vinyl, neatly made with a white coverlet. A few books stacked on the wooden stool that served as a side table. A plain, polished wooden table and chair. No dust, no clutter, no decorations. There was something almost aggressively absent about it, nothing of him in the room, other than that pile of books. On top was a collection of poems by Elizabeth Bishop.

My knees suddenly buckled, as can happen when a pig skull slams into them.

Shaggy tried again to shove past me into the room, but I blocked him with the door. There followed a struggle, with me pulling on the knob and him pushing his head against the wood, squealing in frustration, until he finally huffed and took himself off to Rupert's room. He flopped onto the mattress on the floor.

This is ridiculous, I thought, making sure I heard the latch click when I closed Francis's door. I didn't want to touch anything outside of his room, even to breathe the air in this house. I was already twitchy with imminent pink eye. It wasn't worth it, just to earn a few extra bucks.

I didn't want to leave abruptly, but had to get outside. In Abe's back seat were some pots of asters that I'd picked up for Mum at the nursery on my way to work. She would be annoyed if I came home without them. And then what? She'd send me out for more.

"Hey, Rupert!" I called. "I've got something for you, if you can tell me where the shovel is."

I planted the asters around the front steps. It was such a relief to be out in the fresh air and working with my hands. I was digging a hole for the last of the flowers when the shovel clanked against a hard surface.

Rupert was at the kitchen table, reading the newspaper with the magnifying glass that I'd found inside the fridge earlier. I held up an old Canada Rye whiskey bottle filled with a clear liquid.

"What in the—Where'd you find that?"

"In the ground. By the steps."

"Well, well! I couldn't tell you how old that is. Decades probably."

"What is it?"

"It's not water."

"Is it . . . is it moonshine?"

He tried not to smile, but his whole face crinkled.

"You make moonshine?" I don't know why I was whispering. Wilfred the Electively Mute Parakeet wasn't going to talk.

"Used to bury it around the house. Used to be drunk when I buried it around the house. Never could remember where I put them all. Tell you what, you can keep that."

I set the bottle down on the table. "I'm good, thanks."

"Don't you tell me that you and your friends don't have a drink sometimes."

"Isn't moonshine supposed to make you go blind?"

"Doesn't go bad. Maybe if it was off to begin with, but that's good stuff. Now, you take it and give it to your boyfriend if you don't want to drink it yourself. I bet you'll have an easier time getting around the law in your house than I would in mine. Mind you, it's better than closing up shop and living in a nursing home, like my daughter's always telling me to do."

He spat on the floor.

"Rupert!"

"I was demonstrating that I don't like the idea of dying in one of them places."

I took a tissue from my pocket and wiped up the gob. The floor was now cleaner in that one spot, the gold pattern of the linoleum coming through. "That's what you call a spit shine," Rupert said.

Next thing I knew, I was on my hands and knees scrubbing. Brushes and rags quickly turned soot black and I went again and again to the sink to rinse them in scalding water and vinegar. I couldn't stop. The spreading gold was addictive.

"Rupert, do you mind if I ask how old you are?" I lifted up each of his feet and scoured the floor underneath.

"Old as my tongue and a little older than my teeth."

"And when did you stop farming?"

"After my heart attack. Ach, don't look so alarmed. I was home from the hospital that same day. I was glad, even. Yes, glad to know I've got a bad ticker. Means the end could come quick. Matter fact, if you ever see me doing this . . ." He clutched his left arm. "You walk away, let nature take its course."

"Most people want to go in their sleep or surrounded by loved ones. Like in a movie."

"Now, that's why *I* say that if I had less religion, I'd go by my own hand and be done with it. Imagine, people standing around your bed, staring at you, jumping every time they think your soul might have got sucked out of you, *wishing* it would already because they've got better things to do? I don't want my last vision of this earth to be my daughter going . . ." He leapt to his feet, shaking grit from his shoes onto the clean floor.

"Rupert?"

"Yes, honey?"

"Before you get dramatic again, take off those shoes and let me give them a scrub."

After I finished the floor, I set Rupert up with what he said was his favorite dinner—beans and wieners—and wandered through the fields and down the ridge toward the lighthouse.

The light was gray-tinged, the wind hurrying clouds across the darkening turquoise above, grass rustling in waves like the surf washing over a beach. And then, out of nowhere: something pure white and set ablaze. It looked like a small hot-air balloon, maybe two feet tall, its fire burning brightly against the dimming sky. Soon there were more, at least a dozen launching from the other side of the lighthouse, it appeared, and floating across the fields and up the mountain like ghosts. They flew higher and higher, spreading out and disappearing beyond the tree line.

It was nearly dark by the time the last balloon had vanished and I turned to go climb back to the farm. Someone was standing on the slope above me. Francis. Was he watching me too? I couldn't tell. I felt the lake stone in my pocket, the one from Lake Victoria that he'd given me that night at the bar, smooth and warm against my palm.

After what seemed like a long time, he began to walk slowly toward the house, the soft gray of his uniform barely visible in the grass. When I got to my car, he was nowhere in sight.

FIFTEEN

And so it went for the first week or so, me running off to the farm after school on the days I had less homework, and beating it out of there before Francis got home, sometimes passing him on the driveway as he was turning in.

Until he arrived early one night. When he pulled in, I was outside feeding Shaggy kitchen scraps. I flipped the bucket over so Shaggy could snuffle the remnants out of the dirt, hung it on a peg at the side of the barn without rinsing it, and started for Abe.

"Hang on a sec so I can pay you," he said, getting out of his car. "Unless you'd rather take Rupert to the bank so he can settle with you directly."

I held out my hands, and he counted the money into my

upturned palms. "Twenty-forty-sixty-touched-your-boob-one-hundred."

Neither of us spoke, just stared at the small pile of bills. My left boob had a sort of Day-Glo feeling where he'd accidentally grazed it.

Finally, I said, "That's worth at least another ten."

"I pay you and then I have to arrest you for solicitation."

Rupert stuck his head out the porch door. "Oh, look what the cat dragged in. You going already, George? Stay for dinner, why don't you?"

"Thanks, but I'm not hungry," I said.

My stomach chose that moment to sing out like a baby humpback whale that has lost its mother.

"Stay," Francis said. "I'll cook. And I"—he lowered his voice—"I won't assault you again."

After changing into jeans and a well-worn sweater, Francis poured a jar of yellow powder into a pot with salt and milk, set a pan of water to boil, chopped a bunch of vegetables and herbs, and drizzled oil over them. The quick, confident movements of someone who'd done them many times before. As he worked, I caught myself going over the boob-tag story in my head, as though I were going to tell it to Lisa. One of those habits I was having trouble shaking, like looking over at her in class whenever a teacher said something funny or lame. Except, I realized, that even if we were speaking, I probably wouldn't tell her that story because it wasn't the same if you didn't know that my boob and his hand had a history, and how could I trust her again with a secret like that?

Within twenty minutes we were sitting in front of steaming bowls of yellow porridge he called "polenta" with roasted veg and poached eggs. He grated a hard cheese on top, which turned out to be Parmesan. I'd never seen Parmesan that didn't shake out of a plastic container.

"Son, if you'd told me a few weeks ago that I'd be satisfied without a piece of meat on my plate, I wouldn't have believed you," Rupert said.

"I picked up a few tricks working in kitchens."

"George, honey, pass me that paper over there," Rupert said. "You read 'Tales From the Dispatch'?"

I shook my head. That was the local paper's weekly account of the more entertaining emergency calls made to the police. I got the highlights at home.

"'A man loitering on Main Street in a samurai costume was questioned by police in Veinot.' Obviously waiting for a drive to an early Halloween party."

"No, sir, he was not," Francis said.

"Huh. 'An unattended foil package was found on campus at the University of Noel. It was determined to be a donair.'"

"Six hours," Francis said. "We had to bring in the bomb disposal unit. And today a woman called because another woman gave her a dirty look at Dairy Queen."

"Yeah, sorry again about that," I said.

I'd been pretty quiet, and the sound of my voice seemed to startle Rupert and Francis.

"Oh, George is being funny," Rupert said. "Very good."

Francis didn't smile. "And after *that*," he said, twirling his fork on the tabletop, "we had a call about a stolen pickup parked in someone's driveway. Dispatch said to go up the one-oh-six, get off at Bishops, swing a right down Old Porter Road at the United Church, six miles from there. If you hit the river you've gone too far. I retraced my steps again and again, and I couldn't even find the damn church."

Rupert and I looked at each other.

"What?"

"That church burnt down," Rupert said.

"Burnt down when?"

"Going on ten years!" Rupert guffawed so hard he hiccupped. "Come on, now, son. Dispatch probably didn't think of it."

"By the time I happened upon the place, the truck and the guy who stole it were long gone."

"Did you try his mother's house?" I asked. "It's just, my dad says you always check the mother's."

"Alright, I'll do that. Any more job advice? Or any sort of advice?" His tone had flipped from grateful to challenging in the space of a second. "Kids grow up so fast around here, you must be a wellspring of flawless decision making."

"Don't get me talking," I said coolly. "I can be quite a handful."

The faint percussion of Francis's foot under the table stopped.

Truth is, people had been calling my dad about him. Not that he was doing anything wrong according to the rule of the law, but as far as the unspoken rules of the valley went, he was screwing up regularly.

"Go on, George," Rupert said.

Shaggy had wandered into the kitchen, and now came over to rest his chin on my lap. I used my napkin to scrub the dust from his snout, which I suspected came from breaking into Wilfred's birdseed. "Well," I said, "don't overdo the parking tickets on Main Street."

"In your town?" Francis said.

"Any main street. I know it seems like you're bringing in cash for the municipalities, but the shops complain about business going down. And maybe drop in places sometimes, say hi."

"I got one," Rupert said, pleased with himself. "Don't worry about that sad woman who hangs outside the Pizza Palace in Veinot."

"Are you telling me she's *not* a prostitute?" Francis asked.

"Sure she is, but she has a kid, so they let her be."

"Okay, free parking for all on Main Street, no hookers with kids, say hello. But I have a question: What the hell is a donair?"

Rupert and I laughed.

"That happens every time I ask, and no one ever gives me an answer. All I know is that it's food."

"A pita sandwich," I said. "The meat is carved from one

of those twirling vertical spit jobs and it has sauce made from condensed milk."

Yes, revolting, and yes, heaven.

"Sounds like a Greek gyro. What type of meat?"

"Nobody knows," Rupert said. "Nobody asks."

When I got home, Dad was sitting in his recliner, the TV blaring. His fake foot was on the chesterfield, and he was still wearing a special sock thing with a pin on the bottom that connected his stump to the calf portion of the prosthetic. Nice to see him trying. For a guy who was so married to his job, he hadn't seemed in a big hurry to get back to it, something I couldn't square. At least people had stopped phoning the house instead of 911.

"Hey, Dad."

He didn't move.

"Dad?" I said a little louder.

"What? Oh. Hi, George."

"Sorry I'm late."

"Are you?" He looked at his wrist, but his watch wasn't there. He felt around his bathrobe pockets, then gave up.

"Not very late," I said. "I did call Mum to tell her I was staying at the farm for supper."

He turned back to the TV. Sweat beaded his forehead.

"You look like you hurt." He also looked like he hadn't slept properly in a week. His skin was sallow and he had huge pouches under his eyes.

"I just . . . I hit the leg."

"On what?"

"Uh, the wheelchair."

The wheelchair was tucked into the corner by the vase filled with old peacock feathers, well away from the recliner and the sofa. "But it's on the other side of the room."

"Let it go, George!" He was staring at the seam between the wall and the ceiling, as though anchoring himself to it. "Must have rolled over there when I knocked it."

No, it was neatly parked, as it would be if he had been walking around on his prosthetic.

"Dad, why don't you take more painkillers?"

"Don't want to."

"Are you worried you'll get addicted?"

"They make me irregular and stupid. Can't think clearly."

"So what? It's not like you have to drive. You don't need to think clearly to watch *Coronation Street*."

Dad closed his eyes. "George, go get me my cigarettes. And then go to bed."

SIXTEEN

Lisa kept the cafeteria, the mall, and basketball games. I kept the front steps of the school, where everyone hung out between classes, the movie theater, and the arena. For a few days Nat and Bill had switched between us like a couple of latchkey kids, but pretty soon Nat was only hanging out with me in the classes we had together, and then not at all. There was no big announcement that she was choosing sides, and thank god for that. *Not* being direct was Nat's way of being kind.

Our group may have been divided, but by the grace of Bill, some cool people on the fringes, like Doug the stoner, and a few horny and hopeful jocks, I wasn't so much exiled as hanging out on my own sweet island close to the mainland. The Grunt was still neutral territory, though it didn't feel like it as I slid into the booth where Bill was plowing through a large basket of french fries. Nat, Lisa, and Keith were perched at the end of a table that was pulled up to another table that was packed with Elevens being Elevens. If I was being honest—and why would I do such a thing?—it still hurt seeing Lisa like that, so close but so far away, especially when she seemed to be making an effort not to see me.

I snuck a fry out of the basket, and Bill gave me a low warning growl.

"What's with Nat's eyebrows?" I asked. She had a pair of scorched half-moons where the bottom halves used to be.

"Deforestation with hot wax. Not just north of the border."

"For Doug?"

"Why? Do you care?"

"I don't *care* care."

"Like with feelings."

"Exactly."

"Nah, she decided she doesn't want to date a druggie."

"It's not like he's messed up."

"A little messed up. He's not a bad guy, but if they were going out she'd be spending a lot of time helping him keep it together."

Which reminded me: I took Bill's biology binder out of my knapsack. "You left this on the floor in front of your locker."

"Crap. Thanks."

I decided it was Lisa's job to tell him about the stain on the mock turtleneck she'd obviously talked him into.

"So, uh, you know what's happening on Lisa's birthday?" Bill said.

"Oh. Right. She must be dragging you out to the Old or Hard Inn for dinner." I slipped another fry out of the basket.

The Old Orchard Inn. The *C* in the sign had been burnt-out for years.

"Actually, Christina invited us to her cottage for the weekend."

The french fry felt like it was lodged in my throat. "Lisa doesn't like the outdoors touching her."

"Nat doesn't even want air touching her. But I guess we're going."

I swallowed hard and peeked again at the Elevens' table. Christina was sitting with Joshua in the middle; Lisa was barely hanging on to the edge. This wasn't exactly her dream of the perfect senior year, and it opened that tiny chamber in my walnut heart where everything small and mean lived. Maybe if she'd been less eager to be done with me, we could have made up by now and she would be having the birthday she really wanted. Indoors, unwrapping the vintage Broadway poster I'd picked out of a catalog for her back in June.

"I have to work anyway," I said. "Stop feeling sorry for me."

Bill was giving me the puppy head tilt. "Doug said there's going to be a huge shack party out at the Scotch Shore. You should go. You'll have way more fun than us."

"We'll see."

"You know, the rules state ..." Bill opened his biology binder, pretending to read. "She who asks first gets priority, but, uh, that should not stop anyone else from taking her nineteen-year-old-looking self into a liquor store to buy the person, uh, herewith and henceforth, some birthday booze...."

"I'm sorry, I think you just accidentally asked me to buy you alcohol for a party I'm not invited to."

He shoveled a handful of fries into his gob, chewing them with his mouth as wide open as possible.

"Buddy, why don't you ask ..." I was about to say Doug, then remembered the old bottle of moonshine at the back of my bedroom closet. Was it still good, like Rupert said it would be? Or I could do a trade with Doug for something less science-project. After all, that guy across the table—the charmer with the mouthful of masticated potato that he was letting ooze onto his mock turtleneck—had chosen us over Tracy, and since "us" still included me, it wouldn't hurt to do him a favor.

Like a wee karmic bounce for my good intentions, a postcard from Sid was waiting for me when I got home from the Grunt. It had a photo of a hang-in-there kitty swinging from a tree with a penis drawn on its fluffy white front. On the back of the card he'd scrawled:

Never hate your enemies. It affects your judgment.
—Michael Corleone, The Godfather Part III

I dumped wet, heavy leaves out of Rupert's old wheelbarrow onto the compost pile. My back was aching, and I'd had a minor cardiac event when some variety of rodent had dashed out of the leaves and over my feet. I could handle that in the outdoors, but inside the old house I sometimes still got the heebie-jeebies. One evening I reached under the kitchen sink to grab what I thought was a scouring pad, and a mouse carcass disintegrated in my bare hand.

It had quickly become obvious why Rupert had let things get so bad. For all his talk about wanting to go out of this world swiftly, he seemed awfully afraid of overexerting himself. But he kept busy, always had a little project to work on. While I raked, he sat on the side veranda, taking apart an old radio and watching Shaggy root around in the temporary pen that Francis had set up for him. The earth he'd turn up would become a vegetable garden next year.

"Someone's going to need a bath tonight," Rupert said.

"How does that work exactly?" I asked. "One of you holds him and other hoses him off?"

"Hose?" Rupert put down his magnifying glass. "Girl, the

hose water's far too cold, *far* too cold. No, we do him in the house."

"You mean in the tub?"

"Sure, in the tub. Where else are you going to take a bath?"

"How do you get him in and out?"

"He steps in, and he steps out. You have to put towels down because he's feeling uncertain on his feet these days and he gets nervous stepping on the wet tile. Mostly psychological. He's still spry."

Shaggy was at that moment sinking to his knees before thudding heavily onto his side and sighing. Nap time. I sat in the grass beside him, reaching into the pen to stroke the bristly fur along his back. "You remind me of my friend Bill," I whispered.

He farted appreciatively.

"Rupert, what did you put in that moonshine?" I asked.

"You try it?"

"Not yet. I was wondering how you made it."

"Well, you got to have a still. Matter fact, my still's still down in the basement, in the cold room. The Constable thinks I've lost the key. Suppose we should clear it out before he finds out otherwise."

Did I care what the Constable would make of the idea that was beginning to take shape? What I could do with a working still? No, I did not. He had been such a prick at dinner that I'd gone back to dodging him again. Every time I found one of his soggy herbal tea bags sitting on the edge of the sink, collapsed into itself like a miniature, moss-scented Jabba the Hutt, I thought again of how he'd baited me. *You must be a wellspring of flawless decision making.* It hardly made sense, the way he put it. Besides, that was why he'd come here, wasn't it? To live out a romantic fantasy about living among country people, soaking up their folksy wisdom? Then he got right pissy, as my crazy uncle Burpie would put it, when people turned out to be just like themselves.

"Why don't we go have a look at it?" I said to Rupert.

It took us two hours to locate the key to the cold room that Rupert insisted he hadn't lost, eventually finding it in a trunk in his room where he stored old bedding along with some expired lottery tickets worth about twenty bucks, three silver dollars, and a ballpoint pen. "Burying things seems to be your thing," I said. "What's with the pen?"

"Must have accidentally set it down when I put away something else," he said, tucking it into his plastic pocket protector. "Lord knows what we'll find with all them bodies I buried in the cold room."

There wasn't much to a still, as it turns out. A dusty old electric stove, a bucket, a pot, copper tubing, other odds and ends. "Now, that bottle you found, that was grain alcohol," Rupert said. "But when I was your age, we used to make what they call sugar shine. Cheap as dirt. Cook up some sugar, dump it into a fermenter, add yeast, let it sit."

"That's it?"

"More or less. My buddy Len used to add a good shake of grape cough syrup. For flavor, see."

"What about real fruit?" I asked, and he pondered this seriously. "Not that we'll ever find out."

"Oh, come on, girl. Not with the two of us living with the law."

"Though you could say there's an educational component. Like, the idea about the fruit, that's a hypothesis we could test out."

"And it's not like we're selling it. That's when they throw the book at you." Rupert gave me an impish smile. "I knew you were going to be the good kind of trouble," he said.

We went to three different grocery stores, in three different towns, to pick up the ingredients and glass jars with lids. We didn't exactly look like criminals—in the car I noticed Rupert was wearing mismatched shoes—but he insisted that there were too many people around with long memories, and wouldn't get out of Abe when I bought the yeast.

Once we'd scrubbed down the equipment and finished the initial cook, we had to let the mash ferment down in the basement for a couple of weeks. After that, we finished it off and pulled everything together in the jars, some with peaches on the bottom, some with apples, and dashes of cinnamon and nutmeg. They were so pretty, it was a shame I couldn't show my mother.

"It's yours," Rupert said. "Do what you want with it; just don't let the Constable find out. I never thought a little booze did a kid harm."

I reserved a couple of jars that I hid behind the antique plates at the back of Rupert's old hutch and gave a couple more to Bill. "May you always overcompensate for being a cop's daughter," he said, holding the jar of apple shine up to the light. Then he actually hugged me.

The rest I brought to my fellow delinquents at what became an epic shack party on Lisa's birthday weekend. I got into the finals of a new drinking game Doug invented called Shot Shot Chug, danced my tail off, had a brief make-out session with Skateboarder Brad, and everyone's vomit smelled like granny-baked pies.

I might have been on my own island, but at least I could swim.

SEVENTEEN

I greeted Rupert in the kitchen with a pair of plaid slippers that had a rubber tread. "Gee, I could wear them outdoors," he said. "They're sturdy enough."

That's basically what Bill had said when I'd given him his pair, which he'd been wearing at school with less and less irony every day that week.

"Yes, but you won't because this is how we're keeping the floors clean."

"The Constable, he goes out one door, and the Corporal, she comes in the other."

"Corporal outranks constable, so you'd better listen to her," Francis said, padding into the kitchen. He set his mug on the edge of the sink, taking out the tea bag and plopping it down beside it.

My back teeth clamped together.

I'd walked from the lighthouse after picking up my pay-
check, coming in from the side veranda, and hadn't seen his
car in the drive. He'd started a new shift schedule, something
like five days on, three nights on, three days off. I must have
miscalculated.

"Thought you'd be at work," I said.

"Off today. Can I stick around?"

"Yes."

"Say that again?"

"Yes . . ."

"No, the first time you—"

"Yep. Yup. Yeah. Yay?"

"There's an Elizabeth Bishop poem where she describes the
way people around here say *yes* as they breathe in. It's supposed
to mean something like, *Yes, life's like that. Also death.*"

I'd never heard myself say *yes* like Francis was describing,
but it brought to mind Nat's sighs, what she could say with an
exhale.

That's nice.

That sucks.

He's so dreamy.

You're so right.

If you say so.

Why don't you kill me?

Seriously, just kill me.

"We're all about the subtext," I said, and gave an inner high five to Miss Aker for teaching me to use that word in a conversation.

"You'll stay anyway, won't you, kid?" Rupert asked.

There were about a million other things I'd rather have been doing, and from the way Francis was looking at me, I could tell that he could tell. "Up to you," he said. "Lots to do, whether I'm around or not."

I forced a smile. "Rupert, you got the fish and blueberries out of the deep freeze?" He nodded. "Should be enough for one more," I said to Francis.

"No, thanks. I don't like fish."

I made a deep pot of blueberry grunt for Rupert, sploshing plain flour dumplings into the hot cauldron of sweet berries. After years of watching Mum, it was like whistling an old song, and soon I was doing just that, with Rupert nodding in time to the old Celtic tunes.

As I made the sweet stew, I stewed about Francis, who was in the living room, sewing new buttons onto a jacket. Had I seen a guy sew before? My own coat had a button that had been hanging from its last thread for weeks. I'd also never heard someone refuse to eat because they didn't *like* it. My parents used to make us eat disgusting foods a few times a year—sauerkraut, liver, the chewy seaweed dulse—Dad because it was "character building," and Mum because she was terrified we'd turn up our noses at a meal at someone else's house. If we'd ever done that in front of her, she would have excused us from the table and tearfully wrung our necks.

I moved on to "Something in the Way" from *Nevermind*, which I'd discovered in the cassette deck that Francis had tucked next to Rupert's old record player. Rupert began to sing: *"It's okay to eat fish / Cuz they don't have any feelings. . . ."*

He caught my eye. "I take in more than people think," he said.

Since we were on the subject of fish and had been on the subject of Elizabeth Bishop and possibly because I thought Francis might be listening, I griped to Rupert that Miss Aker had assigned us the poem "The Fish" for homework and I thought it was cheesy. Francis dropped everything, literally, ran upstairs for his collection of Elizabeth Bishop poems and thumped it on the kitchen table. "Cheesy," he said. *"Cheesy."*

The poem, if you haven't had the pleasure, is about this woman—or this person, I don't remember if it's a woman—who catches a huge fish. As it's flopping around she sees that it's got fishing lines in its mouth from tearing itself free in the past, like ribbons hanging down from war medals. Relics of former battles. But she's caught the fish, and this could be the end of the line for it, so to speak. Except . . .

"She lets the fish go," I explained to Rupert. "I know she comes to appreciate it, to see it differently and all that, but . . . she lets it go."

"Sounds like you're not big on a happy ending," Rupert

said, "and Mick here is."

"She said cheesy, not happy."

"Cheesy because it was the obvious thing to do," I said. "It's like, why does every romantic comedy end with someone running through the rain to tell someone they love them? Why can't, for once, people just shake hands and wish each other well?"

"So it would have been better if Bishop had defied expectations?"

"It would have been more interesting. Nervier."

"But maybe she chose that ending *in spite* of the fact that it seemed like the obvious choice."

"How's a person supposed to know that?"

"Does anyone read a poem without asking themselves what it means? It's poetry, not reportage. There's subtext."

"It's sentimental, Francis."

"Yeah, it is, Frances. That's what makes it brave."

The rally over, I became aware of how long I'd been looking into Francis's absurdly blue eyes. I didn't want to be the first to look away, was determined not to flinch—until Francis grinned. "Why don't you give it another chance?" he said.

I read the poem again. Near the end, she describes how she "stared and stared" at the fish, this veteran of at least five previous battles, and begins to understand the size of her victory as a pool of oil spreads a rainbow around the engine that soon encircles the entire boat—

—until everything
was rainbow, rainbow, rainbow!
And I let the fish go.

"Well, maybe," I said. "I hadn't thought of it that way."

I read the lines again, nodding. The important part seemed to be *before* she let it go.

Rupert squinted at the book. He couldn't read much without his magnifying glass and we hadn't yet made the daily rediscovery of it. "So *no one* eats this fish?"

I escaped with Shaggy to the soft-floored tack room of the barn. It was steeped in the deep scent of old wood and hay and the earth itself behind a stone wall sculpted around the hill slope that intruded inside. A few dusty bridles still hung from nails. Miscellaneous trash had gathered in corners—piles of yellowed newspapers, empty pop bottles, paint cans, rusted tools. I reached for a silver lozenge tin overflowing with ancient cigarette butts, meaning to dump it into the garbage bag I'd brought with me, but then thought better of it. It was like a still-life painting, a picture of Rupert before he had his heart attack and gave up smoking, before he started leaving his magnifying glass in the fridge or on the side of the tub and in other improbable places. I could almost see him leaning against the corner of the stable, cigarette dangling from his lip, in his baggy jeans and suspenders and a soft flannel shirt with its plastic pocket protector, which always held two pens.

Shaggy announced Francis's arrival with a loud squeal. He could be like a dog sometimes, as excited to greet you after you've come back from the bathroom as he would be if you'd returned from months at sea.

Francis scratched him between the ears then took a ten-dollar bill from his back pocket and handed it over. "Rupert can afford to buy his own slippers. Believe me, I've helped him with his banking. But you know this is a guy who lived through two world wars and the Depression."

"My mum's like that too. Frugal for life."

"You're his biggest extravagance. His only extravagance. He knows he needs you if this whole staying-at-home thing is going to work."

"Can I ask you something? Why me? Why not post an ad for a housekeeper?"

"He wanted you. Just you. Said he could tell that you're a real firecracker and a great defender of pigs."

The mention of firecrackers silenced us both. I remembered again the weight of Francis on me, my shoulder blades pressing into the cool mud as colors rained down from the black sky.

"Hyperbole, but I'll take it," I said.

"I don't think . . ." He hesitated.

"Does *hyperbole* not mean what I think it means?"

"No, you're right. But it might be pronounced *hi-PER-bolee*." I'd said *hyperbowl*.

I wasn't a blusher. Lisa couldn't answer a question in class without red blotches appearing on her neck, and when she was truly mortified, she looked like someone had been hanging her by the ankles. Not me, sayer of anything, if not everything. As it turns out, not always correctly. I could feel the fire creeping from my collarbone to my cheeks. What evolutionary purpose could this be serving, announcing to the world that a person knows she's humiliated herself?

"Sorry, that's a dick move," he said, "correcting someone's pronunciation. I never know whether it's worse to let people keep saying things wrong, or—"

"No, no, it's fine. Fine. *Whew*, I don't feel very well." I rubbed the back of my burning neck, fooling no one, not even Shaggy, who was staring up at me with profound pity. "I'm gonna splash some water on my face."

I was seething at the hose by the side of the barn. Not at Francis, at myself. God, I must have sounded like Mum. Was verbal dyslexia hereditary? I'd always had a problem with *laborious*—though it *should* be *layborus*—and *ethereal*, a frothy white dress of a word that my mouth was determined to turn into *ereethral*, which sounds like the end of an angel's urinary tract. Worse than my fumble: the pathetic attempt to pretend that I wasn't embarrassed when I so clearly was and should be.

This is why you are here, I reminded myself, patting my face and neck down with water, to earn money to go to a university where you will learn to be less of an idiot. Someday, maybe,

I'd have a grown-up conversation where I said all of the words correctly and someone could bring up the history or politics of a random faraway place and I'd know—really know—what they were talking about. I used to fantasize about getting into a debate with an Ivy League grad at what appeared, in my imagination, like a kitchen party at Woody Allen's apartment. *Oh, that's a rather simplistic way of looking at it, don't you think?* I'd say. *What about the long history of turmoil between the Frodites and the Schmirnites? I believe the native word for it is . . .* And everyone around us would smile into their wineglasses. How did you become a person like that when you were from a place like this? Could you?

I gave Shaggy a drink from the hose. He chewed at the stream of water, then put his head into it and shook like a dog. I gasped as the cold water splattered all over me.

"Okay?" Francis was leaning against the corner of the barn chewing a piece of straw, the same pose I'd pictured Rupert in earlier.

I pulled my wet shirt away from my body. Navy, thank god. "I think it's passed."

"Look, what you said before—"

"Oh, please don't—"

"No, a while back, about finding the guy at his mother's house. You were right; that's where he turned up. I should have been more grateful for the advice. I guess I hated that I needed it so much."

"Don't worry about it."

"There's this other thing I wonder if I should do. That is, I wonder if you think I should do it."

He was looking over at a giant pumpkin sitting on a skid by his car.

"Where did *that* come from? Are you—"

"From the Johnsons' farm up the road. And yes, yes, I am. Pumpkin regatta-ing, on behalf of the force. Or I'm supposed to. Do you think I should?"

"I think you should have made up your mind before you did whatever it was you had to do to get that pumpkin over here." It was, well, large enough for a grown man to sit in.

"The Johnsons have a forklift."

"So, you're asking me if you should disembowel that pumpkin, decorate it, take it down to the bay, climb inside, and race it in the freezing-cold waters?"

"Why, you make it sound so impractical."

I turned the hose on him.

"Holy *shhhh*—!"

I hit him again.

This time, he ran at the tap—*"Ha! Ho! Ho! Ha!"*—and wrenched it off.

"It'll be a touch colder than that," I said.

"Only if I tip over!" He shook the water out of his ears like Shaggy, then leaned over to catch his breath. "Is that a no?"

"No—I mean, yeah, I think you should. It's like Dad said, let the community see you."

"That's what I was thinking."

"The race was his idea—did you know that? This is the first time he's missed it in, like, ten years."

Dad had a tradition of always wearing his uniform, plus a little something extra. The previous year it was a purple tutu that collared the top of the pumpkin when he sat in it. He wasn't even planning to watch this year. Said he wanted to be properly on his feet before going to a public event, and none of the people who'd called to coax him into making an appearance had been able to change his mind about that.

"I know," Francis said. "That's why I want to do it."

He walked down the slope a ways. "Every day I wake up and open the window and I can't believe how beautiful it is. Look at those trees."

I joined him, the water from our clothes dripping onto the ground like raindrops from an eaves trough after a storm. The valley was alight with fall colors, Rupert's blueberry patch a lava-like spread of deep pinks and reds. "You've seen better trees than this, I'm sure."

"I know it's hard for you to believe it, but in this one way, it's better here. And it's better in there"—he nodded toward the house—"because of you. And better at work too. So thanks."

EIGHTEEN

It started with "The Fish," I think, and got stronger at the pumpkin regatta, but really took hold when I went to clean the bathroom sink.

It wasn't Rupert's fingernail I found there. He liked to sit in an old rocking chair on the side veranda and file his nails while he looked over the fields. And here's the thing: If you see a fingernail in a rose-colored bathroom sink—or anywhere—and you do not want to murder its owner for the offense of leaving it for someone to find, when not too long ago that same person's tea bag crimes were enraging, and if sweeping said nail into the garbage can feels intimate and homey and leads you to wonder if he has any dirty laundry you could take care of, then you are in a new kind of trouble.

Each week the temperature had dropped one degree

outdoors and warmed one degree between me and Francis. We no longer moved around each other like accidental contact would be nuclear, though we were still a smidge too polite, a touch too agreeable—not like people who had made out but also not like people who were *over* the fact that they'd made out.

I'd watched him race for the detachment at the regatta—a fierce contest, with accusations that the fire marshal's vessel was leaking because it'd been tampered with, possibly by the handbell choir. Francis had to give him a tow, and still came in second. When he climbed out of his giant pumpkin, his uniform sopping wet and covered in pumpkin slime, he saluted the crowd before accepting the second-place ribbon and handing it to me in the stands to pass on to my father.

"Lot of people said they missed seeing you this year," I told Dad when I gave it to him.

"They'd still be missing me if I'd gone," he said, "seeing as I'm not myself."

That stuck with me, and I noodled it again as I finished cleaning Rupert's upstairs bathroom. Did Dad think that people only wanted him around if he was being the tough but fair-minded and always reliable Sergeant? I'd always thought people liked him as much, maybe more, when he was strutting along the dock in his purple tutu.

I placed a fresh bar of herbal mint soap—Francis's favorite—in the shower and stood there staring at it. I'd gotten into the habit of doing little things for him, like shining his black work shoes and lining them neatly at the bottom of the back staircase, or stuffing the tea box to overflowing, which finally broke him of the tea bag habit. Just being friendly, right? Can't read anything into a tea bag or a bar of soap.

Bullshite, I heard Lisa say. So clearly, I almost turned around to see if she was standing behind me.

Right. And what would Nat say, if we were exchanging more than the occasional smile? That if Francis and I were real friends, he'd be doing things for me too.

I took the soap out of the shower and brought it downstairs with the cleaning supplies, then went up and put it back and then took it out again.

"Get it together, Frances," I muttered, forcing myself to drop it in the dish for the third time.

Francis came home before I could change my mind again. "I've been meaning to ask you how the chords are going," he said, pulling off the shoes I'd polished for him. He tossed them in the direction of the mudroom off the kitchen.

"Great."

"Show me your left hand."

I held it up, and he crossed the freshly scrubbed linoleum and touched the pads of his fingers to mine. I'd backed into the kitchen counter as he came toward me, and a drawer handle was now digging into the back of my hip. I could also feel a faint throbbing in my hand—was it his pulse or my pulse? Maybe he felt it too—or standing like a pair of mimes got too awkward.

"No calluses," he said, heading for the fridge.

"I don't callus."

"Not if you don't practice, you don't."

I escaped upstairs again, where I had nothing left to do, so I changed Rupert's sheets sooner than they needed it. I crept down, slipped the pink tennis shoes I'd taken to wearing around the farmhouse into my bag, and grabbed my coat from the banister. The top button, the button that had been hanging loose for weeks, was tightly sewn in place. My mother or . . . ?

Francis was in the doorway, holding two guitars. "Hey. Thanks," I said.

He shrugged. "Before you go, come in here and show me what you've been doing."

I put the coat back on the banister and followed him into the living room, where Rupert was dozing in his yellow rocker. "Oh!" he said, jerking awake. "Very good."

The cheery wood guitar Francis handed me was so much better than my old beater. Not only did mine not have a good sound, there was also the rack situation. If I tucked my chest behind the guitar, I felt like I was miles away from the strings and my shoulders and ribs would begin to ache within minutes. The alternative was to use the top of the guitar as a breast display shelf. This guitar of Francis's was thinner, slicker, accommodated my chest behind the instrument, and it rang out beautifully.

"For starters, you're holding too tight," Francis said. "Pull your wrist down. Now let's see B-minor."

I couldn't get my fingers to stay in the right place on the fret, and whistled the note as I strummed to cover my flubbing.

"I've never heard anyone whistle like you do. Who taught you?"

"No one, that I can remember. I can't make both hands work at the same time on the piano, and, well, here's how I'm doing on strings. But whistling, you just do it, if you can."

He adjusted my wrist—firmly, nurse-like, somehow still sending a shiver up my arm—then watched me switch between G and D. "Stop doing that with your—"

"I'm not—" I slapped away his hand before he could touch me again.

"No slapsies!" Rupert called over from his rocker.

"I'm trying to help you," Francis said. "When you strum a single chord, it's good, clear. Switching . . ."

"There's no rule that says you have to play more than one chord at a time."

"Set an egg timer and do the switch again and again until you can get through two minutes without grinding your teeth."

As soon as he said it, I felt my teeth clench.

"Or I can give you a simple song to practice, which is more fun than random chords. You like blues? No? What about a waltz? You have this nice background cadence—*dum-dee duh-duh*—and the melody floats up from it."

"Mmm . . ."

"How about . . ." He played a riff on his guitar. "Soft, see? Sweet. And you can add a little dissonance to make it interesting." His fingers trebled over a minor note, and now the shiver raced up my arms to the very top of my head. God, were the hairs on my neck actually *standing up*? I had to start strumming to make it stop.

It took a couple of runs to get the chords even halfway right, and then we started playing the song on repeat. Once I stopped tripping over D-minor, he began to sing very softly under his breath.

> *Here so far away*
> *The ocean is a finger lake*
> *The highway is a well-worn path*
> *That brings me back to you*

"It's a ballad," I said.

"You object to ballads?"

"They're like commercials for relationships."

Francis nodded. "I have no idea what you're talking about. Would it be less disgusting if we call it a lullaby? If you thought of a mother singing this to her child?"

"Yes."

"So it's a lullaby. Look behind you."

In the small window over Wilfred's birdcage, the moon was full and pink.

We kept playing on a loop, and after a while I began to sing too. Under my breath at first, and then a little louder, my voice still buried underneath his. I wanted to see if I could play and sing at the same time, which I could. And then, without warning, Francis switched to harmony. Tricked. Like when you're learning to ride a bike and suddenly you realize that no one is holding the back of your seat. I leaned in and followed his voice like the curves in the road. I wanted to go and go and go.

"I don't want to break up the party, son, but didn't you say you had to meet this lady by eight?"

"Oh. You have a date," I said. "I'm keeping you." I stood up abruptly, giving the E string an accidental twang.

This time, Francis didn't follow me to the hallway. I slipped on my boots, picked up the bag holding my tennis shoes, and stopped. Why did I always bring them home? It was silly, wasn't it? To cart them back and forth every time, these very pink ladies' tennis shoes?

Bullshite, I heard Lisa say again.

Ignoring her, I set the shoes on the landing of the staircase, off to the side so they wouldn't trip anyone but would still be plainly visible to, say, a guy and his visitor going upstairs to one of the bedrooms.

NINETEEN

A week later, I was no better. I found myself playing Yahtzee with an eighty-two-year-old on a late Saturday afternoon, hoping to hang around long enough to see if Francis was going on another date after his shift. I'd spent three days looking forward to my next trip to the farm on the off chance I would see him, however briefly, because seeing him had come to define whether it was a good day and not seeing him left me with a void I couldn't fill, not with food, not with obsessive chord practice that left my ribs bruised and my fingers dented and stinging, and most definitely not with anyone else.

"You planning to get up to no good tonight?" Rupert asked.

"Probably."

I'd need to leave soon if I wanted to catch Bill's hockey game against East Riverview. I didn't think he'd mind if I missed it, especially after he said Nat was planning to go, but I could see he was disappointed when I told him that Rupert might need me to stay late at the farm. Maybe even hurt.

"Do you want me to set up dinner before I leave?" I said to Rupert. "Or is Francis coming home before he goes out tonight?"

Rupert shrugged. If he knew something, he wasn't saying.

The phone rang. "That could be him now," I said, reaching for it.

"Good, you're still there," Dad said. "The old man in the room with you?"

"Yeah, right here." I mouthed to Rupert, *My dad.*

"George, try to fix your face so he can't tell what I'm about to say to you. Can you do that? Can you stay calm?"

"Course." I got up and wandered as far from Rupert as the cord would let me go.

"I just got off the phone with June. McAdams responded to a nine-one-one call that came in from the Scotch Shore as he was passing through. Someone saw a man stranded on a boulder out in the bay. Caught by the tide, probably."

It was getting dark. The water was freezing.

"He wouldn't go in after him."

"She thinks he did. You want me to tell the old man what's going on?"

"No, I'll do it."

"Better wait to until there's something to report. Can you spend the night, if need be?"

"I will. Thanks, Dad."

"Try not to assume the worst, kiddo."

I hung up. Took a breath. Found a lower gear inside me. Steady.

"What'd your old man want?" Rupert asked.

"Oh, he was talking to June—you know Constable Basque? She mentioned that Francis has to work late. He thought he'd send that on in case you didn't know."

"That's what passes for exciting gossip in these parts. Well, you don't have to stick around. There must be a nice fella who wants your company tonight."

"Actually, you'd be doing me a favor if I could stay here." I made a mental note to call Bill in the morning. "Dad said my mum is having people over for oysters and sauerkraut tonight."

Rupert coughed. "There. I have a bad cold and need a nurse."

We gave Shaggy a bath in the tub and fed him oatmeal and Rupert beat me three more times at Yahtzee before he went to bed with Shaggy in tow.

I was just about to call my dad again when I saw the lights turn up the drive.

Francis came in wearing what looked like a borrowed sweat suit, much too big. His hair was wet, face gray and blotchy, eyes haunted. He held a duffel bag in one hand, a paper bag in the shape of a bottle in the other.

He looked startled to see me. "George."

"How are you doing? You didn't drive yourself."

"June brought me home."

Should I ask? "And the man?"

"We got him."

I breathed a sigh of relief.

"But his wife . . ."

Francis leaned against the wall in the entryway as though he couldn't keep himself upright.

"His wife was there too? In the water?"

He nodded, then shook his head.

"She didn't make it."

I don't know what I intended when I went over to him—to hug him, help him make his way all the way inside—but he put up his hand.

"You can go," he said. "It's so late."

"I already told my parents I was staying over. I'll curl up on the couch. You can sleep in and not worry about what Rupert is getting up to."

"Okay. Okay, thanks, George."

When I heard the shower upstairs, I called Dad, who'd gotten word that Francis was heading home. He said the couple were tourists and the emergency responders didn't know about the woman until Francis dragged the husband to shore. They didn't expect to find her—or most likely, her body—until it was light out.

"He saved one of them," Dad said. "Going into rough water like that, this time of year . . ." I could practically hear him shaking his head. "It's what the staff sergeant would call 'stupid courage.'"

I couldn't tell if that was a compliment.

"Keep an eye on him tonight, George. Call me if you need to."

After throwing another log on the fire, I lay on the old red chesterfield under an afghan. I was just starting to doze off when I heard the creak of the floorboards. Francis was in the doorway, holding a bottle of whiskey and two glasses. "There's a pig on my bed."

I patted the arm of the green bong sofa that was kitty-cornered to the red chesterfield. He placed the bottle on the steamer trunk that served as a coffee table, sat on the sofa, and pulled a throw over himself. We didn't speak for a long while. I could hear every breath he was taking, and was conscious of my breathing too, which suddenly seemed mannered and excessive.

"A life-and-death experience makes you think about hard truths," he said, pouring whiskey into the glasses. He handed one to me.

"I can imagine."

"Like how outdoor swimming pool water is always slightly too cold, except in the rare instance when it is unsettlingly pee warm."

"That *is* a hard truth," I said after a moment.

So this is what shock looks like, I thought. Maybe he shouldn't be drinking.

"You go," he said.

My mind was blank and I said so.

"What were you saying to Rupert the other day about corn?"

"Just that baby corn shouldn't be considered a vegetable."

"Because ..."

"Because, scientifically speaking, it's Satan's tiny, floppy penis."

He sort of half laughed, took a swig. "My turn. George, you are crippled by your horror of earnestness."

Under different circumstances, I might have gotten a little yelly. He made me sound like the Elevens. But this conversation was taking turns that I couldn't follow, and I didn't dare try to lead.

"You don't like ballads," he said. "You think 'The Fish' is cheesy."

"I changed my mind about 'The Fish.' Anyway, I think it's more that I don't like cheap emotion. I don't care if someone is enthusiastic about something."

"So you wouldn't mind if I got up and started dancing earnestly?"

"What does that even mean, 'dancing earnestly'?"

He was up in an instant. There was some lip-biting, a lot of punching the air.

"Stop! Oh god, please stop. What was *that?*"

"I call it 'Serbian disco.'"

He flopped down on the sofa again. Then he began to cry. He pressed his face into the crook of his arm and his whole body shuddered, and I didn't know what to do. I let my hand drop to his head and stroked his hair. It had grown in a bit, and as it dried from his shower it was settling into soft black curls. If I reached a little farther, I could rest my hand on his neck, slide it down to the top of his back.

I said, "My dad says you have stupid courage."

"That means I don't think before I act."

"You make it sound like it wasn't brave."

He sat up, stared at the last few drops of liquid in his glass. "He was screaming for his wife. In the water, in the ambulance, at the hospital. *Kate, Kate, Kate . . .*"

"We don't have to talk about it."

"Your voice is the only thing drowning it out. So to speak."

I moved over to the green sofa, refilled his glass, and took a long sip from mine. The whiskey felt both sharp and warm going down. We leaned back and watched the fire. "Now I can't think of anything to say," I admitted. "I'm scared I'll make it worse."

"You don't seem to be scared of much."

"I'm a good faker."

"What are you most afraid of?"

Of making a fool of myself. That some people are nice to me only

because they're intimidated by me. That I'll never get out of here and I'll
turn into my parents.

"Bears."

"Come on, Frances. . . ."

"What reasonable person isn't scared of bears, Francis?"

"That's not what you're *most* afraid of." He smiled. "Do you know that when you're not sure how to answer a question, you look up at the top corner of the room? And if you're really unsure, your eyes travel down to the bottom corner. And if you're really, really unsure, they go all the way around the room and back up to that first corner."

"I'm *thinking.* I can't look at someone while I think."

"And what are you thinking?"

That I'm afraid I'm not smart enough for you. That I'm okay at a bunch of things but not exceptional at any of them. And for a couple of hours there, and probably from now on, that something will happen to someone I care about.

"I'm thinking that I might be most afraid of hurting someone's feelings," I said. "Someone who can't take it, and not being able to undo it."

"Have you?"

"Yes. Oh, I heard it that time, the Elizabeth Bishop *yes.*"

"That's from a poem called 'The Moose.' I reread it the other day."

"How's it go?"

180

"*Life's like that. We know it (also death).*"

We were not lingering on that. "What about you?" I said. "What are you most afraid of?"

"Bears."

I swatted him.

"Alright, my thing is I'm scared I'll make a small mistake, the kind people make every day—forgetting to unplug the iron or to do a shoulder check before I switch lanes, hitting the brakes instead of steering out of a skid—and it'll ruin someone's life. That's my biggest fear."

"You don't think you did that tonight, do you?"

"I'm not sure."

I thought of what my father had said: *That guy ain't police.* "Is this what you want to be when you grow up?"

"It has to be. I don't want to fail at this. Too. I don't want to fail at this too."

"You're not failing."

"Would you tell me if I was?"

No. Maybe. I don't know.

"Yes."

I moved back to the red chesterfield and we stretched out under our afghans and talked into the night about the stupid-hard F chord, the different accents on the north mountain and south mountain (not different at all, to my ear, but I went along with it), where the fictional George and Francis would go on their third adventure after they'd conquered New York and the Serengeti, and other easy things. When I opened my eyes in the morning, Shaggy's snout was rifling around my armpit, looking for who knows what, and the green sofa was empty.

TWENTY

A couple of weeks later, I went to fetch Dad's cigarettes from his bedroom and came back to find him missing from his recliner. He was on the floor, writhing in pain.

"Oh my god, what is it? What is it?" I started grabbing at him, lifting his arms, patting his legs, checking behind his shoulders.

"My foot," he gasped. "I need you to massage my foot."

When I reached for it, he gripped my arm. "The other one."

There was no other one. Just his stump in a compression sock that helped keep the swelling down.

"I don't know what you mean. I don't know how."

"Please!"

I faked it as best I could. It was ridiculous, like I was pretending to be a baker kneading dough, and somehow the pretending was weirder and more uncomfortable than actually touching him.

Whether it worked or the pain began to subside on its own, I couldn't tell. I helped him to his chair, which was crazy hard. It was only then that I saw how much weight he'd gained, how soft he'd gotten. He was soaked with sweat and didn't fight me when I brought over a cloth and gave him a wipe down. Face, shoulders, arms. He leaned forward so I could do his neck. I worked as quickly as I could. All business. The cloth made a scraping sound against his three-day-old beard.

He was now completely without emotion, like his pilot light was blown out. "What were they thinking?" he muttered.

"Who were what . . . ?"

He waved off the question.

I placed a pack of cigarettes on the side table with his pain-killers and a glass of water. "Where's Mum?" I asked.

"Store."

Right. I'd heard him ragging on her about running out of artificial sweetener for his tea—the tea he drank to wash down his new afternoon cookie habit—and she was so quick out the door, you had to think she was grateful to have a break from him. "Do you need anything else? Where's your prosthetic?"

He shook his head, not looking at me.

"Alright, well. I have to go to work."

Matty was sitting outside the family room, his arms wrapped

around his knees. I gave him a hand up and we went to the kitchen.

"I think it's something called phantom pain," he said as I poured him a glass of juice. "I read about it at the library. It happens a lot, feeling pain where the limb used to be. Like, probably most of them have it. Sometimes right away, sometimes later. Sometimes for a while, sometimes forever."

"You'd think they'd have warned him."

"They must have; it's in all the pamphlets. I don't know why he's trying to hide it."

"Because he won't cop to psychological problems."

"I don't think it *is* psychological. I think it's really real."

"He won't get the difference." I wasn't sure I did either. If you felt a pain in a limb that wasn't there anymore, how could it *not* be psychological?

"Do you think Mum knows what's going on?"

Mum wasn't exactly savvy about health issues. Like how she would give Dad insulin in the morning and then serve him dessert at lunch, as if that were the solution. Her whole side of the family was like that. I remember Nan telling Mum that she was depriving us of vegetables because she wouldn't let us eat potato chips for lunch, and my great-aunt Hester rasping, "Screw the doctor. Any fool can hear my asthma gets better when I smoke."

"Wouldn't matter if she did," I said. "Not when he's ordering her around like he's King Louis of France."

"What should we do?"

I tipped a little more orange juice into his glass. "I will go to the farm. Dad will snooze in his chair. Mum will make him tea when she gets home and let him eat cookies. And you will practice the tuba and do your homework and save us all."

Francis's room usually looked like a monk's quarters, every surface clear, few signs of modern life, so it was strange to see his bed unmade, his clothes piled up on the desk chair. I sniffed one of the shirts. Under the scents of soap and fabric softener was something warmer, muskier.

"What are you doing, honey?"

Rupert.

"I was wondering if I should add this to the wash."

"If it suits you."

"I think I won't. He might not want me touching his stuff." I put down the shirt and started collecting tea mugs from the windowsill. "Except I'll take these."

"He's not sleeping," Rupert said. "He thinks I don't know, but I'm an old man. I get up to pee. I spend a lot of time considering whether I will get up to pee before I do it. As I'm considering, I listen to him pacing in his room." He picked up a stray mug from the desk. "I'm hoping this woman will take his mind off things."

My breakfast rolled over in my stomach.

"That same woman he was going out with before?"

"He's started seeing a new gal from town. Lorissa something."

Lorissa. Of course her name was kind of foreign.

"Oh. That's nice."

"Yes, he needs some fun. More time with people his own age."

Maybe that was why I'd hardly seen him over the past couple of weeks. I'd thought he'd just been hiding at work.

They'd found the wife's body in the morning, which was awful, but no one blamed Francis. He had been transformed from a Come From Away rookie cop into a local hero overnight. The farmhouse filled up with houseplants and baked goods that people hand-delivered from up and down the valley. A third-grade class had written individual letters to thank him for protecting the community. Rupert said he returned to work after only a couple of days' leave, but the acting sergeant was sending him on the easier calls when he could. He was finding it less stressful sitting in his car off the highway with his speed radar than waiting for the next knock on the door.

Francis came home as I was pulling on my boots. He'd cut off his curls again, which brought out the hardness in his face, made his expression that much more severe. "You're still here," he said.

Something about the way he said it suggested he'd put off returning until he was sure I was gone.

"I was just leaving. How're you doing?"

"You should be going out with your friends, not spending

all your time out in the boonies. You do have friends, don't you? Know a few boys your own age?"

I felt as though I'd been slapped.

"Don't worry about me," I said, reaching around him to snatch my coat out of the closet. "I'm the most fuckable girl at school."

It was stupid and it was juvenile and I didn't stick around for him to tell me so.

A light, floating. A dingy in the night water.

I rubbed my eyes.

I was looking through a window, the lighthouse window. The dot of light was on the ridge above.

Slowly, I reoriented myself. I'd been so pissed when I left Francis, stomping to my car like a brat only to remember that I had nowhere to go. Not home, not before I had to, and Bill was out with Nat. So I went down to the lighthouse, turned on a reproduction oil lamp and brought it over to the desk, where there was an old black rotary phone with a too-short cord. I sat with my hand on the phone for a very long time.

Chances were, Lisa wouldn't even take my call. But if she did, and we got through whatever needed getting through to set things right again, she might have something to say about how to deal with a hopeless crush. She might say the thing that would make Francis melt into a puddle of wax. What would that cost me? An apology? It's not like I'd have to tell her everything.

"Bullshite," I said aloud.

I fell asleep in the old rocking chair by the potbelly stove, and when I woke up, my hands had gone numb from sitting on them.

The floating light, was it Francis? Now that the sun set so early, I sometimes watched him from the lighthouse walking the fields with his flashlight. But this light on the hillside wasn't bobbing along as usual; it was swirling, spinning.

I threw on my coat and ran outside.

I covered my eyes as the flashlight beam hit my face. Francis moved it off, and I blinked to readjust to the darkness. He was sitting on the ground, old meadow grass in his hair.

"Found the hooch," he said, holding up a glass jar. "And a big rock found my foot."

I didn't laugh.

"I know Rupert couldn't have done this without your help. What I want to know is, why would you help him run a still under my nose? Why would you put me in a position like that? Why would you do that *again*?"

"You decided to drink the evidence?"

"Well, you know, fuck it. Not going to make things worse, is it?"

"It's not that I blame you for feeling sorry for yourself, but you don't get to get drunk and yell at me about it."

"*Why*, George?"

"Man, I dunno. We were just having some fun, and it was only one batch. I got rid of all the equipment afterward."

"It's good. Peachy. No wonder Rupert tore the house apart trying to find it."

"What do you mean, tore the house apart?"

"He said he was looking for stamps, but the stamp drawer was full of them. Didn't you know he used to have a real problem? Why do you think he used to make it himself?"

"Because he's cheap?"

"More likely he didn't want the boys at the liquor store to know how much he was going through. That's why his wife left, you know."

"His wife died."

"She left with their daughter and then she died."

No wonder it had been so easy to talk him into reviving the still. "Jesus. Did he drink the shine?"

"No, I poured it all out—at least, what I could find. Except this one. Poured out the rest of that whiskey we were drinking too."

"Well, maybe you should go home and sleep it off."

"I can't sleep."

Francis lay back in the grass. He flicked the flashlight off. On. Off. "You know what?" he said in the dark. "He told me to let go of him."

"Who, Rupert?"

"The Come From Away. James. He said he was the stronger swimmer. And I could see her—I thought I could see her, in the water. But I was so scared. Seems I can be brave only when I don't have to think about it."

On. Off.

"That doesn't make what you did any less—it makes it *more* heroic. What if you had listened to him and you couldn't get to her? You could have all drowned."

"I'm not handling this so well."

"Who would?"

"Your father, for one. Hell, you'd handle it better than this."

Leaving the flashlight on the ground, he got himself to his feet and staggered over and grasped me by the shoulders. Then he pushed me away, a bit roughly. "I think I hate this place, and everyone in it."

"You like Rupert. And whoever this woman is you're see-ing."

"She's . . . It's nothing. I like Rupert. And I like you. I really like you. And you're a fucking teenager."

"I get it, okay? I'm *months* away from being someone you feel comfortable having a conversation with."

"The thing is, the sick, *sick* thing that ties me up every time I see you, is that's possibly what I like best about you. I don't just mean because you're young. I'm not—I'm not a perv. I don't chase girls. My father spent his whole life with women who were too young for him—he died of a stroke with one of them under him, for Christ's sake—and I *swore* I'd never be that guy."

"So switch to margarine."

"No, I'm not letting you do that. Make a joke. Deflect. You have to stand there and hear it. For a long time I told myself that *this*, that it's in spite of your age, and it's all some cosmic cruelty of bad timing. That's not true. Yes, you're *smart* and you're *funny*—"

He had a way of making this sound like an accusation.

"—but also the world hasn't messed you up yet. We can have a conversation about something that you thought you had a solid opinion about, and while we're talking, you change your mind. You just, *change your mind*. Because you're still becoming who you are. Or maybe, maybe age has nothing to do with it. Maybe who you are is someone who's willing to change her mind. I still change my mind. I can't stop changing my mind. Only, I can't get over that woman I met three months ago at the lighthouse."

"Well, this is the real me. This stupid, pissy person."

"You're not stupid. You can be pissy. I'd still want to stay up all night talking to you."

He was turning away, but I drew him to me.

Have you ever tried to kiss someone midrant? In the movie version of my life, it'll be romantic, how his hands went from flailing to resting on mine, how he leaned into me, but our mouths didn't quite meet and his breath was like peach-flavored nail polish remover.

"Don't be so heartless, George."

He was still holding on to me.

"Let's say you're right," I said. "Let's say you're not supposed to be a cop. But it got you here. To Rupert. To me. What if *this* is what you're supposed to do?"

"I'm supposed to do . . . you?"

I shrugged. "Do I look like a poet?"

That was his cue. When he would remember that I'd said that before I kissed him at the lighthouse. When he would say again, *As a matter of fact, you do*, and light up the sky with fireworks.

He pushed me away. "I'm not just older, I'm in a position of authority. Do you get that? No, you don't. You've probably never seen me like that."

"I'm trying to say that, you and me, we might not be people who are . . . who *are* anything. I'm not an artist or an athlete or a tugboat captain. I don't know if I'll ever have something like that. Sometimes I wish I did, but I don't see what was so terrible about you doing all those cool jobs and traveling to all those cool places other than not having someone to do it with."

He stepped around me and picked up the flashlight, and this time I didn't try to stop him.

"Where are you going?"

"The bar. I told the guys I'd play onstage tonight."

"You can't drive."

"Bobby's coming to pick me up. He asked about you."

"That's slightly terrifying." I hadn't forgotten the sight and sound of Bobby slamming his bandaged hand against the table at Long Fellows.

"He thought you might want to come along, whistle us another tune. I had to say you were sick. How could I tell him that I can't get you past the door? Do you know how bad it must be if you don't want to explain it to a guy like Bobby?"

"What happens out here is between us. No one has to know." I could hear desperation in my voice and it pained me.

"George, we can't."

Right. Of course not. Don't be silly, Frances. "Are you going to be afraid to be around me now?"

"I'm not afraid of you," Francis said as he turned away again. "I'm afraid of myself."

TWENTY-ONE

I sat in the parking lot for a long time, listening to the bass line thrumming from the bar. I didn't dare try to sneak in again. The bartender struck me as a guy who wouldn't be fooled twice, and Francis wouldn't hesitate to toss me out either. What was I even doing? Mooning around like a petulant little girl.

I fished my cigarettes and lighter out of my purse and left the car. A dusting of flurries, the first of the season, was coming down under the orange lights. I paced around as I smoked, then wandered around to the back of the bar, where a window was cranked open. It was the one directly behind the stage.

I sat on a flattened cardboard box beside the trash cans under the window, lit another cigarette, and listened to Francis singing alone.

Here so far away
The ocean is a finger lake
The highway is a well-worn path
That brings me back to you.

It had been a couple of hours since our fight on the ridge, and from the clear high notes and the assured way his fingers were moving over the strings, it sounded as though Francis had sobered up. At some point I started singing along, but I figured no one could hear me there, behind the stage, behind the speakers. No one could hear how our voices entwined, his a little coarse, mine a little sharp, a concrete wall with aluminum siding between us.

After the set, I sat a while longer in the silence. The snowflakes were fatter now, settling thickly on my jacket and my hair. I might have let myself disappear beneath them had "Sweet Home Alabama" not poured out the window.

He came around the building as I was brushing the ash and dirt off my jeans. He was frowning in the orange light when he grabbed me, and suddenly we were tangled up together, his back sliding down the brick wall, me sliding onto his lap, biting into each other under the canopy of my hair. And then we were in it. We were so, so in it.

THE CHEESE STANDS ALONE

TWENTY-TWO

JANUARY 1993

Snow fell steadily outside the classroom window, shin high already. We'd had a green Christmas, which my mother kept apologizing about as though it were somehow her fault, and then the new year came, thick and furious.

Miss Aker had invited the editor from the local paper to talk to our class, a balding middle-aged guy with a thick, tidy moustache that rested heavily on his upper lip like a page-boy haircut.

"How many of you want to be writers?" he asked.

A few hands went up, none of them mine. Shelley-with-an-*E* was waving hers confidently, as though she expected him to ask her to stand up and give an inspiring monologue about her true calling.

"Reporting is not for you," he said.

Her hand dropped into her lap.

"It's not about your story. It's about *the* story. It's about recording the truth, without shaping it into what you wish the facts could be. Clearly. Accurately. Precisely."

"*His mouth has bangs,*" Lisa whispered to Bill, and I barked a loud laugh before I could help myself.

Shrunk down in my seat, I pretended to take notes, starting with a clear, accurate, and precise sentence: *I would rather be anywhere but here.*

I was on my feet as soon as the bell rang. I had to get up the highway to a parking lot behind an abandoned building to meet Francis before his shift started at six thirty. This was our only chance to get together before Saturday, when Rupert would be around. It wasn't like we could call each other if we wanted to talk, not if we didn't want to be found out.

There were weeks when all I could expect was a hand resting briefly on my back or a slight rub of his hip against mine as he moved past me in the farmhouse kitchen. One afternoon when we were standing over Rupert—who had managed to get himself down on his knees to show us how to clean Shaggy's ears—I felt Francis's finger barely grazing the inside of my wrist. I don't want to get overly poetic here, but give me an inch of Francis's skin brushing against mine over a chesterfield jackhammering by some East Riverview boy any day.

Francis and I hadn't had sex yet, didn't have a place to do

it or enough time to make it special. He knew I wasn't a virgin, but seemed to think it needed to be a more tender event than I was hoping for. That afternoon I planned to set him straight.

"George?" Miss Aker was sitting on the edge of her desk wearing a pale denim jumper, argyle knee socks, and a look of kindly concern.

"Sorry about the laughing," I said. "I just remembered this joke I heard."

"What was it?"

"Actually, it wasn't that funny."

"I see. Well, George, I was wondering what you thought of our guest speaker. I saw you taking notes."

"I liked what he said about telling the truth."

I wasn't sucking up. The truth was starting to sound real good to me: no subtext, no double-talk, no trying to impress people, just the facts. Lying had stopped being fun a long time ago, once it became something I had to do constantly.

Miss Aker smiled, a very pretty smile apart from her two perfectly yellow canine teeth. "A better fit for you than poetry, I expect. Although your exam essay—that *wonderful* idea that being sentimental can be brave—was very nicely articulated. I hope you're doing as well in all your courses."

"I am, thanks."

Sort of. My first-term grades had been solid, thanks to all those hours with my textbooks open at the lighthouse and all those nights when it was Lisa and Nat's turn to hang out with

Bill. Mum cried when I sent off my applications to Noel, Aurora, and two other city universities; I had a real shot of being the first person in her family to get a degree. Even Dad looked a little misty. But lately I'd been spending more time on the logistics of being with Francis than I had studying.

On the other side of the window, the snow fluttering around him like he was inside a giant snow globe, Bill held up a plastic lawn chair.

"George, is everything alright?"

I snapped my focus back to Miss Aker. "Yeah—absolutely."

"You're distracted lately."

"Um, just family stuff."

She nodded. "I'm sure we'll see your father back at the regatta next year."

I quickly got my things from my locker and jogged toward the school entrance, stopping at the distinctive sound of valley hooliganism on the other side of the auditorium door. Inside, Lisa was sitting onstage, cross-legged, staring at a script in her lap, while twenty, thirty Elevens were practically swinging from the rafters.

Lisa used to say that a theater production was all about the director's vision for a play, but when had she ever had an original thought? She got her style from magazines, her music from the radio charts, and she parroted back whatever our teachers said. It didn't seem like she had a blueprint for this circus play, or anyone trying to help.

Now that we'd been apart for so long, and now that I had Francis to remind me every day that high school wasn't forever, it was easier to feel bad for her. But what could I do? She'd chosen her stage manager. Christina was sitting on the edge of the stage, kicking someone on the floor below her, and gave me a smug look when she spotted me in the doorway.

"I WANT TO PLAY OUTSIDE!"

I closed the door and gave Bill a two-knuckle punch for startling me. He'd brought the plastic lawn chair inside and was shaking it at me. It was strapped to a pair of children's skis. "I'll let you take the first ride," he said.

"Where did you get that?"

"They made it in shop class this morning when the power was out. There's loads more."

I resisted the urge to check my watch, but could feel it ticking on my wrist. "I gotta get out to the farm."

"Aw, come on. You said the old guy doesn't care when you show up, but you're always bailing on me to go to work."

"Not always."

Just when I got an unexpected chance to see Francis.

"Nat'll go sledding with you."

"Where is she?"

"I dunno. Lisa's in there."

"She throws up when she runs in deep snow. Besides, I'll never get her out of rehearsal, and she's always in rehearsal, and please can we go play? *Please, please, please* . . ."

I felt the watch tick again. "Okay, Billy. For a minute."

All manner of sleds were shooting down the steep hill beyond the school fields. The makeshift magic carpets—mostly cardboard wrapped in a garbage bags—were getting the best distance, judging from the number of kids wrapped around trees at the bottom.

Bill launched me in the chair with a big push. I made it about three-quarters of the way down before wiping out, sending someone else arse-over-teakettle with me. He raised his head out of the snow: Joshua Spring.

"Geez, sorry," I said, crawling over to him. "Are you hurt?"

"It's cool."

He shook the snow out of his hair, and without thinking, I brushed it off his cheeks. They flushed pink. Not a guy who could hide his feelings, Joshua. Some people weren't built for secrets.

"Do you . . ." He glanced around—for Christina, no doubt. "Want to try that again? I mean going down. Down the hill." He flushed redder.

"Sorry, I can't," I said. "I've got to—"

"Okay. Yeah, whatever."

"No, I would, but I have to be somewhere." A bead of blood

had appeared on his lower lip. I pointed to my own lip. "I think you bit yourself."

He put his hand to his mouth, then looked down at the red blotch on his mitten. "Great."

"Here, let me . . ." I took a tissue from my pocket and reached over, but he blocked me with his monster-sized mitt.

Enough. I waved to Bill and power-walked to my car. I couldn't phone Francis, had no way of letting him know I would be late. Our dates often went sideways, usually because he got caught up at work. I was used to that, unfortunately. When I was a kid, how many times had my dad sat down to dinner only to be called back out again? It got so that I'd get stressed out if the phone rang on special days, like when I had a soccer game or a school concert. He missed my sixth birthday because of a house fire, and my ninth because someone was murdered. I guess you're not supposed to complain about that.

Now Dad spent most of his time snoozing, reading, and watching TV, Mum waiting on him hand and foot. So to speak. He rarely bothered to patrol me anymore. With my two jobs and good grades and all the Saturday nights I'd spent with Rupert, he had little reason to doubt that I was playing Yahtzee when I was actually slipping away to meet Francis, who didn't always show. So, there was a lot of sitting in cold cars, fretting about whether he'd come and gone and how long I should hang around to be certain.

It was well after four and getting dark when I arrived at the parking lot, and there was no sign of Francis. If he'd made it, he must have given up. Stupid, slow-moving plow.

I drove on to the lighthouse and sat in the dark car. It was tempting to go to the farm, make up some reason to check in on Rupert, and see if Francis had gone home, but I was trying not to do too much of that, and maybe he'd gone somewhere else before his shift.

I let myself into the lighthouse. In the wintertime I was only there half days on Saturdays, spent most of my time cleaning already clean things and doing homework, so that the air would have hardly thawed before I turned down the heat and locked myself out again. It was especially chilly within the glass walls surrounding the lantern, where I could see the farmhouse lights beckoning from the ridge. I went down a level to the service room and flipped the switch, remembering again Francis's mischievous look when he'd put his hand on the wrong one. Then I wound my way down the metal stairs to the keeper's quarters and waited.

My truest, most visceral memory, the one I can still feel on my skin today, is the moment the lighthouse door opened. A half hour had passed. I'd already turned the lantern off and was zipping up when Francis appeared with a gust of cold air. As we stumbled back into the lighthouse, Francis wrestling off my coat, his mouth warming mine, I understood why people said it was like a part of them was missing when someone they loved went away. Everything felt right again, like all of the pieces of the world had snapped back into place with a resounding click.

We had sex, for the first time, in the lighthouse, is what I'm saying. Sweaty, clamoring, splinters from the wooden floors, drinking each other in the moonlight sex. I do apologize to all members of the lighthouse heritage society for what we did on the hardwood and possibly *to* the hardwood. Afterward, we lay under a rough wool blanket that I remembered was in the closet after the fact, our skin quickly cooling, the grandfather clock ticking down the last few minutes before Francis had to leave. I drew a sentence on his arm—

There is nowhere else I would rather be.

"This might be the happiest I have ever been," he said. "And I did some serious drugs in Peru."

"Me too. Happy, and relieved."

"Thanks for the vote of confidence."

"I was just scared you'd have more hair than I'm used to."

He kissed my forehead and mumbled something into my hair. It might have been: "I was scared you'd have less."

TWENTY-THREE

I never thought I'd be that girl going down on someone in a car on the edge of an empty parking lot. I certainly never thought that I'd be the one to turn the keys off in the ignition, reach over, and unbuckle that someone's belt. (And absolutely never when he was in uniform, because that would be gross, except those two times after work when he happened to still be in uniform.) Nat and Lisa always made it sound like this was something you did for a guy because he whinged you into it. But I liked it, and I liked what Francis was doing to me, things high school boys couldn't learn from watching porn. "I need to spend quality time with my friend," I'd say. "Feel free to listen to the radio." If you locked me in a room without food and water for long enough, I might have admitted that I wished there was a girl I could talk to about it.

I started having this irrational fear that people could read my mind and everyone knew what filthy thoughts I was having. What if a cross-section of my brain was exposed at an angle that I couldn't catch in a mirror, and I was the only one who didn't know my fantasies were playing like a movie reel for the world to see? One day, some little kid who hadn't yet finished Concealing Knowledge of the Inner Thoughts of George Warren 101 would blurt out, *Mummy, that girl is wondering if she has a weird vagina.*

If you want my body and you think I'm sexy
Come on, sugar, let me know

My mother was sitting at the kitchen table with her beloved seed catalog, singing along with Rod Stewart on the radio in her choir voice, which was about as horrifying as you'd expect. "There's my good girl," she said when I came in.

I was so unlike the person she thought I was. I could still feel where Francis's hand had gripped my hair.

Dad was standing at the stove. He had on his prosthetic for a change, but somehow, watching him eat Bird's custard directly from the pot, I doubted he'd been really going at the rehab. Matty had become obsessed with catching him doing his exercises, and rarely did. I slipped a wooden spoon out of the jar on the counter. "Bit early for planting seeds, isn't it?" I asked.

"Just daydreaming. When I was a girl, Grandad and I used

to read seed catalogs like bedtime stories."

I coated the spoon with the thick, bright yellow custard. "You're always saying you want to start the garden over. What would you do instead?"

"Ornamental grass," she said without hesitating. "Real tall, big beautiful plumes, all sorts."

"Paying for grass is ridiculous," Dad said. "If you want tall plants, get that joe-pye weed. My mother always said that nothing fills a plot up like joe-pye weed."

Mum gave Dad a ferocious glare. He may have taken over the house, but the garden was still hers, and had no place in it for his opinion. "It might be ridiculous, but I have a credit at the nursery to use up," she said.

"How's that?"

"Back in the fall I helped a customer and she ended up relandscaping her whole yard. Andrew was so happy, he gave me store credit. Said there's a job waiting for me if I want one."

"I hope this Andrew understood when you told him you have your hands full at home."

"Well, no, I didn't."

"Why, because you've already made up your mind that I'm not going back to my old position?"

"Haven't *you*?"

Dad took the pot from the stove and clanged it into the sink.

I was cowering in the corner, but Mum didn't flinch. How long had she been working up to telling him about this?

"I have not," Dad said.

"I'm glad to hear it," Mum said. "But we have a mortgage to pay. Two kids near ready for university—"

"Why don't you bring in some sewing?"

"No money in that."

"So talk to Beryl about selling Tupperware. I don't see why you have to be running out to the nursery every five minutes when you can have the ladies over here."

"Well, Paul, because that won't do it."

"Do *what*?"

"Get me out of this house. It isn't big enough. It just isn't goddamn big enough!"

My mother had grown up in a cabin with three brothers, her parents, and for a while there, a set of grandparents. Now she lived in house with more bedrooms than people. She didn't mean she needed more space. She meant our house was too small to be sharing with *him*.

Dad grabbed his walker and did his best to storm out. He paused in the doorway. "George, did you say you're going to the farm tonight?"

"Yes."

"Why not Thursday?"

"I don't always go on Thursdays."

"When will you be back?"

What was he playing at? Were we going to pretend that he suddenly had a clue, any clue at all, when my earlobe had just

211

been in Francis's mouth and my hamper probably held traces of his DNA?

"Ten thirty. Maybe eleven."

"I'm holding you to eleven. Marlene, when you've calmed down, I could use a tea."

He lurched onward. Only my father would attempt a grand exit to stage left as though anyone would be sorry to see him go.

Mum stared down at the catalog, lips pressed together tightly. "I'll do it," I said. "You want a cup too?"

Into the silence the radio announcer boomed: *"And finally, a special request for Chad Harkness of Greeeenville! If you're still on your way to the grocery store, please pick up an extra bag of milk for your aunt Delores!"*

Before I met Francis I used to think that love was A plus B equals C. That if you were good friends with someone and you thought they were attractive enough to have sex with, that was love. But C is not A plus B—C is C, and I didn't know how exactly you got to C, but I did know it had something to do with conversation, at least for me, and wanting to take care of that person, needing to know they're okay, plus an almost irresistible desire to snack on their neck.

As I drove out to meet Francis, for a record two times in one day, I thought about the impossibility that my parents had ever had that. It seemed like they'd gotten married for what you might call practical reasons. Dad needed someone to pick up after him, inject his medication, and force-feed his children Solomon Gundy twice a year to build their characters via briny pickled herring. For Mum, being married to a police officer, that was making it. The dangers a cop faced in the valley weren't much worse than what her family had faced at the meatpacking plant, in the forests, at sea. Now she was worried about money and running away from home because Dad had stepped on a pebble.

Maybe we were lucky, Francis and me, not to have a dream about what our lives were supposed to be like or to be sure about what we wanted. If you don't have expectations, you can't let anyone down.

"Say *car*," Francis said, after we'd given the lighthouse floors a good scrubbing, as I'd come to think of it.

"No."

"Say it. Say *car*."

"No."

"Okay, fine. . . . Say *car*."

"Car!"

He rolled over laughing. "I found George's accent. She left it in the . . ."

"*Ugch*. Car?"

He cracked up again.

"Who's the adult here?" I pushed him onto his side so I could draw on his back. "Hey, did you get along with your parents?"

"Uh-oh. Gonna get heavy."

"You never talk about them. I guess I already know you weren't a big fan of your dad's."

"He did introduce me to some good books, I'll give him that. And I, in turn, gave him the greatest disappointment of his life."

"What was that?"

"Me." Francis rubbed his face vigorously. "Sorry, too heavy."

"What about your mum?"

"Am I being interviewed or interrogated?"

"Just curious."

"She's hard."

"Hard to describe?"

He rapped on the wood floor. "Hard. But the family's pilfering of natural resources got me into private schools, so—"

"Ooh, uniforms."

"This is why I don't like to talk about it."

"Do you keep in touch with the people you went to school with?"

"I've moved around too much, and I'm bad about letter writing. There are a few people I'll visit when I can. Not so easy now. Can we change the subject?" He rolled me onto my back and pinned my shoulders to the floor. "Let's see if George can say something romantic."

"She cannot."

"Come on, deep inside I bet you're the most syrupy, sentimental—"

"Get off me, you commie bastard."

I'd learned this in Modern World Problems: You can make any sentence more interesting by inserting the phrase "commie bastard." For example, *President Clinton plays the saxophone, the commie bastard. The drugstore is going to start opening on Sundays, the commie bastards.*

Francis tried it out. "Easter Bunny is coming, the commie bastard. Not bad, Frances."

"Thank you, Francis. The key is to be as random as possible."

"They're giving me a medal, the commie bastards—"

"I mean, you weren't *that* good."

"No, the force. They're giving me a medal for bravery. So that's something." He rolled back onto the floor beside me.

"Why don't you sound very happy about it?"

"I am. It bothers me that you can't come to the ceremony."

Was there a day on the horizon when Francis and I could be together, really together? I had never slept with him—actually *slept* with him. What would that be like? Did he snore? Would he want to cuddle all night? I always slept with one leg on top of the blanket to stay cool; what would I do with a man in my bed? Just lying with him was like snuggling an electric space heater. Then again, what would it be like to not always be watching the clock, not wanting to say, *It's time*, but also not wanting him always to be the one to say it?

I hadn't let myself think a lot about where we were headed. I'd been riding on this blind faith that, somehow, everything would work itself out once I'd graduated. Odds were against that. If Dad didn't go back to his old job in the summertime, there was a good chance Francis would get a permanent position in the valley while I went off to school. And if my dad *did* go back to his old job, they might reshuffle within the ranks at the detachment again, and Francis could be transferred. They could send him anywhere in the country.

"George, you're crying."

"I don't know why . . . It's not like I caught my arm in a car door."

"What are you talking about, car door?"

"I love you." Now I was bawling.

"Oh, I'm sorry. I love you too."

"No, I'm sorry. You're not supposed to say it first if you're not sure someone is going to say it back."

"I did say it back."

"Only because I'm *crying.*"

"George, this is how much I love you. I love you even though you have never embraced the art and the soul of Serbian disco."

I wiped my eyes. "This is how much I love you. I don't mind that you're wearing a T-shirt and no bottoms like a giant baby."

We had been in a hurry to get our clothes off.

"This is how much I love you. I'm here with you. Which is crazy. George, what we're doing is crazy."

"I know." I was really scared.

"That's how much I love you."

My skin was raw where it had been rubbed against his

day-old whiskers, exfoliated smooth and almost hot to the touch. I was going to have to powder the bejesus out of my face to cover it up. I kissed him anyway.

It was after midnight when I got home. I braced myself as I turned into the driveway, half expecting the Sergeant to be waiting on the stoop, but all of the lights in the house were off, even the one over the front door.

No one stirred when I came in or when I tripped coming out of the bathroom and hit the bookshelf in the hallway. In the morning, I woke up with my bedside lamp on and still in my clothes from the night before. When I went downstairs, Dad was alone in the kitchen and the only thing he said was, "Get me my cigarettes."

TWENTY-FOUR

Mum was smoothing down her hair in the mirror of the front hallway, her purse over her shoulder. "Where are you going so early?" I asked. It was only quarter to eight on a Tuesday morning.

"To work."

I was slow to get it. "At the nursery? Dad let you take the job?"

The look she gave me withered my nonexistent balls. I guess *let* was the wrong word.

"Now. George. I'll be doing shift work, which means my schedule will be all over the place. I'll be home by two today; tomorrow, I'll be out all afternoon."

"What will you do at a nursery this time of year?"

"Oh, wreaths, houseplants, seed inventory, bookkeeping . . ."

"Is there anything to eat?" Dad called from the kitchen.

"I'm on my way out the door! Georgie, make your father some breakfast."

"I gotta go too. Bill's all banged up from hockey, so I'm driving him to school, and I promised we'd stop for a donut at the Grunt."

Mum hesitated before she yelled, "Matty!" He appeared at the top of the stairs. "Make breakfast for your father, please. Cereal, toast, and orange juice. Don't let him have jam. Coffee's already made. And if you have time, make him a sandwich for lunch too."

"I don't know where everything is."

I pointed toward the kitchen. "Fridge. Chicken, mayo, lettuce."

"No lettuce!" Dad called. "What about my insulin?"

Mum looked at her watch, then up at Matthew. "You have time before the bus."

"Oh no!" he said. "I'm not sticking a needle into anyone!"

"Your father will help you."

"Why can't he do it himself?"

"You know why," I said, following Mum to the door. "Because he stabs himself like a psychopath."

"This is what they call *exposured*, dear," Mum said. "It's good for you. If you feel weak, you know the drill."

"Head between the legs," Matthew said miserably.

◦◦◦

219

Ernest Burns was one of those people whose hand shot up the moment a teacher asked a question. Some teachers pretended not to see him, or they'd make a lame joke about Ernest being the only person who's taking an interest. Thing is, it's not like Ernest always had the *right* answer—or an answer. Sometimes it wasn't about the subject at all. Like in history he'd go: "I know this is a little off topic, but what's the average life span of the Arctic snow monkey?"

That morning in biology, Mr. Huskins kept rotating between the chalkboard and the opposite side of the classroom from where Ernest sat. Finally, Ernest called out, "Mr. Huskins! Please, Mr. Huskins!"

Huskins slowly pivoted around and said, very wearily, "Yes, Ernest? Do you have a question?"

"No, sir. It's just, Mr. Huskins, my desk is going to fall apart."

Then it did. Out popped the last screw holding it together, and Ernest and his desk collapsed onto the floor.

No one moved.

"You probably want me to ask the janitor for a new desk," Ernest said.

Mr. Huskins just nodded and turned back to the board.

"That's your answer about nurture versus nature right there," Bill said as we crossed the hall to the lab. He was back in his old plaid shirts again. Maybe Lisa was too busy with the play to patrol his wardrobe.

"You're saying it's in Ernest's biology to have his desk fall apart?"

"I'm saying it's not like he doesn't know what the difference is between cool and not cool—"

"Does he?"

"He must be able to see that cool people don't wear pants that are three inches above the ankles or ask a lot of dumb questions—"

"Or spend so much time on the floor. Shelley-with-an-*E* should create a new yearbook category: most likely to fall into an open manhole."

We snickered. *Open manhole.*

"That's his deal," Bill said. "Can't fight nature. Tracy hooked up with someone."

He slid it in there so slickly that I almost didn't catch what he'd said.

"Oh, buddy." I tried to hug him, but he was already turning away to check the equipment at our station, so we ended up in an awkward T-shape position.

"What is happening?" Bill said.

"I'm not sure."

"You're squeezing my bruises."

"I'm sorry." I flicked donut crumbs off his collar and let him go. "Who'd she hook up with?"

"My cousin Kenny."

"Geez."

"It doesn't matter."

"Isn't that breaking some kind of code, for both of them?"

"Yup."

I couldn't read him at all, so I just said: "I guess sometimes good people do bad things."

"Uh, *no*. Bad people do bad things." He flipped open his binder so violently it flew off the counter and hit the floor with a loud bang.

"Oops," I said to all the eyeballs now looking at us, jarred and otherwise.

"Doing bad things is what makes people bad," Bill said as I set the binder in front of him. "That's the *only* thing that makes them bad. Here's a biological fact: No one who was born bad just hasn't gotten around to doing bad things."

Maybe, but bad was in the eyes of the beholder. All hell would break loose if anyone found out about Francis and me, and there would be nothing we could say to make anyone understand, but there was also nothing anyone could say that could convince me that what we were doing was wrong.

"Just out of curiosity," I asked, "how many bad things do you have to do to officially become a bad person?"

"Are you saying that Tracy doing Kenny is a gray area? Whatever. We're broken up."

For now, I thought, but there was always a chance they'd get back together. In the end, it wouldn't work out, that I was sure of, because whatever force it was that kept dragging those two toward each other, it wasn't real love. Real love is deeper. Stickier. Bigger. Francis and I were big-time in love, and we were navigating our whole crazy situation with sharp, practiced strokes, while Bill and Tracy and everyone else at school splashed around in circles like they had no idea they were paddling giant pumpkins. A whole lot of drama that wasn't getting them anywhere.

Huskins tossed a dissection tray on the counter in front of us. Fetal pig.

"You'll have to make the first cut," I said to Bill. "That looks too much like someone I know."

"You need to get better at projecting your anger," he said, taking the knife I held out to him.

Francis was leaning on his cop car in the school parking lot. The final bell had rung, and the students streaming out of the building were giving him a wide berth. He gestured me over.

I slipped past Nat and Doug, who were sitting on the front steps, talking heatedly. Bill had said that he was meeting Nat in the library to study, but it seemed like he'd be waiting a long time. She was poking Doug's shoulder with her twiggy finger.

"I had to give a talk about drug-free schools to the tenth graders, so I brought your pay," Francis said. The envelope he passed me was empty. "Could we meet somewhere to talk?"

Something was wrong. Very wrong. One of Francis's legs was crossed over the other, all casual, except his foot was vibrating almost violently. He was having trouble meeting my eyes. All my animal instincts told me to run.

"Sorry, I have a biology quiz to study for," I said, shifting my weight heavily onto my heels, as though that would tether me to the ground.

"Okay." He smiled, sort of. "We'll talk on the weekend."

"Did the medal ceremony go alright yesterday?"

"It was nice. I met the brass. I'll show you the, you know."

"The medal?"

"Yes, the medal."

"Constable McAdams?"

"Frances George?"

"What's going on?"

His foot stopped twitching. "Let's not talk here."

I knew our love was precarious, every moment as dangerous and delicate as raising the mast of a ship in a bottle, but I'd had this strange confidence that the only thing that could end us before next fall would be getting caught. It hadn't occurred to me that we could break it off voluntarily, not after we'd said we loved each other. I'd never considered that it would be just like Francis to change his mind.

"Are you . . . not wanting to do this anymore?"

"George—"

"Don't make me worry about it for days."

He looked over at Mr. Humphreys, who had appeared on the steps near Natalie and Doug, then met my eyes and said, "I think I have to make a decision, yes."

He sounded so sober and grown-up.

"I thought you had."

"Let's talk about it on Saturday. I'll come by the lighthouse in the afternoon."

I turned to walk away.

"Don't . . . don't go slamming your bedroom door."

"Slamming my bedroom door?"

"Storming off like a kid."

"I'm just leaving," I said. "I didn't know there was a wrong way to do it."

Mr. Humphreys's big arms were folded across his chest. "Problem, Warren?" he said.

"No, sir. Forgot something in my locker."

"You were talking to the RCMP officer."

"Yeah, I work for him. Sort of."

"Gone over to the other side, have we?"

"Gone over . . . Oh no, I'm not some druggie snitch." I followed his eyes to Doug, who was standing up to leave. He and Nat weren't quite out of hearing range. "Of course you aren't," he said.

"No, really, I clean his house. Do the laundry, make dinner. Feed the pig."

"Feed the pig." He rocked back on his heels, then began slowly trailing Doug down the steps. "I like that," he said over his shoulder. *"Feed the pig."*

TWENTY-FIVE

Lisa got dumped once. Dumped hard.

It happened at a shack party in tenth grade. Lisa and Whatshisname disappeared soon after we got there, and the rest of us ended up hanging out with the skateboarders. (Who doesn't love a skateboarder? They're like the cheerfully demented love children of the Goths and the jocks.) The next morning, my mother said, "I think you'd better check the machine."

Lisa: "Hi. Uh. Sorry. I . . ."

And then she lost it. It was the saddest, most wretched thing I'd heard in my life. It made me burst into tears all thirty-two times I heard it—thirty of them because I was testing a theory that I couldn't *not* cry while listening to it—until my father yanked the plug from the wall, picked up the machine, and walked out of the house with it. We never saw it again.

When I let myself into Lisa's bedroom, she was sobbing into her pillow. Every now and then, she would lift her head and move her mouth as though she was trying to form the word *sorry*, but her face would contort as the heaves welled up and she'd be down for the count again. Her mum came in and put a glass of water on the bedside table. "What do I do?" I whispered.

"Just make sure she doesn't get dehydrated."

As bad as I felt for Lisa, part of me—the bit that lived in that dark chamber of my heart—wasn't totally buying it. Like when you see ladies in labor on TV and they're wailing and clutching their husbands so hard the men fall to their knees. It seems like if someone has it in them to be that dramatic, it couldn't really *hurt*-hurt, right?

Losing Francis *hurt*.

Watching my friends' relationships bust up, even breaking up with Lisa, hadn't prepared me for this. I had no idea how exhausting it would be. All the not-eating, imaginary confrontations, darting out of stores when the wrong songs came over the speakers. I'd always had a superimmunity against ballads, but now the first three bars of "Against All Odds" left me completely unhinged. I couldn't get through the breakup scene in *The Godfather Part III*, which I put on the VCR to soothe an honest-to-goodness pining for Sid, who was always pretty good at making a person laugh when the going got rough. When Andy Garcia said, "Love somebody else," I cried so hard that Dad made me turn it off before I could see Sofia Coppola get shot.

I couldn't believe that Bill had gotten back together with Tracy so many times only to go through this all over again, and felt awful that we'd all told him he was better off without her. Who cared about "better off" when that person had decided that *they* were better off without *you*? Someone collects information on you for weeks or months or years, and after studying all the data, they drop you into a bin to become someone else's sloppy seconds.

Something I learned about myself that week: I do not enjoy a wallow. If you like a wallow, no judgment, but I didn't want to lie on the floor listening to Kate Bush and examining the nature of my pain. There were things to do: study, help my dear sainted mother, spend quality time with Bill. A large karmic deposit was due for all the times I'd said I was doing those things and was actually pressed up against the barn wall, fumbling under Francis's winter clothes to find bare skin.

I drove out to the bay after school that Friday, after telling Rupert that I was too sick with a cold to go out to the farm. The wind was bitter through my jeans as I sat on Abe's cooling hood and looked across the water at a distant island whose name escaped me. This was the horizon that I couldn't see from the lighthouse. Maybe Francis had taken this route into town, hugging the shoreline en route to what he thought would be a simpler life. I put my hand in my pocket for a tissue and felt the lake stone he'd given me that first night at Long Fellows, which I carried around like a good-luck charm.

You could sink a ship with all the lies I'd told lately. The biggest were the ones I'd told myself. Like, the only reason I'd taken the job at Rupert's was to make some extra cash. That good people sometimes do bad things. That I kept forgetting to take the stone out of my pocket.

I peeled off my mitten and rubbed the smooth, shimmery pink surface. Then I hopped down from the hood, picked my way across the rocky beach, and threw it into the water.

Two things happened next: number one, I felt immediate and profound regret before the stone even broke the surface; and number two, I'd just become the kind of girl who would dramatically throw a love symbol into the ocean.

If we were ending, Francis and me, it shouldn't be like this, with half a conversation in a parking lot and a *ploink* into the bay. Not our love. Not us. But I didn't know what to do about it, and there was no one I could ask how a person was supposed to get her head out of her brown dot.

So I decided to do what I did best: shake it off at a shack party.

When Bill and I arrived, I slipped out of my coat and tossed it onto the pile in the corner of the bedroom with the grace of someone who knows they look good. I'd lost the weight that had been bothering me in the fall and then some, despite having given up running over the winter. After the last time Francis and I had slept together, he'd touched my hip bone and said, "Where did this come from? Did you always have this?"

"I think it's meant to keep my lower part from collapsing in on itself."

"Don't disappear, my love."

I grabbed the bottle of Screech that Bill had set on the windowsill, and checked myself out in a cracked mirror. My hair was falling just so, and I was glad I had chosen the vintage ballet sweater that crisscrossed my front and tied around my waist. Behind me, Bill was staring.

"Dude," I said.

"You're wearing something that makes guys think about how to get it on and off."

I spied Lisa's hot-pink feather key chain on the floor and instinctively reached down, but before I got my hand on it, Bill said, "Alright, that's enough." He closed the door. "Stand up. Put your ass away."

"Why did you close the door?"

"I like you, but you're not going to seduce me."

"Uh, no, I'm not. Also, who says *seduce?*"

"Not that I haven't thought about it. You have a good rack, you do. There's a nice curvature on the left one there in particular. But Sid and I swore a pact that we'd never get together with any of you girls, even if you begged us."

"Even if we *begged* you?"

"It's been pretty obvious. You're always 'finding my binder'—"

"You're always leaving it somewhere—"

"Making sure I get to class on time. Remember when you brought me *cake*?"

"You were just complaining about me bailing on you."

I looked down at the key chain on the floor. Maybe there was more to it. Probably wasn't a coincidence that Bill and I got closer after Sid left and Lisa and I broke up. Like those nicotine patches that Dad's doctor couldn't convince him to try, we helped each other kick our best-friend habits. And he was also sometimes my Francis patch, holding me over when we couldn't be together.

"I'm sorry," I said. "I'm sorry that I've been doing too much for you, and I'm sorry that I haven't always been around to do more for you. Does that cover it?"

"Yes. Are you going to get emotional because I don't want to have sex with you?"

"No."

"Good."

And that, right there, was the best thing about being friends with a boy. Wasn't a lot you couldn't work out in two minutes or less.

"Gotta whiz," Bill said.

I tossed his jacket to him. "I saw a couple of Elevens go into the bathroom together. Think they'll be a while."

He was partway out of the room when he turned around. "Lisa's here."

"And?"

He fiddled with the door latch. "She had a bad week. The play is . . ."

"She needs to fire half the actors."

"I tried to tell her that, but then she looked like she was going to cry." He shuddered. "She said she wished she could talk to you about it."

"No, she didn't."

"Okay, she said you'd know how to do it, which is basically the same thing."

"What do you want me to do? Start firing people for her?"

"I'm just saying that if you think you might want to start talking again, this might be a good night to do it."

The party was at someone's uncle's oversized lake cabin on the far side of the south mountain. The music was loud, and practically everyone was already messed up. "How's it goin'?" Doug asked. He'd sank deep into a gigantic armchair, his hat tipped over his eyes.

"*Comme ci, comme ça.* You?"

He peered at me from under the hat brim. "Nat's avoiding me."

"I can't figure you two out," I said, perching on the arm of the chair. "Are you dating?"

"Naw."

"Do you *want* to go out with her?"

"Uh, *yaw.*"

233

"Enough to stop smoking this?"

Doug gazed down at the joint in his hand like I'd told him it was a terminal puppy.

"Oh, give me some of that," I said. "We can be pathetic together."

Just as my fingers wrapped around the joint, a third hand came out of nowhere and knocked it onto Doug's lap.

That was the fastest I'd seen Doug move since—ever.

Lisa was standing in the doorway by the chair, straddling the line between slushy and surprised. I had a feeling she'd punted the joint without thinking. Maybe she'd developed a muscle memory after years of trying to keep me away from the stuff.

She half smiled. "No one wants to see you high."

It was the first time she'd spoken to me in months.

"Well, that's true," I admitted, "but it's been kind of a shitty week."

"Mine sucked too."

"Yeah?"

"Big-time."

"So let's have some of this. Drugs solve everything, right, Doug?"

"Won't make it worse," he said.

Christina called from the sofa, "Couldn't possibly make her sluttier."

A few nervous laughs. Joshua looked uncomfortable beside Christina. Nat was tucked in the corner behind Skateboarder

Brad, pretending to be absorbed in peeling the label off a beer bottle. Doug pulled his hat down so it covered his face entirely and sank deeper into the chair. Lisa just stood there.

The funny thing is, I think the other people in the room *wanted* me to slam Christina, or at least make her flinch. It would give them something to talk about on Monday. But as I sat there considering my options, hoping I gave the impression of deliberately taking my time, I couldn't think of anything to say. Because I didn't care. Real life was out *there*, beyond this cabin, after high school. This was nothing but a holding pen, and suddenly I didn't give a damn about anyone in it—except Bill, out peeing in the snow. Certainly not Lisa and Nat, who were letting Christina bait me.

"This is . . ." I was going to say *boring*, but didn't bother finishing the sentence.

Back in the coatroom, my foot decided Lisa's key chain wanted to live under the radiator.

Bill was doing his thing at the side of the house. I stomped over a snowbank and prodded him in the back. "My privates are hanging out!" he said.

"Just how long have you been peeing?"

"It took me a while to find a place." He shook and zipped.

"I want to go home, buddy. I'm sorry. I should have driven myself."

"You're bailing? Seriously?"

"Seriously, it's getting mean in there."

"Who's picking on you?"

"Christina."

"Fuck that ferret."

The sudden flashing lights of a cop car sent us skittering around the back of the shed. It was something I'd always avoided in the past, getting busted at a shack party, thanks to my early curfew. Usually, the noise complaints didn't roll in until well after midnight, and the cops couldn't be bothered to break up parties before they got out of control, especially out in the boonies. But this cop didn't always follow the unwritten rules.

"Young guy," Bill said. "Do you know him?"

"He's the constable who boards with Rupert."

"Is that a good thing or a bad thing?"

"Bad. Very bad."

"Maybe you can get him onside."

"Of everyone here, whose father is he mostly likely to call?"

Within minutes, the party was out in the snow. Francis was taking names, sending some kids on their way, making the less sober types stay back.

Christina looked terrified. She was inching behind Nat, who hid under the hood of a giant man's parka that she'd managed to nick from someone.

"If I get grounded," Lisa said, "I won't be able to work on the play."

I didn't catch what Nat said from under her hood, but Lisa had tears in her eyes.

Bill gave me a shove, harder than I think he meant to, and I knocked into the woodpile, sending a couple of logs tumbling.

"Just taking a leak," I said as Francis turned in our direction.

I yanked Bill out into the open with me.

Francis could not have seemed less interested. "Miss Warren. What would your father think about you being out here at this party?"

I felt about twelve years old. Christina and Lisa were both crying now. Joshua was off to the side, stomping his feet sulkily, and Keith was giving me the stink eye, like this was somehow my fault.

My pride smarted. I was not like them. I wouldn't let him treat me like them.

"He'd make a big frigging deal of it, but you don't have to. It's just kids having fun." I pointed to Christina. "This one has literally nothing else to live for."

Prodding the bull, as my father would say.

"I mean, if you need to arrest someone to make your night, arrest me. Maybe they'll give you another medal."

He wouldn't. I had too much on him. Mutually assured destruction. But no one else knew that, and I realized that I appeared to be going down on purpose, taking one for the team. People were sneaking off while Francis's attention was focused on me. You could hear the clinking of bottles being tossed into the woods.

"Welcome back, Enforcer," Bill said under his breath.

"Get in the car," Francis said, his voice tight. "We can discuss this further with your parents."

He pointed to Lisa, Keith, and Christina. "And you three. Let's go."

TWENTY-SIX

I was in the front seat, the others in the back. If Lisa and Keith said anything, I couldn't hear it over Christina's bawling.

Lisa was sitting in the middle. She leaned forward and tapped Francis's shoulder. "Sorry. She's pretty upset."

"You don't need to apologize for her."

"It's just, it might look like her family's well off because she lives in a nice house, but she comes from very humble roots. Rough childhood, you know? Some people would say that *mine* was rough, but honestly, not like hers."

Rough childhoods, my arse. Christina came from one of the few old-money families in that part of the valley. As for Lisa, her father was an insurance agent and her mother was a dentist, and they were those lovey-dovey parents who put their hands up the back of each other's sweaters in front of their kids' friends and said things like, *I was telling Dave in the bath last night* . . .

Not that Francis was going to fall for that, but since I was the only one in the car who wasn't about to get in huge trouble, I said: "Sure, rough. You probably heard the rumor about mountain men marrying their daughters."

"Shut up, George!" Christina screeched.

"Easy," Francis said.

After a moment, Lisa leaned forward again and stage-whispered to me, "You know she can't help how she is."

Francis stopped the car about a block from Lisa's house. "You can walk from here," he said.

"You aren't going to tell my parents?"

"Put on a good show."

"Oh, I'll be very convincing. I only had, like, five beers."

"I meant the play."

"Oh, right. Thank you! I will!"

"I know you will."

Christina was next, then Keith.

As we drove on, Francis didn't look at me, didn't speak. It was so strange to be sitting together in upright silence, belted in, staring out the window, when under all those layers of clothes was a body I knew so well that there was no part I couldn't describe precisely, down to the blue veins crossing the double tendon under his left wrist. If this wasn't a police car, I might have chanced it, sliding over so that my leg, just my leg, was touching his. Just to see.

Francis took off his hat, placed it on the seat between us, and ran his hand over his chin. Freshly shaved. Jaw like a blade.

I was still furious with him, but the reasons were becoming murkier as we passed through shadows and streetlights. For wanting to talk about how hopeless this was, was that it? Or for keeping his cool when he saw me and letting everyone off?

"Were you drinking?" he asked.

"Couple slugs of Screech."

"Do you have the bottle?"

"In my bag."

Silence again, my mind working overtime. We were not driving in the direction of my house. Or the farmhouse, the detachment, or anywhere we'd stolen time together. At some point it occurred to me that he didn't know where we were going, that he was just driving, thinking.

Finally, he pulled over by a wooded area on the outskirts of town. He got out of the car, walked around, and opened my door. "Bring the Screech."

There was nothing in his posture that suggested we would be sharing a nightcap as we walked down a rough path into the woods lit by his flashlight. The snow had melted here and the ground was uneven where muddy footprints had frozen. Eventually, we came to a clearing with a crumbling brick bunker surrounded by fallen trees that had been taken out by storms. The shrill call of coyotes in the night.

The flashlight flicked off. I felt Francis behind me, his hand heavy on my back through my jacket. Down my spine and around to my belt buckle. Then he stopped. He waited until I leaned into him, sank into the heat of him, feeling upward to his bare neck, before sliding his hand into my jeans.

On the way back to the car, the bouncing light beam illuminated a large tree that had come up from the roots, its huge base like a secret entrance to another world.

An old man was walking his dog along the shoulder of the road. "Evening," he said, looking bewildered until his eyes landed on the bottle of Screech under Francis's arm. "She won't be the only one you find back there tonight. Unless the coyotes get them first."

As we pulled away from the curb, Francis said, "I had a very long conversation with a woman from the lighthouse heritage society this week. Those window locks have a remarkable history."

"Did you have to buy a ticket?"

"I sure did." He tightened his grip on the wheel. "George, after they gave me the medal, I felt so—"

"Ashamed."

His voice was low and reassuring, but regret was already setting in, I could tell. It was there in the tightness of his hands, the way he kept his eyes on the road ahead.

"Yes," he said. "Ashamed. It was easier when I was far away from you, in the city, to decide to do the right thing."

"The right thing being to stop."

"When we're together, this big gap opens up between who I am and the person I wish I could be."

I wouldn't cry. He was being grown-up and reasonable and there was nothing to blub over. It wasn't like the world hadn't given us solid reasons to stay apart. But to hear him describe us as a wrong thing, saying he was ashamed of himself when he was with me and that I made him feel like he was failing, it more than hurt. It was humiliating.

"I know you don't like yourself when you're with me," I said, looking up at the stars to keep the tears from rolling down. "But I like myself a lot better when I'm with you."

He reached over and rested his hand on my thigh, his hand warm through the denim. "When we got together, I'd already made up my mind that I wasn't staying. I would wait until your dad was confirmed to return to his position or not before giving my notice."

"And go where?"

"Maybe nowhere. Maybe stay with Rupert, get the farm going again. And then they gave me the medal. . . ."

"And you realized that you might be police, after all."

"No. What we're doing is incompatible with wearing the badge."

"But you saw that you could do it, right? Or you could if it weren't for me."

He nodded. "I could make a life here. I like waking up at

243

the farm. It's just ... I'm still not sleeping. Can you understand?"

"What if you did the counseling they offered you...."

"What good is counseling if you can't talk about the most important person in your life?"

I took a second to absorb this.

"That's you."

"Yes." The Bishop *yes*. I heard myself doing it all the time now.

"The fact is, we've crossed a line," he said. "A new line."

"I know."

"I can't be around you and not be with you, George. I end up prowling after you the way Rupert prowls after 'stamps.'"

"I'm your hooch."

"You're my hooch."

I thought he was going to tell me to quit my job at the farm, that I would lose not only him but any nearness to him. Somehow it hadn't sunk in before that I might also have to give up polishing his shoes, his dirty teacups, his scent lingering in the hallway.

"So I guess it's a good thing that you applied to the city schools," he said, "because I don't think I can end this on my own."

He checked the rearview mirror to be sure no one was behind us before he took my hand and kissed it, holding it until the sharp left turn that would return us to town forced his hand back onto the wheel.

TWENTY-SEVEN

In early March, Dad had a state-of-the-union meeting with his division commander, disability case manager, career adviser, and a whole bunch of other people who were monitoring his progress. I wondered whether he told them, after shuffling in with his walker, that napping had become his part-time job.

When he got home, he went straight to his recliner and fell asleep in front of cartoons.

"Dad?"

"Huh—what?"

"Sorry to wake you up."

"No, I was reading." He picked up the book on his chest. "Have you read this yet?"

It was his favorite, the history of the valley, with chapters on the logging industry and the Apple Harvest Parade and equally tedious subjects.

"No offense," I said, "but I think I've had my fill of superexciting local history from superexcited local historians."

"It wasn't written by a historian. It was written by a guy who lives ten miles up the highway. Plumber by trade, insomniac by nature. He used to go down to his basement every night to write after his family went to bed."

I'd never met an author before, never considered that people who wrote books might come from a place like the valley. I thought of Miss Aker with her suitcase full of rejection letters. Had to admire her for trying.

"Good. So, what did the team have to say?"

"Looks like I'm not getting into the history books, which I could have told them back in July. We'll reassess in the fall, but it's safe to say that the dream of having the first peg leg serving active duty is over."

On the other side of the window Mum was furiously shoveling the walkway. She knew, I thought. That *is* why she took that job.

"So then what?" I said, trying to keep cool. "Do they kick you off the force?"

"No, then we'll see if there's another suitable position to be had. Could be civilian."

"I know this isn't the most important thing, but what does that mean for us, as far as . . ."

"Money-wise? It means we are unlikely to be eating squirrel next winter."

How could he be so nonchalant about the fact that he'd sabotaged his big chance to do something important? All he'd had to do was follow the program they'd given him. When had he made up his mind that he wasn't even going to try?

"Dad? Aren't you disappointed?"

He let a breath out slowly. "Well, George, it's like this. The job has certain requirements that I can't fulfill. Nothing to get emotional over; I had a good couple of decades on the force and no regrets. When you get older, you'll understand that none of us is entitled to any more than that."

I thought of how proud I'd been to visit my father at the detachment when I was a kid. I loved the clacking and hum of the typewriters, the smell of stale coffee and the stubby brown cigarettes that the staff sergeant smoked at his desk, talking to the receptionist through the hole in the window that separated her from the public. How people straightened up when Dad entered a room. He was the walking embodiment of responsibility: for your community, your fellow officers, your family, your own personal conduct.

Now, as I watched him light another cigarette, I felt, for the first time, a little ashamed of my dad. Not because he couldn't be an RCMP officer anymore, but for making it sound like it was all the universe's doing, not his own.

&

We used to have a cat named Priscilla. After she got sick and went to the vet for three days, we were never sure we'd brought home the right animal. Gone was the midnight yowler who went mousing at night for balled socks and once almost tore my hand off for trying to take a pair away from her. It became impossible to sit when she was in the room because she was suddenly so full of love that she would climb onto your chest, put you in a stranglehold of a hug, and try to lick your face off.

That was how I felt in the weeks after Francis and I got back together, like I'd had an out-of-kitty experience and was filled up with more feelings than I knew what to do with, even just watching him fork hay across the barn floor.

"How long are you going to stand there watching me?"

"I like what I see. Why don't you give us a spin?"

Well, he whipped around that pitchfork like it was a stripper pole, and I did not want to think about how he could have that move at the ready.

"Change of scenery for Shaggy," he said when I uncovered my eyes. "Poor guy's got cabin fever."

Shaggy had already burrowed into a pile, and his head and back rose out of the hay like a pink crocodile floating in a lake. "Thank god," I said, crouching down to give him a scratch. "Rupert fights me every time I try to let him outside."

I stretched out beside Shaggy and looked up at the rafters. "My dad found out that he's not returning to his job."

I'd been sitting on this for more than a week. I needed time to consider what it meant. That Francis would probably stay, yes, but also how that made him all the righter about our fall expiration date.

"I know," he said.

"You do?"

"Your father called. They might not tell me for a while since nothing is official, so he wanted to give me a heads-up."

"That was surprisingly decent of him."

He joined me and Shaggy on the hay. "Is he upset?"

"Weirdly, no."

"Are you upset?"

"Not anymore," I said truthfully. "This could make things simpler. For us."

I felt around the hay for his gloved hand. "I was thinking, maybe if you stay, I stay."

His hand flexed in surprise, which he tried to cover by giving mine a squeeze. "You've been talking about getting out of here since I first met you."

"The universe has been conspiring against that. With some help from my dad."

"And what does the universe want?"

"For me to go to Noel. I don't want to take off just when it starts to become okay to be with you. The city, and everywhere beyond the city, they aren't going anywhere."

"You know it'll be a long time before anyone will think this is okay."

"I know. But it'll stop being something you could lose your job over a lot sooner than that. In the meantime, I could swing residence if I got a student loan, or board at the farm. In the maid's room. Then it wouldn't be a problem if people saw us together."

"Incremental acclimatization."

"Right."

"And you'd be happy at Noel."

"I think so."

If I got in, and stayed in. I had been worrying about how things were going to average out on my final transcripts. They could send an acceptance letter in May only to send a rejection later.

"Will you have friends there?"

I shrugged. It honestly didn't matter to me anymore. I didn't need anyone but him.

"George, have I gotten between you and your friends? When I busted up that party—"

"Oh, those weren't my friends. I hang with a different group."

Francis propped himself up on his elbow. "You know as well as I do that I could be relocated at any time. Even with a permanent position, I'll still be transferred within three, four years. If I can bring myself to leave the farm, and that's a big *if.*"

"In three, four years, I could be done with my degree."

I couldn't read him. "You've thought it through," he said in a way that made it clear he hadn't.

"I'm sorry. God, it's too much. I'm freaking you out."

He gave me a fierce look. "George, you're the only thing I've ever been sure about. I know that sounds like a line from a shitty love song—"

"It actually *is* a line from a shitty love song."

"But it's true. I don't want you planning your life around me when I can't promise to do the same."

"I'm not." I sat up. "I'm *not.*"

"Okay. You're not."

"I wish . . . I wish we could get out of here, just for a while."

He'd be able to picture it better, being together. We'd see who we were away from the valley.

He saw me struggling, the floodwaters rising. "How about this," he said. "I know someone in the city who's gone to Guatemala for a year. She gave me a key to her place in case I wanted a break from the countryside. I don't know how we'd both get away the same weekend without people putting two and two together, but—"

"Leave that to the professional."

At this, Shaggy made a noise like someone was letting all the air out of him.

"You're not coming," I said.

"So you and I will go," Francis said. "And we'll figure this out. Because I love you, George. You commie bastard."

"Well, get in line, son. My friend Bill says I'm the girl all the boys want to haul into their boat."

As I said it, sunbeams poured in through the barn windows. Francis stared at them and he stared at me. "What?" I said. "I didn't do it."

If anything, it was the gods stating their approval. Then I noticed the rainbows, dozens of them all around us from the prism-shaped sun-catchers in the windows. "That might be over-the-top," I said after we watched them, mesmerized, dancing over the rough wooden planks, the hay bales, and the walls.

Francis said, "I need you to say something to me before I go."

"Where are you going?"

"Work. Say something incredibly romantic."

"Never."

"Do it for all the star-crossed lovers, George." He wasn't joking now. "I know you have it in you."

"You're . . . *Ugch.* You're a part of me."

"And?"

"I'm a part of you. And for the record, you can't follow someone who's a part of you."

He took off one glove and one of my mittens and held my bare hand in his. "Thank you."

TWENTY-EIGHT

Rupert thought I was working on a big journalism assignment all weekend, and since Francis would be in the city until Sunday night, he arranged for Bobby the Biker Crooner to look in on him. He was worried that Rupert would find the timing suspicious, but Rupert was too huffed up about the suggestion that he couldn't make do on his own to be making connections.

I couldn't come up with an artful lie for my parents. There were so many ways for them to poke holes in my story if I said I wanted to visit relatives or go on a school trip or any other excuse I might concoct. The simplest thing, I'd decided, would be to just drive away. Leave a note on my bed that said I was going somewhere on a bus, then meet Francis over at Mr. and Mrs. Dempsey's place. They were elderly neighbors who'd gone to Florida for the winter, so I could park Abe out of view in the driveway behind their house. If we took Francis's car, no cops could set their sights on Abe's license plates—though, if the note said I'd be back by Sunday night, my father probably wouldn't send the troops after me. He wouldn't announce that he couldn't control his own kid if he didn't have to. I'd get a serious grounding, but it was worth it.

That left Bill, who'd been hoping we could hang out that weekend. "*Ugch*, two whole days with crazy Uncle Burpie," I said as we shot hoops after school. I wasn't great at sinking baskets, but pounding the ball against the floor helped settle my nerves. "You've got, like, twenty minutes to give me an injury that gets me out of it."

More like nineteen. I had to make an appearance at home before meeting Francis at eight.

I passed the ball to Bill and he immediately threw it back to me—or *at* me. So hard, my fingers snapped back.

"I was kidding!" I said.

"Sorry."

"Are you?" He looked right pissy, as he had all day. "What's wrong?"

"I was talking to Lisa."

"Okay . . . ?"

"She told me she tried to call you."

"When?"

"The day after that cop drove you home from the shack party."

"Oh. I don't think I was around."

"She said you weren't around the first time she called, but Matthew told her you'd be home at eleven, so she called you back."

Matty had taken the message before he went to his friend Tim's. I was out getting milk for the barrel of coffee I'd need after lying awake all night, replaying my conversation in the car with Francis, and Mum and Dad were staying in the city for my cousin Junior-Junior's birthday party. The phone went off right at eleven. It must have rung a dozen times. It rang again when I got out of the shower, again after lunch, and when I was doing my homework in the late afternoon. Then it stopped, and when I went to school on Monday, Lisa had kept her distance as usual.

"I went out to the farm," I said. "She didn't say anything to me, so what did you want me to do? I don't get why this is on me."

It was on me because something that had seemed permanently frozen had thawed slightly—and I couldn't do it, be Lisa's friend again, not after I'd gotten back together with Francis. I'd never be able to keep it from her. The choice had been made even before I knew it was going to be put to me; it was made when I followed Francis into the woods.

"It's on *all* of you, and I'm sick of it," Bill said. "Man, you're the worst friends."

"Buddy, Lisa and I haven't been friends for a long time."

"Not to each other, to me! I feel like the only real friend I have left is four thousand miles away."

"That's not true."

"You know, after Sid moved, none of you girls called me to see how I was doing. Lisa barely spoke to me for a week."

"You know why she was mad at you."

"Yeah, because I panicked."

I thought back to when we said good-bye to Sid, how Bill's throat was working when Sid gave him that shoulder punch boys do instead of a hug, and I realized that you could only blurt out something as stupid as Bill had—that thing about there not being other black kids at school—if what you were feeling was too big to say to a guy in an Eddie Murphy costume.

"I guess we just assumed you were okay because, well, you're always okay."

"Then Tracy and I broke up, and where were you guys?"

"I brought you gingerbread," I said. "And Nat brought you date squares, and Lisa got you that stupid shirt. . . ."

"Sure, I had a little harem going for, like, ten minutes before you all disappeared."

I shouldn't have, and I'll regret it forever, but at the mention of minutes my eyes went to the clock on the wall above his head.

"Unbelievable," he said.

"I'm sorry—"

"Go on, if you've got somewhere to be. I could use a break from you."

I had a few more minutes, but he wasn't going to cool down, so I tossed the ball over to him. He let it hit him on his chest and roll away.

"There she goes! Where to, nobody knows!" Bill said to my back. "Just off somewhere being George, doing George things."

The ball slammed against the gymnasium door after I closed it behind me.

When I got home, Dad was, as usual, asleep in his recliner—head tipped back, openmouthed snoring. Matthew was watching *Coronation Street* with the volume turned down. "Does it seem like Dad's been sleeping a lot?" he whispered.

"He doesn't even wake up when I come home at night," I said. "He could be back to taking pain meds."

Matthew gnawed on his knuckle. "His stump shouldn't hurt that much anymore. Unless it's that phantom pain."

We listened to him snore for a minute. Matthew pointed to a box of Benadryl next to Dad's cigarette pack. "Maybe he's sleepy from the Benadryl. I got him some for a rash on his leg."

"I think that's the box I bought a few days ago."

"He shouldn't have gone through the stuff I bought already."

"I put another in his bedroom too."

We quietly got up and went upstairs. Another box of Bena-dryl was on Dad's bedside table where I'd left it.

We hunted for the third box. Not on the dresser or in the drawers. "Not in the cabinet either," Matthew said, returning from the bathroom.

There didn't appear to be anything in the wastebasket beside the bed but tissues and dental floss. Matty turned and gagged as I plunged my hand in. Three empty blister packs were at the bottom.

"Got to be overdoing it," I said. "Have you seen this rash? Is it that bad?"

"Nope."

I looked around the bedroom at the cluttered surfaces—ashtrays overflowing, stacks of crosswords and *Reader's Digest*s lying around. "He could be using it to put himself to sleep."

Dad's voice from downstairs: "George! Get my cigarettes."

"They're on the table next to you!"

"There's only five left!"

Did I want to get into this thing with the Benadryl before I left? No, I did not. Francis and I were driving to the city in a few hours. We were spending two whole days together and sleeping in the same bed and when I woke up in the morning, he'd be there. We'd get to see if we'd run out of conversation. If we were sure no one we knew was around, we might even hold hands in public.

"I'm going to a movie with Bill tonight," I said, handing

Dad a fresh pack. "We'll get a bite at the Grunt."

"You'll have to cancel. I've decided that we're having a sit-down family supper when your mother gets home." He rose inelegantly from his chair.

"I promised Bill—"

"Call him."

Did he know? He knew. But how could he? I'd hidden my bag in Abe's trunk before anyone else was up that morning, had been careful to buy a new toothbrush and toiletries so nothing went missing from the bathroom. So why the sudden desperation to have a sit-down dinner?

We followed Dad into the kitchen and watched him moving awkwardly around with his walker, opening cupboards, tossing things onto the counter.

Because he had something to prove, is why. Maybe he'd heard us talking upstairs.

"What are you making?" Matthew asked.

"Stew."

"Doesn't stew have to cook for a long time?"

"Soup."

Dad stifled a yawn as he piled vegetables around the cutting board. The man had tranquilized himself at horse level.

"You're holding the squash wrong, Dad," I said. His fingers were splayed across the butternut squash, perilously close to the knife blade. Francis had taught me how to do it properly. "You're supposed to put your fingertips in, knuckles out."

"I don't need your advice, thank you."

Matthew gripped the back of a chair, as though steeling himself. He was going in. "Dad? We noticed you're taking a lot of Benadryl."

"I have a rash."

"Can I see it?"

"*You* want to see my . . ." Dad frowned. "No," he said. "No, you may not see my rash."

"We're wondering if you might want to talk to the doctor or something."

"You focus on keeping your grades up, not on me."

"But, Dad—"

"Mind your own damn business!" Dad shouted.

Matthew's lip was trembling. He was trembling all over.

"You don't want to admit you've got ghost pain or whatever they call it, fine," I said. "Don't take it out on Matty."

Dad turned to glare at me. "Let me clarify a few things for you. We are not discussing my private medical condition. We are not inspecting my rash. We are not rifling through my garbage. We are not going out tonight. We are having a sit-down family supper, and we are staying right *here*!"

He slammed the knife for emphasis, his eyes meeting the cutting board just as the blade made contact. Then he looked back at me, and his expression changed from one of fury to a mild *On second thought . . .*

Matthew screamed. Not a horror movie screech, like an

alarm going off—*"Aaagh! Aaagh! Aaagh! Aaagh!"*—before he crumpled to the floor, while Dad and I stared at the river of blood streaming onto the board and down the counter from the space between the top of his index finger and the rest of my father's left hand.

TWENTY-NINE

I don't know why I took my shirt off, given that there was a pile of freshly laundered dish towels on the counter. Once I'd set myself in motion, it all happened so quickly: pulling my long-sleeved T-shirt over my head as I crossed the room so that I was wearing only an obscenely small tank top that I'd shrunk in the wash, accordioning the body of the shirt and pressing it onto Dad's hand, tying the sleeves tight around it. Then I looped his other arm over my shoulders and we staggered over to a chair at the kitchen table. His breathing was rapid and shallow as I lowered him into the seat. What if he was about to go into shock, and what the hell was I supposed to do if he did?

"George—"

"I know exactly what to do, Dad. We covered this in health class."

We had not covered this in health class.

"Just let me get my keys and I'll get you out to the car."

Matthew shouted, "Ice!"

He had woken up, dragged himself through the blood on the floor, and was now sitting with his back against the cupboards, holding the fingertip up like it was the Olympic torch. "Put it down, Matty!" I said.

"We need to—put this—on ice!" He was fighting so hard to stay conscious. "And wrap it—"

"That's correct," Dad said, closing his eyes. "Wrap it in something so you don't damage the skin. . . ."

"Neither one of you is allowed to pass out," I said.

I grabbed a paper towel from the stand on the counter, nearly going arse-over-teakettle sliding in the blood. I held the towel open and Matty dropped in the fingertip, cut just below the nail bed, then I rolled it up like a corn dog and went hunting for a container to put it in.

I'll say this for my mother: She didn't skip a beat when she came home to find me half-naked and lugging Dad into the snowy night with a bloody shirt on his hand. Perhaps because she'd seen more than her share of injuries working at the meatpacking plant before she got married. "I'll take him in my car," she said after I'd bleated an explanation at her. "Call the hospital—the city hospital—and tell them we're on our way."

Maybe it was the smallness of the Honda, the fact that he

had Matthew's old Batman thermos on his lap, the fingertip packed on ice inside, or my own shock, but watching Dad staring down at the thermos as Mum backed out of the driveway, I could have sworn he'd shrunk.

Mum rolled down her window. "For goodness' sakes, George," she said. "Put on a sweater."

My mother always stocked the garage with years' worth of supplies, as though she were preparing for a bunker-worthy event, and I must have used half of the paper towels sopping up blood and washing the cupboards and floors with Lysol. My gut told me that if I waited, if I hesitated at all, I wouldn't be able to face it.

What to do about Francis? It might seem suspicious to Rupert if I called the farm as Francis was getting ready to go, and I couldn't take off without knowing what was happening with my dad. What if something went wrong? What if he'd lost too much blood?

Suddenly freezing, I went upstairs and changed into clean jeans and a sweater before checking on Matthew, who was curled up in Dad's recliner.

"How did you do that?" he said.

"Do what?"

"Stay so calm. Maybe you should be a paramedic."

The Forest Primeval: A Journey Through the Valley, Dad's favorite book, was on the table beside the recliner, underneath a cigarette lighter. I still hadn't read it, but knew from Dad that it had a whole chapter about how the original sawmill in our village blew up back in 1919, killing six people. Whenever I saw the new mill, I wondered about the first responders that day: the firemen, the policemen, the closest neighbors. How did you make yourself go, knowing what you would find? My dad had seen some bad stuff, like the time he went out to a farmhouse after a guy killed his ex-wife with a hunting rifle. Was it that it didn't get to him or that he knew how to swallow it? And if this was swallowing it, the numb feeling that I had, did that mean I would turn out like Dad in other ways too?

"Mum was pretty cool about it," I said, sitting on the sofa and willing myself not to look at the clock on the VCR. "I hope I get it from her."

The phone rang and I pounced on it. "He's going into surgery," Mum said, "but just to repair the rest of the finger."

It was his choice. Reattaching the tip would have meant a longer surgery, days in the hospital, and a good chance the repaired finger wouldn't work as well as a healthy stump.

"You did everything right," she said. "The doctors told me to tell you that. It's one of those things."

I repeated what she said to Matthew, who started to cry.

"Tell your brother that his father's proud of him. You too."

"I will. How's he doing?"

"Oh, you know. He said this was the best his foot had felt in weeks."

"Bizarre."

"If all goes well, he could be home Sunday."

When I hung up, Matthew had his head buried in his arm, like a kid who thinks you can't see him if he can't see you.

"Dad says he's proud of you."

"Mmhmh."

"It's kind of funny if you think about it."

He looked up. *"Funny?"*

"Matty, he amputated his own fingertip. He's just *lopping* off parts of himself."

"Life's a bad writer."

"Exactly."

Matthew took a tissue out of his pocket and blew his nose. "Dad wasn't always a jerk."

"I know. He used to be fun. Doesn't make it any easier to live with him."

"You're not living with him. You're hardly ever here. I've had to pick up all the slack while you're off working and partying—"

"I'm not partying—"

"You got arrested at a party!"

So he'd heard about that. I had to give it to him for keeping it to himself.

"Not arrested. Constable McAdams drove a bunch of us home because some people had been drinking. No one's stopping you from going to parties, by the way."

"Easy for you to say. You get to check out, and Mum has checked out. No one cares about all the shit I've been putting up with."

It hadn't occurred to me that I might have made things tough for Matty. Or to tell him what a good job he was doing taking care of Dad, as much as anyone could take care of him. And I was honestly about to apologize when he added: "Do you know I have to help him take baths now? As in, he's naked. As in, things *float*. And when he does that throat-clearing thing in the morning? You've never seen anything grosser."

I mean, if you have to make it a competition.

"No, I have," I said. "Remember when we were little and had the flu at Christmas and we needed the bucket at the same time? You got there first, but I had to go. Oh man, all those cinnamon buns and sausages and hot chocolate. Remember how it got into your hair and your ears? It slid right into your *head*. And it's still there, isn't it? Because once you go that deep into the ear canal, there's no getting it all out. You don't have great hearing, buddy, and you know it."

It took a good ten seconds before he broke and grinned. "I hate you."

"I know. I'm sorry I've made things hard for you. Thanks for picking up the slack."

The time on the VCR read 7:50 p.m. If I left now, I could catch Francis and at least explain.

"I put my clothes, the bloody ones, down by the washing

machine," Matthew said as I pulled myself to my feet. "Could you do them? Or should we toss them?"

"I'm going out for a bit. I'll take care of it when I come back." I gave his head a little rub. "That's probably enough *exposured* for one night."

Mum called again just as I was leaving to remind us to eat, and so I had to drive faster than I should have to the Dempseys, given the snow coming down, but managed to pull into their driveway by 8:20. Francis wasn't there. I prayed the roads had slowed him down.

While I waited, I stewed—or souped. Worry bumping up against anger getting stirred up with fear. Of course Dad had found a way to ruin our weekend, but he couldn't just, you know, *catch us*. No, sir, not when he could drag Mum and Matty and an innocent kitchen floor into it. Then I remembered how he'd closed his eyes, how small he'd looked in the car. Because he'd slammed the knife into himself while soused on Benadryl! What kind of job could he do with a prosthetic foot and a messed-up hand? What if Mum decided she couldn't take it anymore? I thought maybe I *would* go to the city, get a break from him, and then the worry circled around again.

Francis was very late, and it was getting chilly inside the car. I turned the engine back on, waited for the interior to get warm. Turned it off again. Turned it on. The snow was accumulating on the hood faster than Abe could melt it off. I stopped bothering with the wipers, and the windshield was soon covered and it was very dark.

Nearly two hours passed before I gave up.

On the way home, the streets were so empty and quiet. The house was quiet too. It was far too late to call the farm, and besides, Francis wouldn't have turned around and gone home. He would have had to carry on to the city alone, and I didn't have the phone number of the apartment where we were going to stay.

I sank into the chair by the phone in the kitchen, unsure of what to do. The air was heavy with cleaner fumes. For years afterward, I thought of Lysol as the official scent of disaster.

THIRTY

Saturday was the longest day there ever was. I hovered near the phone for updates from Mum and maybe, maybe a call from Francis, if he felt like taking a chance. Had I any idea where the apartment was, I'm sure I would have gotten in my car and gone after him, but there was nothing to do but pace my room and wait for the sun to take a thousand hours to move around the house.

Dad was in a good mood when he got home on Sunday, which may or may not have been drug related. I half hoped he'd had an out-of-kitty experience when he rested his bandaged hand on my shoulder. He even gave Matthew a hug and didn't say anything smart when Matty had a little cry.

The call from Rupert came in soon after Dad and his hand had settled into his recliner. "The pamphlet says you can't smoke," Matty was saying when I came back into the family room. "Right here. It's bad for healing."

"George, get my cigarettes," Dad said.

So, not so out-of-kitty.

"Don't you dare," Mum said.

"I'm staying out of it," I said. "And I'm sorry, but I have to go out to the farm to help Rupert."

"Like fun," Dad said. "Don't you have a French test next week? Go forth and conjugate."

Mum was giving me big eyes. "Your father just got home."

"I know, and I wouldn't ask, but his pig escaped and he can't find him. He's having a meltdown."

"There's no one else who can do it? A neighbor?"

"I have no idea. He was hardly making sense."

Yes, I wanted to get out there in case Francis came home early, but the truth was, I'd never heard Rupert so upset. His sentences were disjointed, and he kept repeating, "You'll bring the old boy back, George, won't you? You'll bring him back," until I said I would.

"I could go out there with her, Paul," Mum said.

"How are you going to lasso a rogue pig out in the snow?"

He pointed to her with his bandaged hand. He'd been gesturing with it constantly since he got home, and I thought the old Dad—the Dad who wore a purple tutu while paddling a pumpkin, the Dad who used to terrorize Matty by making Halloween decorations out of frozen cows' hearts that he picked up at the meatpacking plant—might have had a lot of sick fun with a quarter less finger.

"I meant that someone should clap their eyes on this old gentleman," Mum said. "He doesn't sound too good. Maybe his mind's gone."

"Just to be clear, there *is* a pig," I said. "The same pig that got out before. The last time this happened, I found him, so."

"Georgie, go," Mum said. "But for god's sake, be careful on those back roads."

As I turned into Rupert's long driveway, I passed a bearded man in a black hat and motorcycle jacket. I was nearly to the house before I took in that it was Bobby.

A gray-haired woman came round the barn as I got out of the car. "You Georgia?" she said.

"Yeah. Well, George."

"George—sorry. Thank you for coming out, and I'm sorry for that phone call. Rupert insisted that if anyone could find this damnable pig it was you. I'm Janet, I should have said. Live up the road."

"I can try, but I found him accidentally the last time."

"Do you know how to get hold of Mick? Apparently, he just up and left on Friday night. . . ."

"Oh, no, he went to the city for the weekend. I don't have a number, but he should be back tonight."

"Thank god. Rupert made it sound like he was lost to the

wind. Never mind. He's not all there at the moment."

She took my arm and we crossed the icy driveway together.

"Did I see Bobby?" I asked.

"He was lucky enough to drop by in the middle of this ruckus, yes. My husband and my boys are out looking too, and the Johnson family—except the one inside. By god, that girl is useless."

The useless Johnson girl—a blond blob arranged in the vague outline of a human—was sitting at the kitchen table with Rupert, reading a magazine, apparently oblivious to the crumbs and sticky splotches around the plate of whatever she'd helped herself to and the tears hovering at the edges of Rupert's eyes. I kicked my boots off and rushed in to hug him. "What happened?" I asked.

Short story, really. Back door open. Pig gone.

"Have some tea," I said, pouring him a cup from the pot that was simmering on the back of the stove. I loaded it up with milk and sugar. "Have you eaten? You've probably been too worried."

He nodded and took a few long sips.

"Better?"

He nodded again, and he did seem better. "Oh, George, he's been smelling awful these past few days. I blame myself. Switching him to powdered milk to save a few dollars. *Stale* bread. *Canned* peas." He whispered, "I may have accidentally given him some canned *ham*. You know what that could do to a mind as fragile as Shaggy's?"

The Johnson girl rolled her eyes and flipped another page of her magazine. I brought my fist down on the table just for the satisfaction of seeing her jump. "I have an idea," I said. "This might sound obvious, but did anyone check Francis's room?"

"'Course," said Rupert, but he looked doubtful, then worried.

"I'm sure you would have heard him," I said.

"Can you imagine? I got all those people out in the cold—"

"I'll run up. He's *not* there, but I'll run up."

I had an alternative motive, which was to leave something for Francis in one of the books that he kept on the stool by his bedside, in case I had to go home before he returned. A lock of hair, a note—just to show I'd been at the farm and was thinking of him. But the stool was empty, like the other surfaces in the room, which was in its usual monk mode. There was nothing in place to be out of place—nothing but a large pig softly snoring on an old striped mattress.

It took some coaxing to get Shaggy off the bed, and a back knee buckled when his hooves hit the floor. He glared at me accusingly through his long lashes. "Yes, you're very delicate." I pointed to the door. "Downstairs."

Janet's husband rang a triangle-shaped dinner bell to call in the search.

I was sitting on the veranda with Shaggy, his head in my lap. It had taken all of his effort to get down the stairs and now he seemed a bit feverish, his breathing shallow. Janet dropped an afghan over him, whispering, "I think a call to the vet and to Rupert's daughter may be in order."

While I took care of the four-legged patient, she went inside to deal with the two-legged situation. Rupert had burst into tears when he'd seen Shaggy, from relief or embarrassment, I don't know. I could hear Janet through the door saying again and again, "It was no trouble, dear. No trouble at all. It's not like the rest of us thought to check upstairs."

In the distance, Bobby's leather-clad form was traveling along the highway, moving quickly, awkwardly, his gait strange, off somehow. He reminded me of the White Rabbit from *Alice in Wonderland* going, *I'm late, I'm late . . .*

"We got him, Bobby!" someone called.

He didn't respond. He stopped partway up the drive, bent over, weight on his thighs. Then he crouched down, hands clasped behind his head. And then he sat right on the frozen ground, which is when people started running.

They must have thought he was having a heart attack or something, but it didn't look like a heart attack to me, and he didn't look like a man who'd walked too fast and just needed to catch his breath. He looked like a man who had been moving as fast and far as he could before despair overtook him.

A sharp pain shot through my chest, like the flare I'd felt the day I met Francis—except this was fear, sudden and stabbing. I wrapped my arms around Shaggy, and pulled his warmth into me. I felt his shallow breathing, in and out, in and out. Steady, boy, steady.

LULLABY FOR THE CAT

THIRTY-ONE

April 1993

When I woke up the morning light was slanting through my window. I could hear newspapers rustling downstairs, the kettle settling back on the stove, Mum's continuous murmur. Was she talking on the telephone, or were Dad and Matthew just not responding? My brother's low grumble interrupted the flow of words. Silence, then Mum again.

The sharp pain that had run through me at the farm was now faded and had been replaced with something like a hum. I placed my hand in the square of sunlight on my chest, felt heat. It seemed to be coming from under my pajama top, from inside me, not the sun, as though my palm were cooking over a low flame. I closed my eyes again and felt my heart's slow burn.

"Georgie, could you come downstairs, please?"

My family was sitting at the kitchen table, oddly arranged to one side, as though they'd pulled their chairs closer together.

"Are you alright?" Mum asked.

I nodded. A little too vigorously.

"Did you see it?" Matthew asked. "Must have been . . . I mean, it was probably . . ."

Mum put her hand on Matthew's arm and gave him a warning look.

"It" couldn't be seen from a moving vehicle up on the road, not that many people had gone by over the past couple of days, given the weather. Only someone on foot, walking alongside the guardrail with his eyes peeled for the unusual, could have spotted Francis's car down in the ravine, partially covered with snow. Any skid marks next to the start of the guardrail had disappeared under the ice and the gravel they put down out there instead of salt.

"No, I didn't see it," I said to Matty.

Janet and her husband had driven me home in Abe, another neighbor following behind in their car. I hadn't said much since Bobby went down on the driveway, was almost as preternaturally calm then as I was now in front of my family, but it was dark by the time the officers from the New Oban detachment finished taking statements and it had started snowing again, and I kept pulling cold, damp air into my lungs so sharply that my body would occasionally jerk as though I'd jumped into the frigid bay. Janet hadn't asked me if I wanted a drive, just steered me to my car and opened a back-seat door.

She turned around in the front passenger seat as we approached the emergency vehicles on the side of the road. "They're pulling the car out of the ravine," she said. "Don't look."

She held my eyes.

I needed to look.

"Don't look, dear."

She faced front again after we passed. I immediately turned my head, but could see only blurry lights through the back window. Blue and flashing. Orange and steady. Red and blinking. On. Off.

"Georgie, you must be hungry."

On. Off.

"Georgie," Mum said again. "You want breakfast?"

My family was staring at me like I was a carnival act. My stomach pinched, but with the burning in my chest, swallowing wasn't doable. "No, thanks."

"Sometimes I forget how lucky you and Matty have been. By the time I was your age, I'd buried one of my brothers, aunts, uncles, all the grandparents. But it *is* shocking when someone so young dies, isn't it? Though I suppose to you he wasn't that young." She leaned forward and peered at me. "Maybe I don't know what I'm talking about."

"No, that's it," I said, trying to approximate the sound of someone who is okay yet not unfeeling and not at all in the grip of an endless F-minor chord vibrating from her core. "That's exactly it."

"Would you like to go to the service? I doubt they'll have the funeral here, but surely the force will have a memorial of some kind, won't they, Paul?"

My father's nod was so slight it was almost imperceptible. Something you learn early on when you grow up in a police household is that there is nothing more somber and steadfast than the force in mourning for someone who has served.

"I don't think so, Mum." I wouldn't be able to get through a service without the kind of violent cracking up that leaves a person permanently drooling. "Can I see Rupert, though? Is someone with him?"

The last thing I heard Rupert say before he collapsed and had to be put to bed was, "I encouraged him. My god, I told him to go."

"We called over this morning," Dad said. "His daughter drove in from the city last night."

"She's the one who's always trying to get him into a nursing home."

"That's between them."

"What's important," Mum said, "is that he has family to help him through the shock of all this. And she arrived in time to be there when the pig went, thank goodness."

"What do you mean?"

"Terrible timing, to have to put a pet down on top of every-thing else."

"They put down *Shaggy*?" My voice broke as a sob came roaring up.

Dad opened his mouth to speak but Mum clasped his arm. Now she was holding on to both my father and my brother like she was about to rodeo-ride a pair of wild ponies, and it was plain they all thought I'd lost my mind, which I had.

"More like they just . . . helped him over the line, dear. By the time the vet got out to the farm, his heartbeat was very faint."

"Shaggy's dead? He's *dead*?"

Through the blur of tears, I saw my father remove some-thing from the table with his good hand, which he appeared to be holding on his lap. I became aware of the smell of bacon.

"You know he was quite old," Mum said. "And he'd had a good life, sounds like. He slipped away peacefully with loved ones around him."

"It's so unfair!"

"Do you want to go to *his* funeral?" Matthew asked. "Ow, Mum, you're cutting off my circulation."

I sniffed and wiped my nose on the sleeve of my robe. "Are they having one?"

"Why don't you go back upstairs to bed?" Mum said. "You've had a big shock." I nodded. "Okay? Off you pop, then. Don't hurry back down."

"So, she isn't *completely* heartless," I heard Matthew say before Mum shushed him. "She can get right emotional over a pork chop."

THIRTY-TWO

"What's wrong, baby?" Keith asked.

Homeroom, ten minutes before the bell. Lisa and Christina were huddled over a newspaper, Nat sitting off to the side with another copy. Lisa held it up, tapped the headline. *RCMP Hero Killed: Deadly Accident.*

There was no photo, so it took Keith a minute with the article to put together that this was the cop who had busted up the shack party.

"Holy crud."

"He saved that tourist in the bay last year," Lisa said. "I wish I'd known that was him when he drove us home. Remember when he told me to put on a good show? I was like, *I have a play,* and he was all, *I know it'll be good.* That was the last thing he said to me."

She smiled bravely and Keith put his arm around her. "I remember," he said. "The next morning you were like, *I know what I have to do.*"

As Sid often complained, one of the worst things about girls was how there wasn't a tragedy they couldn't make about themselves. Not that I doubted Lisa felt sorry about Francis; it was just the way she needed everyone to know she did.

I was sitting sidesaddle at my desk, my knapsack warming my lap, not knowing what to do with my various parts—where to set my hands, how to position my mouth like a normal person. I used to watch people go into stores and shovel their walkways and sit behind the wheels of their cars and thrill to the fact that they had no idea that I, George Warren, the supposedly heartless girl, was in love—sometimes, at that very moment, still throbbing with sex—and now I wondered how anyone could be in a room with me and not detect this never-ending vibration, like a single bass note sounded on a piano. Alone in my bedroom, it was almost comforting. Now I had to move around in the world as though the hum weren't there, and try to focus on the problems in front of me. How to dress myself. How to get to school. I'd left Abe in the driveway that morning, sleep-walked to the bus stop, following the path that Matthew made in the snow.

I wasn't going to get through the day. I needed a reason to go home—flu, allergies, political dissention. I'd think of something by the time I got to the office. I would impale myself on the metal divider in my pencil case, if need be.

Lisa caught my wrist as I passed her. "How well did you know him?"

She obviously wanted to keep talking about it, this little brush she'd had with celebrity, which was irritating only because she didn't know what she was scratching at.

"Not well," I said.

"But you worked for him?"

"Mostly I helped out his landlord when he wasn't around."

Nat was shaking her head at Lisa, who released my wrist and leaned back into Keith.

"He was nice. He didn't have to let us go," Christina said, grabbing her bag and following me to the door. "'Course, George probably sucked him off."

I'd never hit anyone before and had no idea it would hurt so much. Hurt *me*, that is. I assume it hurt Christina from the noise her face made as my fist made contact and the way she gasped and Lisa crying, "You *bitch*!" I looked down at my throbbing knuckles, astonished that they had done what they had done.

"We do not tolerate violence in this school, as you well know," Mr. Humphreys said over the sound of my mother's weeping. "But . . ." He sighed. "There are two sides to every story, and experience tells me that students, especially female students, rarely lash out like this without being provoked."

We were sitting in his office, my mother and me on hard

wooden chairs designed for maximum discomfort. The back on mine felt like it could eject me at any moment.

"No, I deserve to be suspended," I said a little too sincerely.

Shit. Now he was looking at me with even more interest.

"Mr. Humphreys is giving you a chance to explain yourself," Mum said. "So explain yourself."

I shrugged. "Christina has had it in for me all year cuz her boyfriend used to have a crush on me. I got sick of it."

The truth is, just before my knuckles slammed into her cheekbone, it registered that Christina was sort of smiling when she said what she said. The tiniest possibility that she had been teasing was threatening to sink in.

"Mrs. Warren, do you know what the other students call your daughter? The Enforcer."

So that was a thing. Bill and Sid were the only ones who called me that to my face.

"Because her father is in law enforcement?"

"It's a hockey term. Means the heavy. The tough guy. But enforcers don't pick fights on the ice for fun. They're usually protecting someone."

"Who were you protecting, Georgie?"

I had nothing. The easy lies, the quick comebacks—gone.

"I'm trying to help you," said Mr. Humphreys.

"Thank you, sir. But I just want to go home."

He sighed another Nat-like sigh, so drawn out that he

seemed to be emptying his lungs entirely. "Two weeks. You'll apologize to Christina in this office on the day you return."

"You will *not* leave the house," Mum said in the car.

"Fine."

"You will not make phone calls. You will not have guests."

"No problem."

Mum was a nervous driver, terrified of taking her eyes off the road, and her furtive, machine-gun glances at me were almost comical.

"I'm glad you're taking this so seriously."

"Whatever you want to do is okay by me. I'm not going to start drinking the Listerine as soon as your back is turned."

"Why would you drink the Listerine?"

"For the alcohol."

"How would you know that?!"

"I said I *wouldn't* drink the . . . Never mind. God, I get into one fight and suddenly I'm a delinquent."

She pulled over. "Not suddenly. Not suddenly at all. You've been acting strangely for months. Out all the time. Your grades up and down and up again. Look at your clothes falling off you! I would say you were in knots about your father's situation except you don't show any compassion for him, not anymore. Nothing seems to affect you—except that pig. And don't think I haven't noticed that we never see Lisa anymore."

"Did it occur to you to ask me what's wrong, if this is all such suspicious behavior?"

"What's wrong? What *is* it? Is it drugs?"

"I'm probably the only person who gets peer-pressured *not* to do drugs."

"Then what? What?"

"I'm just . . . tired. Tired of being here. School. The valley. Dad. All of it."

She turned on her signal light to pull back onto the road. "I'll tell you what," she said. "For someone so hell-bent on getting away, you're doing a very good job of jeopardizing your future."

There was nothing harder than Dad's anger. Hard like a slab of thick, cold glass. You could see in, but you couldn't get past it; you didn't even try. You watched him talking with Matthew at the dinner table and gesturing to Mum with his bandaged finger to pass the scalloped potatoes as though you were watching a TV show about a place you'd like to travel to but couldn't afford. You dug your socked toes into the shag area rug and told yourself that you'd had a good run, but sooner or later the law catches up to everyone. Like Al Capone getting sent up for tax evasion, the suspension was just the thing that helped the Sergeant bring you in. It sucked, but you couldn't do anything about it. You told yourself that, though you didn't quite feel it in your bones.

A chore list was posted on the refrigerator: scrub toilets and garbage bins, pull hair out of drain, and so on. All of it nasty, none of it for Matthew. But Dad quickly lost interest in monitoring the prisoner, which put me in his sight line too often and required him to get up to check my work. It was disturbing, how he hardly moved from his recliner at all. He wasn't pretending to do his rehab exercises anymore.

On the third afternoon, I placed a pack of cigarettes beside him and slipped upstairs to my bed, staying there for the rest of the day and the next. And the next. And the next. I spread my textbooks and notebooks around so it would look like I'd been studying, which I did, but also to make it less obvious if I drifted off, which I did.

I wasn't allowed to talk to anyone, including Rupert. My mother had told his daughter, Sarah, and the heritage society that I had mono or something and would be out for a couple of weeks, and Sarah said that she might have him into a nursing home by then. The thought of it made my chest burn hotter.

My eighteenth birthday passed without the cards or gifts that were put away until after my suspension, though Matty did smuggle me one from Sid that had a picture of Charlie Chaplin wearing an old-timey prisoner's uniform (*I bet Joshua Spring would pay you a conjugal visit.*). Soon, I was no longer coming out of my room to push food around on my plate. Every time I crept back into my warm, safe cocoon after being forced out to use the bathroom, I was nearly giddy with gratitude. I would lie in bed for hours with my hand resting on the mattress in the space where Francis never was but I always wished he could be, and I would fall asleep that way.

When I woke up, that's when it came rushing at me in waves. Had he died instantly? Or had he survived that long drop into the icy ravine and waited for help that didn't come? Had he called out? For me? The thought of it was so intensely and ruthlessly and relentlessly painful that it felt like a long, silent howl.

In between were the dreams, some of them joyful and full of touch and scent, caresses and sweat and callused fingertips, but there were also the bed-like toboggans careening around trees and skirting crevices, and the recurring image of the lake stone lying among the debris at the bottom of the bay. I was so afraid Francis's face would stop visiting me in my sleep and start slipping away. I didn't have a single photograph of him, no letters, no ticket stubs or playbills or locks of hair or old T-shirts or any of those things that you were supposed to have and hold on to when you were in love.

Then one night, I couldn't sleep anymore. We were having one of those surprise mid-April snowfalls, and as the hours passed and the snow piled up, the darkness pressing against my window grew blacker, scarier. I slipped down onto the floor to crawl under the bed, like I did when I was little, but it was crammed with all my kid things. Even if I pulled it all out, I wouldn't be able to squeeze between the frame and the floor. Curled up on the rug, I began to panic. What was the point of

being clever, or at least quick, if I couldn't wriggle out of this one? Couldn't talk my way out of it, couldn't outrun it, and I no longer fit under the bed.

I heard Matthew's slippered feet padding down the hallway, followed by the *shooft* of a piece of yellow construction paper sliding under my door. He'd scrawled: "Something for you on the front stoop."

"Matty?"

The soft click of his bedroom latch.

My legs, once I got them under me, were like a newborn calf's. Just walking down the hallway felt precarious, never mind the stairs. Matthew had turned out the lights behind him and I left them off. I didn't want to wake up Mum, who was snoring in the guest room with the door half open, or alert Dad, watching TV in the family room, that I was up and available to fetch him things.

I eased the front door open, stepped lightly across the creaky porch, and opened that door too. On the stoop, nestled in a clump of snow, was a single rose in a glass bud vase. The yard was marked by two trails, one a deep track where the snow had been kicked up and tramped down, the other made of enormous footprints, spaced well apart and pointing toward the road, as though a giant had taken off at a run.

THIRTY-THREE

"**G**ood morning, sunshine." My mother was standing at the foot of my bed, wearing a forced-looking smile. "You know what would be fun, Georgie?" she said. "Let's get you washed up right here!"

What? No. Weird.

I shook my head and it began to throb. I could feel my pulse in my face.

"Like a spa! Wouldn't that be a—"

I'm thinking she said *hoot*, but she was already down the hallway.

I closed my eyes, drifting off for a moment, and when I opened them again she was sitting beside me on the bed, gently wiping my face with a warm washcloth. She'd placed a second one on the bedside table along with the water cup from the bathroom. "Your father would be so jealous if he knew you're getting the royal treatment."

Her expression turned grim as she swabbed my nose and chin, grimmer when she got to my lips. They seemed stuck to my teeth. "I'll do it," I tried to say, but my mouth was full of goo and crust.

"Shush-shush," Mum said. "Spa, hospital, tomayto, tomahto."

Slowly, she worked her way to the inside of my lips, ignoring my flinches and whimpers, and started wiping my teeth and gums. "Done," she said, handing me the cup. "Swish some water around. You can spit it right back in."

I filled the cup with brown flakes and a stream of red then reached for the makeup mirror on my bedside table. Mum said, "Just don't . . ."

She didn't finish the thought. Because there's no point in telling someone *don't get upset* when they're about to be confronted with what happens when you hit the floor without breaking your fall.

A brick-red carpet burn seared the skin over purple-brown bruises from my nose to my chin. My bottom lip was gaping where a tooth had sliced into it. "Oh my god," I said, and I started laughing. My face was raw from the wiping and it was pounding, pounding, but I couldn't stop.

"What's going on?" Matty called from his bedroom.

"Don't come in!" Mum said. "Georgie had a little accident."

"I fell on the way back from the bathroom last night," I said, calming down. "Or fainted?"

I remembered the scratchy rug against my cheek, my fingers digging into the fibers, the long crawl back to my room. I hadn't wondered at the time how exactly I'd ended up there. It was just, *Excuse me, floor. I'll be going now.*

I touched the oozing space between my nose and upper lip. "Oh, that's bad."

"You're lucky you didn't knock your teeth out," Mum said. She felt my forehead. "No temperature. Do you feel sick?"

"I feel like I face-planted."

"Were you sick last night?"

"I don't think so. I got up to pee."

"Is it your monthlies?"

The heat under my sternum radiated upward. "Yeah, maybe that's it. Or maybe I got up from the toilet too fast."

"Well, this is the first chance I've had to take care of you for a long, long time."

She looked over at the rose on my dresser.

"Someone left it on the front step last night," I said. "It might not even be for me."

"Must be a birthday gift. Are you feeling grown-up?"

"Not this second." I stretched until my blanketed toes touched the fading Disney stickers plastered across the foot-board of my bed.

"When you started nursery school you were so small, doll-sized, and here you are, eighteen, a half foot taller than average.

Force of will, I say. Always trying to push yourself out of the nest."

"Sorry I've been such a jerk. I didn't mean what I said."

"I knew something was wrong. I said to myself, 'Marlene, she's at that age where kids start to have a drink and get into trouble. But you were always so responsible. And now you're drinking the Listerine." Her eyes were glistening. "Do you think this is funny?"

I tried to stop smiling. "I don't drink the Listerine, I promise. Wouldn't Dad of all people have known if I was an addict?"

"You have always managed to work around him when you wanted to—don't think I am completely unaware. Although he could have been too loaded up with Benadryl to notice."

She laughed, and, oh god, what a relief. When Mum let herself get mad at us, it was awful. When she blamed herself, it was the worst.

"I won't say I haven't tried anything, but honestly, it's true what I said about getting peer pressure in reverse. No one wants me to get high."

"What happened with Lisa, dear?"

"I hurt her feelings. And some other stuff."

"Is that all that's been bothering you? I know you can't be friends with your kids, but I always wished . . . well, I wish you would at least let me mother you."

There were so many words that wanted out of my crusty mouth.

It hurts to eat.

It hurts to breathe.

It hurts to wake up in the morning.

I don't know how to break my fall.

She touched my face so tenderly, and it seemed impossible that I could ever tell her about Francis. Her heart couldn't take it.

"That's all, Mum."

"Alright, I've got to go to work. Did I tell you that Miriam is convinced I waited on Rod Stewart the other day? At first she thought it was just some fella *impersonifying* him, but . . . Never mind, I'll bore you with that later."

"Doesn't sound boring."

"It's a long story. When you feel up to it, put my mind at ease and *eat some breakfast.*"

I hadn't really thought about telling people what it meant to me that Francis was gone. I guess somewhere in the back of my mind I assumed I would when I was ready, whenever that was. He no longer had anything to lose and neither did I, and I didn't believe he was up in the clouds watching to see if I'd break my promise. But after talking to Mum, I could see all too easily what would happen if I told my parents. About 10 percent of the conversation would be spent trying to reassure her that she wasn't a bad mother for not intuiting my moral failings, and reckon another 15 percent on the logistics of getting around

Dad, the hows and wheres and whens. The rest would be spent defending Francis. I'd have to defend him to anyone I told, even Bill, if we were still speaking. Especially Bill, who thought only bad people did bad things. I couldn't see how that would make anyone feel better, least of all me. It was easier to stay in the habit of the secret, though when I put on my jacket to go to school, I kept reaching into the pocket for the stone that was no longer there.

Dad wouldn't let me stay home the first day after my suspension, so I was slathered in foundation that I'd pinched from my mother. (Colors that match my Irish paleosity hadn't been invented yet.) I wore a turtleneck to cover the place where the foundation and my skin parted ways. I could feel the makeup sliding south as I climbed the school steps and pooling in the collar of the formerly tight sweater that no longer hugged my frame.

Matthew hopped out of Abe, couldn't get away fast enough, leaving me to slouch inside on my own. Double takes, a snicker or two. The only person who approached me was Shelley-with-an-*E*. She put her hand on my shoulder, squinted at my face, then just sort of backed away.

I searched for Bill in the hallway, but locked eyes with Joshua instead. I'd punched his girlfriend and he'd bought me a birthday gift. What did I owe him: *thank you, sorry*, or *you're welcome*? I decided to lead with *thank you*, but before I could get all the words out, he fled like an impala that's spotted a lion in the grass.

So things were off to a good start.

During homeroom I had to go to the principal's office for my official smackdown. There was a little speech to give, which Mr. Humphreys had basically written for me.

"Violence," I began, "is not the solution—"

"I'm sorry about your face," Christina said.

"You're sorry about . . . *my* face?"

The area under her eye still had a large greenish-brown bruise that must have been pretty gruesome two weeks earlier. Unlike me, she hadn't tried to cover it up with makeup. I looked over at Mr. Humphreys, assuming he'd put her up to it, but he was as taken aback as I was. He gave me a go-on nod.

"I'm sorry too," I said. "Violence is not the solution to our problems and also not in the spirit of our school motto, 'Courteousness, Cooperation and Consideration For All.'"

Christina seemed rattled, staring down at her hands. For a second I thought maybe Joshua had dumped her. Hopefully not for me. Again. But then she met my eyes and had a look I'd never seen before on her ferrety face. She felt sorry for me.

What did she know?

"Matthew said . . ."

Matthew!

"He said . . ."

Something told me that I should act like I knew what she was trying to say, so I sat back in my chair and knitted my eyebrows together and swallowed a sour taste that was rising in my throat.

"What about Matthew?" Mr. Humphreys said.

"Nothing. I don't want to cause any more trouble."

"Good. So now you two can put this behind you. Christina, you're excused. George, I need you to sign this pledge form. The PTA believes students are less likely to re-offend if they promise not to."

The pledge was printed in a scroll font on top of a picture of a sunset. "'I pledge to be honest and always true. To treat each day as bright and new. To honor my teachers and my classmates too . . .' I feel less violent already," I said as Christina fled the office.

Mr. Humphreys handed me a pen. "I feel the opposite."

I tried to keep my head down in Modern World Problems, but could feel eyes on me. Maybe Nat's. Maybe Lisa's. I instinctively glanced up when Doug dropped his books onto the desk in front of mine, and I think he started laughing before his brain had computed what was so funny. Hey, it's nice to make a person's life in one nanosecond. Because while everyone else saw some kind of mysterious accident, all Doug took in was my half-cracked attempt to cover it up. I'm not sure he noticed the sharp look from Mr. Gifford, just got up, tipped his hat to me, and marched himself out of the classroom, still laughing.

Mr. Gifford seemed to feel the same as me: like the day had already defeated him. He popped a tape into the VCR and babysat us with news reports about the Bombay Riots, leaning back in his chair with his fingers pinching the bridge of his nose. I slid down in my seat and cupped my hands around my temples, as though cutting off my peripheral vision could shut out the buzzing worry about what it was that my baby brother and the person who had told everyone about the East Riverview guys knew—basically asking the good people of India to distract me with their immense suffering.

I'd watched a lot of horror movies, no problem, so it wasn't the blood. Or the bodies lying in the streets, the shouting or the sirens. It was a woman in the corner of the screen, squatting, her hands reaching up in despair to God, one of her thin arms bent at an unnatural angle. What was her story? What had she lost?

I dreamt. About what, I can't remember now. Something curious. Violent. Then whoever was sitting behind me kicked the bottom of my seat and I was back in the classroom but somehow also still in the dream. It pulled on me like a bath of molasses, and I couldn't climb all the way out.

Slowly, faces appeared, gawking at me with huge grins. You'd think they were witnessing a Christmas miracle: *Thank you, Jesus, for bestowing this spectacle upon us, we surely do believe.* And it could have been Christmas, for all I knew. I couldn't have told you my own name.

"Wake UP," said Mr. Gifford, I suspect not for the first time.

"I . . ."

I retched. More specifically, I *belch-retched* in front of the entire class, and now scenery was flying by—desks and classroom walls and lockers and posters and mirrors and stalls—and then I was staring into a toilet bowl where bobbed a tidy wad of paper in a bath of very yellow pee. I retched again, brought up bile, and broke into a cold sweat.

I sat on the floor with my back against the metal stall. Lisa was gazing down at me.

"Are you okay?" she asked.

I nodded.

"You were snoring."

"What? *No.*"

"And not just a little. Big-daddy dinosaur snores."

Closing my eyes made me dizzy again, so I focused on the toilet paper dispenser. "I think I fainted." I pointed to my subnasal disaster zone. "Last night too."

"Did it hurt?"

"No. I broke the fall with my face."

She didn't laugh. "When you came to, you were the wrong color," she said. "Besides the shite makeup. Are you sick?"

"Sort of."

"Do you . . . do you think you might be pregnant?"

What made her say *that*, when I'd gotten thinner, not heavier?

"No chance."

Anymore.

"Sorry if that sounded . . . My cousin Deanna fainted a lot when she was in her first trimester. Remember her? She was in the skating club."

"Yeah, I do. That brown cow bitch knocked me down during 'The Farmer in the Dell.'"

I said it jokingly, but in the back of my mind I heard the echo of what Lisa said when I hit Christina. *You bitch.*

And yet Christina had apologized. If that was because she knew about Francis and me, wouldn't she have told Lisa, if not the entire school? But Lisa wasn't looking at me with that same pity, only worry. It was enough to make me hope that Christina had been talking about something else.

"You were totally going to skate in the Olympics if it weren't for Deanna," Lisa said.

"One hundred percent."

She smiled, then caught herself and cleared her throat, the concern in her eyes retreating. "I'd better take you to the office."

"That's alright."

"Come on. Oh, and sorry about your sweater."

As she pulled me up I saw my sleeve was out of shape where she'd grabbed me and dragged my arse to the bathroom. Knowing Lisa, she may have meant that she was sorry that I'd worn it—except that her own sweater was ratty, and her hair was pulled into a tight ponytail with a regular elastic band, as though she'd just rolled out of bed. She hooked my arm in hers and we walked too fast, considering, saying nothing more. A silent march toward the school secretaries, who took one look at me and closed in. I felt Lisa release my arm. "Lise—wait," I said. She was already walking away.

THIRTY-FOUR

Since my mother couldn't be reached at work and my dad couldn't drive even if he were picking up the phone, Matthew had to come home with me in case I got woozy again. What he was supposed to do when I fainted at the wheel was unclear, so basically, it would be a two-for-one special if I wrapped the car around a telephone pole.

Which suited me fine. "Why are we going this way?" he said as I turned the car onto the old highway.

"It's my fault you're missing band practice," I said. "Let me make it up to you."

Matty was one of those winter ice cream people. I wasn't, but the vanilla sludge at Dairy Queen felt good sliding down my throat. "It's tasty, yeah?" he said, licking chocolate sauce off his spoon. "There's no such thing as good food or bad food.

Sometimes food just makes us happy."

"Why are you talking like a *Schoolhouse Rock!* message?" Oh. "Do you think I have an eating disorder?"

"No, I . . . You don't eat much lately."

"You're the one who kept saying I needed to lose weight."

"Not really, though," he said. "I was only kidding." His face twisted with the regret of a thousand butt jokes. "You don't need to be on a diet."

"Aw, buddy, I'm not. Promise. I've just been kind of stressed out. You know what would make me feel better?"

"What?"

"If someone could tell me what's going on with Christina."

His spoon hovered in front of his mouth. "What do you mean?"

"I don't know, she was being weird this morning. Did she and Joshua break up?"

"Someone said she dumped him for Skateboarder Brad."

That was disappointing. Skateboarder Brad was the best of the Brads, a baby-faced bruiser with a confusing haircut. He deserved better. "Poor, dumb Brad," I said.

"Yeah. But lucky Joshua, right? Better off without her."

"Right, right. Here's what I can't work out. What it is that you, Matty, said to Christina to make her feel bad for me."

"What *I* said?" He did a pretty good job of pretending to search his memory. "Can't think of anything. Maybe now that she and Joshua are done, she's sorry about being mean to you."

I pulled his bowl out of reach. "Don't bullshit a bullshitter, son."

"Okay, I—I told her that I was on her side after what you did. Sorry, threw you under the bus."

"And?"

"That's it." He tried to grab the bowl. "And . . . I might have also said I did that to you."

"What, this?"

"I saw her by the principal's office this morning, and was all like, 'I took care of it; she won't be bothering you again' or something like that."

"Why?"

"The Elevens would have kicked my ass a long time ago if you weren't around. Well, next year you won't be around."

I pushed the bowl toward him. "So you decided that it would be better if she thinks you're a psycho. And she believed you."

He drank the puddle of melted ice cream, wiped the chocolate moustache off his cupid's-bow mouth, and tried not to smile. "Getting better at bullshitting, I guess."

I got to the end of the week without any more public retching, but it had been clear almost from the moment I went through the school doors that I couldn't go back to leading my double life. My stupid body was trying to rat on me. The only reason Mum hadn't been able to force me to the doctor yet was because he was on holiday. When he got back and couldn't find something physically wrong, how long before people started connecting the dots? It'd be so much better if you could be sad part-time. Go into a chamber, get zapped with a thousand volts, scream into the void, come out and go for a nice run.

Lying curled on my bed that Friday afternoon, the panic started rising again. Should I tell Bill, just to get it over with? We hadn't said a word to each other since our fight, and he'd been out all week with a stomach bug. I didn't know if we weren't talking or hadn't had a chance. If not Bill, who? If not telling, what? What do I do? What do I DO?

I'd always felt like there was a point I was moving toward, small, vague, and distant, but *there*. For a long time the plan had been all about leaving with my friends (I mean, I'd chosen Aurora for them, not me), then I'd hung my future on Francis. Now what? Did I even *want* to feel better? This burning in my chest was all I had left of him. If it went away, it might be like he never was. I had nothing else to hold on to.

I didn't, but maybe someone else did.

When I got to the farm, I half expected the house to be dirty and neglected and moldering back to its former state, and of course it wasn't. Rupert's daughter, Sarah, was staying there when she came to visit Rupert from the city, and seemed to be keeping things up for the time being. A small suitcase was parked by the staircase. But the house felt hollow. Rupert's yellow rocker had been moved out, and his TV and VCR, his stereo and music, his afghans and Wilfred's birdcage. The fridge and cupboards were nearly empty. The composition of the air itself had changed. It was lighter and stale.

I'd tried calling Rupert when my suspension ended, and was told he wasn't seeing anyone but family. A nurse explained that the combination of an infection and "upset" had left him confused. "He was probably putting on a good front before. Sometimes at this age, when dementia is starting to creep in, the body gets sick and the mind goes too. He'll be more like himself again when the infection clears up, and then you can have a nice visit."

I knew someone might have already shipped Francis's belongings to his mother in Calgary, and had prepared myself for the sight of his empty drawers and closets. It was seeing Shaggy's old mattress on Rupert's bedroom floor that nearly set me off again. So I began my search for a keepsake to replace the lake stone in the other upstairs rooms. They couldn't have gotten every single thing, I reckoned. Something would turn up—a shaving brush, a cassette tape, a shoe, or maybe—oh, please—a photograph. I went through all the closets and cupboards, the desk, the hutch, and medicine cabinet. I got on my knees and looked under the beds and chesterfields, and did a forensic search of the barn. I even checked the garbage pails and the tub and sinks for a sliver of Francis's herb-mint soap. After three hours, I'd found only two pairs of black socks that were probably-but-not-for-sure Rupert's.

Swallowing tears, I went back up to Rupert's bedroom, the

one room I hadn't thoroughly scoured, stepped over Shaggy's mattress, and started again. It just wasn't possible that I was leaving with only an old man's socks.

I was elbow-deep in Rupert's underwear drawer when someone said: "Are you George?"

A woman in her late forties was standing in the doorway gripping a fire poker. She dropped it to her side. "You are. I recognize you from Dad's description," she said.

Sarah.

"I'm sorry I scared you," I said. "Funny, I didn't hear you coming up the stairs."

"I got lots of practice sneaking into the house when I was your age."

Sarah wasn't at all what I'd expected. There was a black-and-white photograph of her as a blond-haired girl on Rupert's fridge, and this woman had the same narrow nose, same deep-set eyes, but I'd always imagined she'd grown up to be a skinny, hard-edged, urban business lady. The reality was pink-cheeked and plump, with intensely chestnut-colored hair. She wore no makeup and was dressed in a brightly patterned sweater and large, dangly earrings.

I eased my hands out of the drawer, no easy lie at the ready about what I was doing. "I bet I know what you're looking for," she said. "Found it when I was turning the house upside down for his magnifying glass. Hang on a sec."

She returned with a small package wrapped in brown paper.

"I've been carrying it around in my purse," she said, handing it to me. "Been meaning to drop it off."

My name was written on the outside with a fountain pen: *Ms. Frances George Warren*. Francis's handwriting.

"You'll never guess where I found it." Sarah pointed to the far corner of the room, and I finally saw the too-obvious: the large trunk in the corner that held Rupert's old bedding, his lottery tickets and silver dollars.

"I'll put tea on," she said. "And I'm going to make you eat some pie. I have a desperate need to put meat on those bones."

I sat on the edge of Rupert's bed and drank in the sight of my name as Francis had set it down. He always used a tidy, well-spaced mix of printing and cursive—a restrained curl on the *G*, a little extra on the *W*. The handwriting of someone who thought it mattered how pen met paper.

What was inside—a book? It felt like a book. Maybe it was the Elizabeth Bishop collection that had been missing from his bedside. That would be like Lisa's father giving her mother *Cooking for Absolute Beginners* for her fortieth birthday, but I didn't care. I had something, and that was all I wanted.

I peeled back the paper carefully, and there she was, Elizabeth Bishop. Not the collected poems; this one was called *Geography III*. It was an old hardcover, secondhand from the look of it. When I slipped it out of its clear plastic covering, a bookmark fluttered to the floor. I held the book by its spine to see if I could find the place it had been tucked. Seemed to be a poem called "One Art."

> the art of losing's not too hard to master
> though it may look like (Write it!) like disaster.

I read the whole poem and then I read it again, trying to make sense of why Francis had marked this particular one, if he'd marked it. It was as though he'd had a premonition that he would hit black ice that night and was telling me that I would get over him one day. The possibility that he had gone into the ravine on purpose briefly glinted, but no. Francis was too interested in the world to leave it sooner than he had to. He might have just tucked the bookmark at random, or it hadn't been holding that page at all.

I flipped to the front of the book. No inscription. No, he wouldn't want anyone else to read the message. But there, on the back of the bookmark lying on the floor, was that same tidy handwriting.

G— A memento. A promissory note. A ticket. xF

A teapot leaking steam, a store-bought rhubarb pie, and two forks were waiting on the kitchen table. I sat in my old place across from Sarah, who was in Francis's chair, my wheels turning. If only Rupert weren't sick; I had so many questions. Why hadn't Francis given me the book himself? Why had Rupert tucked it away in his hiding place? Was it meant to be a birthday present? What had Francis said when he'd given it to Rupert? What I most wanted to ask was what the message on the bookmark meant. A memento I sort of understood, but not a promissory note, a ticket.

"How did you hurt yourself?" Sarah asked, pouring the tea. "Your face, honey."

"Oh, just a carpet burn. I tripped."

"Listen, I was sorry to hear about Mick—Francis, whatever his name was. Expect you knew him pretty well."

"Sort of."

She raised her eyebrows. "Dad said he wasn't the best influence on you."

I took a sip from my mug, burning my tongue, and hoped it covered any surprise I was reflecting back. "What did he mean by that?"

"Something he said in passing, never explained. But, hey, I'm grateful to the guy. Dad and I have always been like cats and dogs, for no good reason. I couldn't have taken care of him like that. I'm grateful to you too."

"I miss him. Rupert. I'll go see him when he's better."

"Do you know how the French say *I miss you*? It's *tu me manques*. Think about that." She lifted a forkful of pie straight out of the middle.

"You—you are missed by me."

"Literally, you're missing to me. Isn't that beautiful?"

It was exactly right. Losing Francis had been like losing part of myself, the best part—and I know that's ripe cheese, but goddamn it if it wasn't true, and if he wouldn't have been thrilled to hear me admit it. He'd made my hard little heart swell and pulse, and now it was burning itself out like a charcoal briquette. If this was what phantom pain felt like, I thought, no wonder Dad medicated himself into a semicoma.

"Didn't mean to upset you," Sarah said, and I realized my eyes were leaking.

"Sorry," I said. "My boyfriend and I broke up and I'm kind of a mess."

"Say no more. My husband and I are separating, so I too have been feeling feelings. Who knew you could long for a man who flosses with his credit card?"

I laughed, and dabbed my eyes with the napkin she passed to me.

"Lonesome, isn't it?" she said.

"Yes." The Bishop *yes*.

"Just remember, you were lonesome when you were with him too."

All this time I'd thought of Sarah as Rupert's nemesis and so mine by association. She was more like an insta-friend, or a psychic. Because she was right again, this lady forking the pie to death, being with Francis had come with a side helping of lonesomeness, though I hadn't thought about it before. It wasn't like I could bring him to the school dance, so I didn't go to the school dance. There was a lot we couldn't do together.

"How did you guess?" I asked.

"Relationships can be lonely places at the best of times." She pushed the other fork across the table to me. "Do you mind if I ask what was in the package?"

"A book Francis left for me. We like the same poets."

"Awfully considerate of him, considering."

"Considering what?"

"I talked to him a few times on the phone, seemed like a decent young man. Suppose he had to have been. He was an RCMP officer, for god's sake. But at the same time, this was a guy who could . . ."

I wasn't sure I wanted her to finish that sentence.

"Well, who could just pack up his car one night, with everything he owns. No notice to the employer, no notice to the landlord—who considers you a friend, maybe even a son. I don't know. I guess I shouldn't be mad if Dad isn't. Are you going to let me eat this entire pie?"

THIRTY-FIVE

A be accelerated through the twists and turns of the old highway, darting around the few vehicles on the road.

It had taken me too long to put it together, but the facts
were finally presenting themselves.

Francis hadn't gone off the road on his way to meet me
that night; he was leaving. The valley, Rupert, me. He'd taken
all his things, Sarah said, which meant he had no intention of
coming back, and she'd also told me that he left hours before
we planned to meet at the Dempseys. That old book in my bag,
that was supposed to be good-bye, and he wasn't even going to
give it to me himself.

I pressed harder on the accelerator and an oncoming car
flashed its headlights at me.

The first time I saw Francis, drifting through the fallow

meadow like a life raft, a flare had shot through my chest. A beacon, I thought. Or a warning. That was how it began. Was this really how it ended, with seven words, three of them *A*?

A memento. A promissory note. A ticket.

When had he made up his mind?

I just don't want you planning your life around me, he'd said in the barn. *I can't promise to do the same.* That was the last time I saw him. Maybe he never meant for us to go to the city together. Or he went to pack a weekend suitcase and kept on packing. Maybe he told himself that it was better to slip away because he didn't want to hurt me. God forbid she cries! So instead of hitting me with it straight, he quietly hooked me up to the back of his car, got in, and started driving. That's what it felt like, the not-knowing, the non-good-bye, like being dragged behind him.

A small shadow darted in front of my wheels. I swerved and the car fishtailed wildly, hit gravel on the side of the road and skidded toward the ditch, stopping right at the brink. I could feel how close Abe's tires were to the loose edge. I set the emergency brake, forced myself to breathe.

Rabbit.

It's true what Nat had said, that I was both a liar and a fortress. Loyal keeper of secrets, promises, and lighthouses. But the real reason I didn't tell anyone about Francis, the absolute truth, is that if I had, they would have pointed out the too-obvious. That there must have been something wrong, something broken

inside him. That's what Lisa would have said. She might try to put it nicely, but it would boil down to this: *If he wasn't broken, why here and why you? Did you really think your whistling was so damn charming?*

I'd been playacting at being a grown-up with this person I hardly knew and had turned into the very thing I'd accused Lisa of being: a girl who would sink everything for some guy who was always going to be a passing ship. Worst of all, it was that guy who'd shown me that I wasn't cold-blooded. Now I was alone and felt like I was literally dying of heartsickness, like a karmic clobbering with a big cliché stick.

I've never been able to make myself believe in any of the gods, but as I idled on the side of the road, gathering myself, I said a prayer. Please let it end now. Let me put this down and drive away. Let me forget, so that when I'm as old as my parents are, I won't be sure whether this happened. Do me this favor and I will believe and I will behave and I will be forever benevolent toward all of your creations, even baby corn.

For just a second, I thought the hum in my chest was gone, and then it began again.

Carefully, I shifted the car into reverse and released the brake, inching backward with more caution than necessary until I was on the road.

By the time I pulled onto the new highway, the western sky was a mess of Easter colors between the mountains. Every tree branch was in relief against the low clouds and dome of darkening blue above, like those delicate paper illustrations, the silhouettes you see in old children's books with the funny German name. The woman in a rocking chair. The boy and girl under the apple tree.

My exit was coming up, but I decided to keep going, head over the mountain and drive along the bay. I rolled down the window an inch, shrugging my jacket loose. The darkness was inkier now, the sun a gold thread hemming the horizon. I passed a pair of transport trucks without cargo, like insect heads that had lost their bodies, and a magnificent willow. Its canopy against the blue-black sky had such otherworldliness that you might have believed this was a road on a desert island or some other faraway place, not an ordinary rural highway that ran from here to nearly somewhere, then circled back on itself like an empty promise.

THIRTY-SIX

My friends and I never knocked at each other's houses. When I let myself into Bill's, it was quiet except for the shower running upstairs and his off-key singing.

"Sometimes the snow comes down in June. Sometimes the sun goes round the moooooooon . . ."

I waited in his rooooooom.

His robe was open when he came in, his wrist wrapped in a tensor bandage and swinging by his side like a club, and when he screamed, he found that note he hadn't been able to hit in the shower. "Jesus," he said, collapsing on the end of the bed. "Where did you come from?"

"Sometimes it's all a big surprise."

Thank god he had boxers on. He pulled his robe closed and took a good look at me. "Nice face," he said.

"Nice wrist. Is it broken?"

"Just sprained."

"Thought you had a stomach thing."

"I did. And this. I came to see you when you were suspended, but your parents wouldn't let me in, so I had this idea that I could get to your bedroom window from the garage roof."

"God, how did we not hear you?"

"I did a trial run on our garage roof." He picked up an old duffel bag from the floor and started rifling in it. "I wanted to bring you something. Two somethings."

"Aren't we fighting?"

"We had *a* fight." Something One—small, hard, and plastic—sailed across the bed and hit me in the shoulder. Han Solo. I'd given him to Bill in seventh grade, after Han and I had grown apart. "Peace offering," Bill said. This was followed by a baggie filled with five brown-and-green-flecked cookies. "Birthday gift."

"Gee, thanks. Pot?"

"I'm not sure. Doug was clearing out his stash a few weeks ago. The cookie part is stale, but the other part should still work. Go ahead."

"Not right now."

"Why not? Did you drive over?"

"No, I walked, but . . ."

How could I get high, sitting in Bill's room next to his gently bubbling fish tank, like it was an ordinary Saturday night?

"I actually came to talk to you," I said. "It's kind of serious."

I took a breath, located that lower gear inside myself, and looked into Bill's anxious face. Which is when I decided that getting high next to Bill's gently bubbling fish tank was exactly what I needed that Saturday night. If it gave me the courage to say what had to be said, great. If it only gave me a few hours outside of my own head—well, that'd do too.

As a wise man once said, if you can't make it better, you can at least make it blurry.

"How long before these kick in?" I asked, when we'd downed cookie number four. We were alternating between cookie bites and grapes, and the grapes felt like they were expanding in my stomach.

"Beats me."

I stroked Han's tiny black vest. "He was my one true love. Course, I was kinda confused about whether I wanted to be him or do him."

"Is that what you wanted to talk about?"

"Sort of."

"You'll find someone who's not plastic."

"What if I don't?"

Or worse. What if I thought I found someone again, and I was wrong—again?

"See, I don't think you're a person who doesn't find it," he said. "You're a person who people fall in love with at first sight. Maybe it passes for some of them, but not all. Not me. You're

323

like an infection that keeps coming back. Are you crying?"

"A bit."

"Fuck. I meant in a nonsexual way, right? No offense, but it's *all* no-man's-land under that sweater."

He scooched over. Then he scooched a little closer, a little closer still, and when he put his arms around me, I needed that, more than anything, more than oxygen. No one had hugged me after Francis died. No one except Francis had hugged me for a very long time. It wasn't just being held; I needed to hold someone. To feel Bill's curls and neck scruff against my cheek, his sinewy teenage boy undercarriage beneath the Dorito layer, his heartbeat, his breathing. I needed to feel someone I loved alive in my grip.

"There, there," he said. "There, there, there."

That was the moment to tell him. I meant to. I'd gone over there to unleash it all because screw Francis. My grades were down, my body was shriveled, and nobody was there to sniff out my lies or squeeze me when I needed it most. If it hadn't been for Francis, I might have made up with Lisa. I'd definitely have been a better friend to Bill, and I wouldn't let Francis lose me the one friend I had left.

I couldn't do it, though. Confessing was supposed to make it all real, bring it out of the shadows, and shine a holy cleansing light. It always had with Lisa. But Bill didn't want to spend hours dissecting the last year like a fetal pig. I could tell by the way he patted my hair and kept rubbing my face on the cuff of his robe. He'd never seen me full-on cry before and just wanted me to stop—which I did, because being with my buddy again made me feel human for the first time since they pulled Francis's car from the ravine. For now, that was enough.

"Look," Bill said. "The grapes are breathing."

"No, they aren't." I looked at the grapes. "*Ugch*, they are."

"And the guppies are going *dwoop-dwoop*."

I put my hand up. "Stop *saying* things. You *say* things and then they *happen*."

When did he get so annoying, with all the breathing and the blinking and the arm hair? He'd started swatting at something that I'm pretty sure wasn't there.

"Oh my god. I forgot why it's such a bad idea to get you high."

Where to start? With the night at Lisa's cottage when we did hash off hot knives and I spent the whole night shushing everyone because I was paranoid that we were bothering the neighbors, the closest of whom were a mile away? The time we smoked pot by a bonfire at the shore and I was so terrified we'd set the whole beach alight that I kept running back and forth between the fire and the ocean, trying to put out the flames with handfuls of seawater? Some people turn into rock stars when they get high. I turn into your mother.

"We need to go out so that I don't have to deal with you alone." His eyes grew wide. "The play!"

"The plane?"

"Lisa's play! Tonight! Like, in less than an hour. Shit. Shit, shit. I'm calling a taxi."

"*The* taxi."

"George, this play is gonna be a disaster—really, *really* a disaster. After Lisa fired everyone, a lot of people said they were boycotting. We gotta fill the seats."

"Fired who when?"

"Everyone except, like, six people. Couple weeks ago. She's hardly left the auditorium since. *Shit.* Where are my clean pants?"

So she'd grown a backbone and done what she needed to do, just in time to ruin it. Too bad none of her friends—not Christina or Keith or even Bill—had the nads to tell her the hard truth when there was still time to save her.

"Buddy, we don't need to go to this play," I said. "We need to stop it."

I had my hand up, waiting for the high five.

He was back to swatting the air.

We arrived soaking wet after a long sprint in the rain. The taxi driver had ditched us a half mile away, disinclined to have anyone at the school see two frantic, stoned kids doing parachute rolls out of his vehicle.

"This is what's happening," I said to Bill after we bought our tickets. "First, we go in through the front doors here and you cover me while I head down to the stage."

"And then what, you pull the fire alarm?"

I had no idea what came second, but the fire alarm sounded good, which I said loudly enough to bring Nat and Doug running from the makeshift concession stand by the principal's office.

"What the hell, George?" Nat said.

"We need to stop the play. It's going to suck."

"We need to *what*?"

Doug said, "Babe, check out their pupils."

Nat glared at Bill.

"What? I thought she needed to relax."

"Most people get high to lose control," she said. "But the possibility of losing control is exactly what turns George into ... *this*."

I was looking at Nat, looking at Doug, looking at Nat, looking at Doug, trying to figure out how a person was supposed to figure out if they were together without being too obvious about it.

"Oh, come on," Bill said. "Let's see what happens. She's in a totally different movie from the rest of us."

Nat had never been a touchy-feely person, and she didn't seem to know quite what to do with her hand when she reached over to me. She settled for brushing my wet hair away from my face. Then she brushed it the other way. Then she gave up. "George? Georgie Girl? I know you think you're having some kind of a big moment here, but you don't want to ruin this for Lisa."

"I'm going to *save* her," I said. "Because it is going to *suck*."

"No, you're going to embarrass her and get kicked out and the play will go on. You know why?"

"Yes," I said, hoping that would keep Nat from laying one of her truth nuggets.

"Lisa doesn't need you anymore."

I don't know how long I'd been staring at her, my ears ringing, chest flaring spectacularly, when Doug said, "Let's just go in. Maybe you guys will sober up by the time it starts. What did you take?"

"The stuff in the blue baggie," Bill said.

"Oh no, you're not sobering up."

Getting to our seats was challenging, seeing as the aisle kept stretching out to infinity no matter how far we walked. It felt like everyone was watching us, though I couldn't tell for sure because my eyes were blurry with the sting of what Nat had said.

She plunked me into a seat and turned to shush Bill, who was having a giggle fit on her other side.

A long leg nudged mine. "You okay?"

I started so badly at the sight of Joshua Spring that he jumped and hit his knee painfully on the seat in front of him.

"Aw, *why*?" he groaned.

"I'm sorry! Sorry. I'm a little, you know. Out of it."

He gave his knee a last rub, then reached under his seat for a thermos he'd stowed there, holding it out to me. I sniffed it: the infamous Spring family home brew. "I mean, this is going to suck," he said. "I don't think anyone here is sober."

The house lights dimmed and the curtains parted to reveal a single light on a bare stage. Keith stood in the center, wearing a pair of old-fashioned pants with suspenders and a white shirt. His feet were bare. "This is the forest primeval," he announced to the half-empty auditorium.

"*No*," I said, apparently not just in my head.

Beside me, Joshua chugged his home brew.

As the pared-down cast spoke their lines, they leapt around, clamored over a moving set made of entirely of barrels and ladders, tossed one another into the air—athletic and forceful but also graceful and fluid. The stage lights went out and they somehow tumbled with lit candles in the darkness, and my eyes blurred again, it was so beautiful, and because it was so like Francis rolling down the mountain ridge with his flashlight the night I begged him to love me.

> *And the soul of the maiden, between the stars and*
> *the fire-flies,*
> *Wandered alone, and she cried,— 'O Gabriel! O*
> *my beloved!*
> *Art thou so near unto me, and yet I cannot behold*
> *thee!*

Art thou so near unto me, and yet thy voice does not reach me?

So close and yet so far away.

I found myself thinking about how I would have described it to Francis, starting with how shockingly nimble Keith turned out to be. Then I remembered that if Francis were alive, he wouldn't have been around to tell, and if he had been around to tell, I probably would have missed the play.

The applause was as thundering as half an auditorium could be, especially when Lisa took her bow.

"S'alright," Joshua said. Dozens of white balloons had been released from the rafters and were now drifting down to the stage.

"Yeah. S'alright," I said.

Nat and the boys were starting to make their way into the aisle, but I wasn't in a hurry to return to real life. "Back in the fall I saw these small hot-air-balloon-type things floating up the north mountain," I said. "Out of nowhere. It was so strange."

"Paper lanterns. East Riverview science club does it every year."

We watched the cast kicking the balloons into the audience.

"Well, whaddya know, Joshua."

"I didn't know it was your birthday until after I left the rose. I just felt bad about how you got suspended."

"I deserved it."

"So did she."

He took a swig from the thermos, wiped a drip off his chin. "I never got why you lied about what happened between us, George. It's not like there weren't other girls who could vouch for me. But it seems like you paid for it five times over."

I was slow to work out what he was saying, and then I couldn't believe it—he hadn't believed it! All this time, he thought the bad kiss was something I'd made up, the one truth at the center of all those lies.

I suppose I could have set him straight. Maybe his future girlfriends would have thanked me. Then again, Christina might have already sorted him out. And, you know, sometimes the truth is overrated. Years later I convinced Bill that I made out with Bryan Adams in the back of a Greyhound bus, and though he eventually clued in that I was pulling his leg, he still loves to tell people that story.

"I guess I wasn't ready for a grown-up relationship," I said, which was as close to true as we needed to be.

Joshua lightly touched a curl over my ear. Then he passed over the home brew. Unlike some of us, it lived up to its reputation.

THIRTY-SEVEN

Doug dropped Bill and me off at Bill's house before heading to the cast party at the Grunt. I started walking home, but decided to try sobering up first. Two seconds later I found the fifth cookie in my coat pocket, and decided to try not sobering up first. I must have walked for a couple of hours, through the old section of town, past the cat lady's house and around the sawmill, looping back to Main Street, where I became fixated on the store windows. They were like museum exhibits, re-creations of eras gone by. The pharmaceuticals of yesteryear. The hardware of yore.

Dirty dishes and a large chartreuse feather on a key chain were all that remained of the cast party when I peered into the Grunt. I went inside, slipped into a booth, and ordered a coffee, leaving the keys on the table where Lisa had left them. Pushing my damp hair out of my eyes, I contemplated sugar, but the metal bowl with its flip-up lid was looking at me in a menacing way. I tapped it a couple of times, tried to provoke it into action, before deciding to drink my coffee plain.

And then she was there. The atmosphere of the Grunt was golden and luminous in my dilated eyes, making Lisa appear as though she were in the floodlights of some fancy Broadway show. "I love you," I said.

It just slipped out.

"Why are you being gay?"

"People need to stop saying things like that. It's the *nineties*."

I started to cry.

"What's wrong with you?"

"What is wrong with me is that I'm emoting a real emotion for once and I'm ruining it by being high and also having hands that don't want to work *at all*."

I flapped my hands at her until she grabbed them and held them on the table. "Right," she said, sitting down. "You can put the cork back in the bottle."

"Lise, listen to me."

"I'm listening—"

"*Shhhh.* Listen to me. I loved your weirdo circus play. It was so you. I knew it would be good."

"George, I know you tried to stop it."

Now I was bawling.

"It's okay," she said.

"No, it's not. You were right. I'm such a"—here I sprayed her ever so lightly with saliva—"*bitch*."

"I never said you're . . . I said that to Christina, not you."

"You did?"

"For what it's worth, she felt bad about it. She was trying to be funny."

"Who would think that was funny?"

"She thought you would. She's always tried to be like you. No, it's true. Problem is, she doesn't know the difference between being tough and just being mean."

"I was mean to you. I said awful things."

"Yeah. You did."

"I *was* jealous of Keith. I guess I was scared because I didn't have a plan if you weren't in it. And I didn't call you back because I didn't think it was possible for us to be friends again, not because I didn't want to."

"Is that all?"

She knew it wasn't. Of course she did.

I fell silent, transfixed by her hair. It was floating about her head in a halo of red spirals, completely untamed. Her face was thinner, her jaw stronger. There was a raised line winding around the freckles on the back of her left hand, a scar from some long-ago incident I'd missed. (It was wriggling, but I was pretty sure that was the drugs.) She had changed so much, probably all for the better. And I realized that she would never understand what had brought me to this place because it was an impossible thing to understand from the outside. Even on the inside it was nearly impossible.

"I know you don't need an enforcer anymore."

She turned the key chain over in her hands. "You say that like it was the only reason we were friends."

A tap on the window. Keith was on the other side, motioning to Lisa to come out. "I gotta go," she said. "Sorry. See you at school?"

"Okay. See you."

She inched to the edge of the booth, but didn't get out. "Maybe someday you'll trust me enough to tell me the rest," she said.

"It's not that."

"It is that. And I'm sorry too."

THIRTY-EIGHT

"First we should find out if she's missing and if there's a reward for her. Then we can call the police."

"No, first we should find out if she's dead."

"She's dead. Look—"

I felt something tap my heel.

I'm not entirely certain how I came to be facedown under my mother's shrub and subsequently the object of an Encyclopedia Brown investigation. I recall stumbling home. I recall thinking that a little lie-down would be pleasant and that I could make the rest of the journey to my house after I'd rested up. I remember trying to stand and feeling dizzy and the ground coming up.

"I'll take this leg; you and Russ do the other. One . . ." Hands around my ankles. "Two . . ."

"I'm not dead!" I shouted.

I shimmied out of the shrub to see three redheaded boys tearing down the sidewalk. "Dad! Dad!" they shrieked at a man who was power-walking with two small redheaded girls hanging off him like he was a set of monkey bars. The boys got distracted by the urgent need to pummel one another before they reached their father, but the father's attention was fixed on me.

"I'll leave this one to the Sergeant," Mr. Humphreys said. "Be in my office at nine a.m. on Monday."

He didn't even break his stride.

Dad was standing in the doorway of our porch in his old robe, one leg of his jogging pants fluttering in the breeze under his stump. He didn't say anything, and so I sat there, feeling the cold muck seep through my jeans. No excuses. For once I'd been doing exactly what my dad and Mr. Humphreys thought I was doing all the time and they'd caught me red-handed. I was getting grounded, two seconds after the thaw-out with my friends, and probably worse.

Then Dad's face crumpled, and that was easily the most god-awful sight I've ever seen—my father crying, chin to his chest, looking disheveled and trapped and clutching the doorframe like it was the only thing keeping him from getting sucked into a world he no longer inhabited.

My mother was hogging the pay phone in the emergency room hallway, telling everyone she'd called regarding my whereabouts that I was alive in spite of all her deficiencies as a parent. I hadn't been able to persuade her that I'd been asleep in the yard with a little bonus fainting, so now I waited behind a curtain for an emergency room doctor who was a dead ringer for my cousin Buster, down to the black goatee and minor mullet.

I sat on a bed in my wet jeans, Dad in a chair in the corner. He'd come in after my examination but hadn't said a word since we'd gotten in the car to drive to the hospital. "I'm sorry," I said for the tenth time. "I didn't mean to scare you."

"June called me last week," he said. "She saw you driving like a maniac in Scotch County. Would have pulled you over but was on her way to a serious domestic call. She wanted to make sure you'd made it home."

"I was just running late. I wasn't drinking or—"

"I didn't do anything about it." He was blinking hard. "When you didn't come home last night . . ."

Oh geez.

"I checked your room. All your toys and keepsakes were gone. That's often a sign, giving these things away."

"A sign of what?"

"That someone is planning to hurt themselves."

As badly as I felt that I'd given my parents such a scare, this was truly terrible detective work. The book from Francis was in my nightstand drawer, the cigarettes that now hurt my chest to smoke in various pockets. A condom or two could have been turned up, and I wouldn't blame a person if he made a false connection between them and the half-dead rose in the bud vase. All my kid stuff was under the bed. It was almost farcical how much my dad had lost his grip since last summer.

"Dad, I'm not planning to do myself in. I went to a *play*. I got *high*."

"We're in a *hospital*."

There was that.

"Your mother and I, we know you're having a rough time. And I know when you're young it seems like rough times will never end, but they do. So I'm asking you, please, I'm asking you to live with it, whatever it is. Even if it hurts sometimes to be alive."

He was clutching his knee with his good hand, tobacco-stained fingers against his blue jogging pants. Something snapped inside me. Because he wasn't wrong; I did go to the brink. It was very nearly death by rabbit. I didn't know who I was anymore, and maybe he didn't know who he was either, now that he wasn't the Sergeant, but only one of us was trying to put things right again. Every morning, putting on my pants. This was one of the few times I'd seen him beyond the boundaries of our yard since last summer.

"Why?" I said. "So I can watch you fall apart? What are you going to lose next? Your kidneys? Your eyesight? You can't give up buttered donuts for us, but I'm supposed to do what it takes to stay alive for you?"

Was it tough or was it mean?

I meant it, anyway, every word of it thrumming through my body as I looked again at those yellow fingers.

The doctor pulled back the curtain. "Everything okay, Frances?"

"George," my dad said quietly. "She goes by her middle name."

"It doesn't matter, Dad," I said.

"I don't mind calling you by your actual name," the doctor said. "You comfortable having your old man here?"

"I don't know, is it anything embarrassing?"

"No pregnancy, STDs, or drugs he doesn't already know about."

"He can stay." Now was not the time to tell my dad he was being overly parental.

"Then first things first. That's acid burbling around your stomach and up your esophagus. Because you're not eating enough, probably because of the acid, you should be tested for low iron, low potassium, low magnesium, low a lot of things. You been feeling lethargic? Dizzy?"

"Yeah."

"No shit."

Were doctors allowed to say that?

"You said you have pain when you eat," the doctor continued, "and when you're lying down. We can fix that. But tell me

this: Why didn't you get yourself checked out sooner? Were you scared?"

"I thought—I thought it was my heart. Pretty dumb."

He consulted my chart. "Sounded okay, blood pressure's good. Does it feel like it's squeezing?"

"No."

"Palpitations? Fast heartbeat? Shortness of breath?"

"No, just that burning feeling. When I eat, when I don't eat, even when I'm not thinking about it."

"Even when you're not thinking about what?"

"What?"

"That's what I'm asking you. Even when you aren't thinking about what do you feel the acid shooting up? Something stressing you out?"

"Um . . ."

My dad was now sitting forward in his chair. "Maybe you should excuse us, big guy," the doctor said.

"No, it's nothing," I said. "School stress, you know?" Wait a second. "Though it's been hard to stay focused. Because I've been feeling tired. And dizzy. So dizzy. To be honest, my grades have been suffering. . . ."

The doctor had been making notes on my chart as I talked. Now he looked up and his expression said, *Not buying it, but tell you what, I respect the effort.*

"Well! We'd better get you a note for school, then, since this has been going on for a while. Your regular doctor should run the bloodwork to check for the deficiencies, and I'll write you a prescription to help with that acid reflux, which you can start taking now."

"That'll make it stop hurting?"

"That'll stop you from burning a hole in your gut."

"So it's definitely not my heart."

"Your heart is fine, George, but you're on your way to an ulcer. You think you're handling something, but you ain't handling it. That's what your body's telling you." The doctor put his hand on my dad's shoulder. "You'll make sure she takes her prescription."

Dad nodded.

"And, George? Eat some frigging food."

THIRTY-NINE

I was so stupid. I actually believed that if I did what the doctor ordered, I'd get over Francis. Take my medicine, do my schoolwork, practice my chords, eat some frigging food, ask for forgiveness, forgive. Like launching a skiff into the water: a push and a push and a push and a sudden release. That's not how it works.

But it did get easier. One day, when I was working alone in the computer room at lunchtime, I pressed my hand to my heart. Well, my esophagus. The humming was barely there. I pressed harder, knowing that I was losing something painful but also dear.

Someone sat opposite me and unwrapped a sandwich. I peered around the computer terminal. "Hi."

"Hi," Nat said.

"Yeah, hi."

"Are you working on your English essay?"

"News report on Crimea. It's an extra-credit thing for Gifford and Aker."

"Cool."

I pretended to work while I listened to her chew.

"Nat?"

"Yeah?"

"Thanks for stopping me at the play," I said. "Even though I know you did it for Lisa."

"Not just Lisa. If it weren't for you, I probably would have started going with Doug before he sobered up. But I kept thinking about how you'd never settle for a guy who wasn't perfect. Perfect enough."

That wasn't true, of course, so I just nodded and breathed the familiar lemon scent of her hair.

The next day she turned up again. On the third day Bill was with her, and on the fifth day, Lisa. We didn't say too much. Stuff like, "The quiz is on Friday, right?" or "Have my apple." Mostly we studied and ate, and when the buzzer went, we'd go back to our own sides of the classroom. But it went like that day after day, week after week, and slowly the space between us was closing.

Maybe it was the poetry books on the shelf behind Mr. Humphreys' desk—Auden, Lowell, Rich, Yeats, Pound—or as my nan used to say, I could have pulled it out of my pancreas.

"Did you write that poem we read in class?" I asked. "About the two boys who used to be friends? Miss Aker said it was by a local poet, and everyone figured it was her, but now I'm thinking . . ."

Mr. Humphreys kept reading my Crimea report. It'd taken him ten minutes of staring in disbelief at my doctor's note and an interminably long meeting with my parents and he'd insisted that I turn in my extra-credit assignments to him directly, but I had to hand it to him. He and Dr. Buster had really saved my bacon, so to speak.

"Did you hear me? I was asking if you wrote—"

"No."

He wasn't a good liar.

"I liked that line near the end: 'We buried the reason' . . . That's not it. 'The reason was buried like . . .'"

"'The reason buried like a bone,'" he finished, shaking his head.

"It's so sad that you can't remember what made you stop being friends."

"We were thirteen. The reason was probably stupid."

"Do you have any idea when I can expect to stop being stupid?"

"Thirty-six. If you're lucky."

I slipped the book—*the* book—out of my bag. I'd been thinking about asking Miss Aker about the poem that Francis may or may not have bookmarked, which was probably not what the doctor ordered, as far as getting on with things, but not understanding it had been an itch I couldn't scratch.

"Thought you were done with poetry for the year," Mr. Humphreys said.

"Not reading it for school. Do you know her stuff?"

"I do."

"Do you happen to know the poem 'One Art'?"

"'The art of losing isn't hard to master.'"

"Right—oh, good. What does that mean exactly? She can't really be saying that you get better at losing things. Places. People."

"I think the point is she isn't fooling anybody, not even herself. But I'd have to read it again."

I slid the book across the desk to him.

"An oldie." He turned the pages. Frowned. Flipped to the front, then back to the middle. "Where did you get it?"

"It was a gift."

"A first edition. You've seen this, I assume."

The poem was called "The End of March," and below the title was a dedication: *For John Malcolm Brinnin and Bill Read: Duxbury.* Beside the dedication, in the margin, was an inscription scribbled in looped handwriting: *For J.M.B., with affection and bottomless gratitude. E.B.*

"That's her?"

"Seems likely, though odd not to have signed the title page,"

Mr. Humphreys said. "Perhaps she intended to surprise him." He carefully slipped the book back into its plastic wrapper. "George, this could be worth a lot of money. Who did you say gave it to you? They might not have known its value."

A ticket.

"I think he did," I said.

Rupert was sitting on a park bench behind the nursing home, watching the river run.

I sat beside him and passed over a tin of cookies that Mum and Matthew had baked for me to bring. Oatmeal, Shaggy's favorite.

"Hey, Rupert."

"Oh, George. They said you were coming."

His jacket parted and the ugliest creature in the world poked out its head and snarled at me. It might have been a dog.

"You got a new pet," I said. "Don't tell me something happened to Wilfred."

"Wilfred is still alive, still a dick. This is Crystal. She belongs to my neighbor. Say thanks for the cookies, Crystal."

Crystal disappeared into his jacket again.

"How are you feeling?"

"Old as hell. Sarah said I was out of my mind for a long while. Nice to be half back in it again."

"You must miss Shaggy. And Francis. I'm so sorry."

Rupert nodded, then gave me a sidelong look. "Never got

used to you calling him that."

How long had he known about Francis and me? Because he knew, didn't he? Why else would he have hidden the book away?

I encouraged him. My god, I told him to go.

Still, I hoped there was another explanation. "Remember this?" I asked, taking *Geography III* out of my bag.

"Ah, an inheritance from the senior McAdams."

"Francis left it for me. Sarah found it in your trunk."

"Very good."

Either he didn't remember how it had ended up there or was an excellent poker player.

"It might be worth a lot of money."

Mr. Humphreys wasn't sure, but at least a few thousand dollars, he thought. He suggested I take it to someone he knew at Noel who could help authenticate it. Rupert looked only mildly surprised when I explained this to him. "The Constable had money to spare, as it turns out. Lot of money. Most of it was in trust. He hadn't touched it yet, but it was there, part of his grandfather's legacy. And last year he came into a large estate after his father died."

"I'm sorry, but are you sure? This is a guy who darned his old socks."

"Suppose that explains his wandering around. Easier to be a free spirit when you have a big ol' net to catch you."

I was stunned. Francis had made passing references to his

family's business and boarding school, and he'd never made it sound like they were *that* rich.

"Did he tell you all this?"

"Not all of it. I spoke to his mother at length. She is a piece of something."

But why live out here? I thought. Why birth calves in the riverbed, if he didn't have to work at all? I hadn't realized I'd spoken the words aloud until Rupert replied: "I suppose some people need to make their own start."

I wrapped the book in the cardigan that I'd been using for extra protection and returned it to my bag. "You know, no matter what this is worth, it's still a shitty substitute for good-bye."

"Men are cowards. We'd rather face a firing squad than a woman's tears." He chuckled. "A firing squad doesn't talk you into things."

"The problem with that is, now I don't know what he wanted me to do with it."

"Maybe nothing."

"You mean hang on to it, like a memento."

"Could be. Or could have been just a loaner. Or a what's-it. When you don't bring enough cash to the store so you leave something behind to show you'll come back."

"Collateral."

Or a promissory note.

"You know, honey, he was not a fellow to make assumptions. He gave that to you, and it's for you to decide what you want to do with it. I, for one, think some decisions are best made when you're older. So, if you're asking me, I say give it a minute. Something special like that, you could let it go and then change your mind. You think the lady in the poem from way back wasn't wishing she'd kept that fish for supper?"

I was certain then that Rupert had hidden the package to try to keep us apart. He may have thought it would be better for me in the long run to believe that Francis had left without a final word. Or maybe he was trying to buy us time and sober second thought before we worked out what he'd done. I suddenly didn't care. That he thought Francis could let me go and then change his mind meant Rupert believed that he had gotten into his car still loving me.

Rupert was crumbling cookie down his front. His eyes were filmy. He had on one brown shoe and one black shoe. I wasn't sure he remembered what he'd done, and I couldn't muster anything like anger. Sitting in the afternoon sun, listening to the water rush over the rocky riverbed, I was just so relieved there was one person I could talk to about Francis. Hearing him say "the Constable" made it feel, for a fleeting moment, like Francis was in the other room. I hadn't talked to a soul who knew him, really knew him, since he died.

Rupert went to wipe his mouth with a handkerchief and wrapped my fingers around it instead.

"Alright?"

"Alright." I dried my eyes. "Yes, alright. Do you want me to read some of those poems to you?"

"Crystal here is not such a great fan of poetry," Rupert said. "But I don't think she would complain if you whistled a little tune."

I helped Rupert back to his room and tucked him into his yellow rocker with his favorite afghan. Just as I put my hand on the doorknob to leave, Wilfred chirped in his cage—a hot, indignant little chirp, followed by a cascade of swamp water raining noisily onto the newspaper below.

"I mean, at least he's talking to me," I said.

"Wilfred may be a dick," Rupert said, "but by George, George, he's a good listener."

So was Rupert, and I hoped I would become one too, because, for me, love is a conversation, but you have to be able to hear the subtext.

I want you.

I need you.

I'm mad at you.

I misled you.

I love you.

I love you.

I'm letting go of you.

I'll miss you.

FORTY

Dad was right: life is a bad writer. I've thought a lot about whether I'd rewrite my senior year given the chance. I guess this was it. But in a way, that's what I did the first time around. Truth is, I never did tell anyone the whole story, because the facts are a bit mean and I had to work too hard to convince people that I'm alright. Unless you count dreaming of Joshua Spring's tongue filling my mouth like a wet sausage whenever I go to bed without brushing my teeth.

I'm not a haunted person. You can't be followed by someone who's part of you. Though sometimes when I'm back home, especially near the edge of the great basin where the mountains begin, where you can look down at the squares of cornfields and pastures rugging the valley floor and the snatches of woodland and the villages and the sea, I think about the people who've come and gone from this place and I might get a little sentimental.

The punctuation mark at the end of my idiot year, as Dad once called it, wasn't the prom. Please. I sent the others off with some dances they said brought the house down, including Serbian Disco, Seated Floor-Mopping, Speed Skater, and the soulful come-on, I Really Should Have Chewed More Before Swallowing. (Slow shuffle, hand over the heart, deep gulp, remember to maintain eye contact.) But I did go to our all-night grad party, held in an old airfield, wearing Sid's leather jacket. He'd sent it to Bill as a birthday gift, along with three tickets to a summer Tragically Hip concert in the city for Bill, himself, and me.

"He says we need male bonding time," Bill said, reading the card. "Someone might have told him you've turned into a weeper."

Sid sounded like his same old self, but I wondered if he'd changed as much as we all had, and how much that would matter when he came back.

When I got home from the grad party at sunrise, Dad was sitting on the porch floor doing his mirror therapy. His foot was bare, pants rolled above the knee, and he had a three-foot mirror lying lengthwise between his legs so that it looked like he had both a left foot and a right one. The physiotherapist had given him a bunch of exercises to help with phantom pain, like squeezing his toes and flexing.

"You don't look much worse for wear," he said.

I sat with him until he finished his exercises, then told him about my final grades, which would soon be making their way to Aurora. My marks had averaged out well enough to secure my acceptance in the journalism program.

"I'm proud of you. Still sure journalism's the thing?"

"Honestly, I have no idea what I want to do."

"That's what school is for. So now there is just the matter of paying for it."

"I'm applying for a student loan," I said. "I know that will stress Mum out, but it'll be my debt, and I'll get a job in the city. If that's not enough, I'll go to school part-time."

This was mostly true, but I left out the other option that I'd been wrestling with for weeks, which was to sell the copy of *Geography III* and how I would explain where it had come from and why Constable McAdams would give me something so valuable.

"I have a better plan," Dad said. "You'll accept the full-time placement they've offered you and go live with your aunt Joanna."

"She doesn't have space for me."

"She does if Junior-Junior comes and lives with us. He's going to end up in jail or knock someone up or both, if Joanna doesn't do something."

"So she's sending him to live with the Sergeant."

"Hey, you turned out okay, didn't you?" When I didn't answer, he said, "You did, kiddo. You'll have your own space in the basement with a bathroom and one of those electric stove tops, and we'll get you a bar fridge. It's not a free ride. You'll be expected to do some cleaning and babysitting to cover your room and board, sorry to tell you."

It meant living under my family's roof for a while longer, but if it let me hold on to the one thing I had left of Francis, that wasn't a hard choice to make.

"You must really want me to leave," I said.

I wanted him to say no.

He nodded. "You shouldn't choose a school because it's the closest."

"Scary, all of a sudden."

"Good. You should be scared. Life is scary. So is your aunt Joanna. But you won't be there forever, and I'm sure you'll have friends around. Miss Prissy going to Aurora?"

"Lisa? Thinking about it."

That was where Keith was headed, but she was also still thinking about Noel and another theater program in Montreal.

Mum opened a window above our heads. Now that Dad was smoking only outdoors, she'd begun tidying their room, perhaps working up to moving back in. I had come to see my parents' marriage as fragile; I suppose most relationships are. You just don't know it in the beginning, when you're tattooing someone's name on your body.

"Dad, do you believe in love at first sight?"

"No."

"Didn't you stamp Mum's name on your arm after, like, your third date?"

"That is more a reflection of my youthful stupidity."

"So, you don't think you ever just kind of know right away."

"Sounds like foresight, and I don't go for voodoo like that. If you meet someone and it doesn't work out, you say, *Oh well, I lost my head*. If it does, you say, *I knew all along*. Only time will tell. I don't care how smart you think you are, there's no substitute for time."

"So, what do you call it when you have the big feelings for someone you don't know yet? *Lust?*"

He wrinkled his face at me then looked into the top corner of the porch as though the answer lived there. *"Ugch,"* he said. "Hope."

ACKNOWLEDGMENTS

The settings in this novel are similar to the Annapolis Valley, Nova Scotia, but do not exist as I portrayed them here. However, there is an Ironwood Farm on the Avon River, and I highly recommend Rupert and Heather's blueberries.

Because the cheese never stands alone, there are a number of people to whom I owe a large debt of gratitude, including:

My family.

HarperCollins, especially Alexandra Cooper, Suzanne Sutherland, Jane Warren, Alyssa Miele, Janet Robbins Rosenberg, Alexandra Rakaczki, Stephanie Nuñez, Heather Daugherty, Jennifer Lambert, Iris Tupholme, Rosemary Brosnan, Leo MacDonald, Cory Beatty, Shamin Alli, Maeve O'Regan, Sabrina Abballe, Bess Braswell, and Olivia Russo.

Folio Literary Management, especially Emily van Beek, patron saint of patience; Estelle Laure; and Molly Cusick.

First responders Lena Coakley, Kathy Stinson, Paula Wing, and Rachael Dyer.

Michael Devlin, Ronald Sigal, and Kevin Cleary for sharing their expertise (any liberties with facts are my own).

The Cassaday family, whose generous donation of space and solitude made this book possible.

Melissa McCormack, Vikki VanSickle, Kate Blair, Amir Ocampo, Vicki Grant, Lorissa Sengara, Chad Fraser, Amy Harkness, and Andy Sheppard for the fact-checking, feedback, and inspiration.

The *King's County Advertiser and Register*'s "From the Cruiser" column for being funnier than fiction.

Victor Fleury, Karl West, Nelda Humphreys, Bill Wagstaff, Leonard Diepeveen, and the many other teachers whose influences can be found throughout this story and who share some responsibility for turning me into a writer.

Please direct all complaints to the above.